M000012534

Nobody
Else's
Business

ALSO BY BEVERLY HURWITZ

A Walker's Guide to Park City

Park City Hiking Guide

.

Nobody Else's Business

Beverly Hurwitz MD

Surrogate Press™

Copyright ©2019 Beverly Hurwitz

All rights reserved.

No part of this publication may be reproduced, stored in a retrieval system, or transmitted in any form or by any means, electronic, mechanical, photocopying, recording, or otherwise, without written permission of the author.

Published in the United States by
Surrogate Press™
an imprint of Faceted Press
Surrogate Press, LLC
SurrogatePress.com

ISBN: 978-1-947459-24-3
Library of Congress Control Number: 2019931505

Book cover design by: Beverly Hurwitz
Interior design by: Katie Mullaly, Surrogate Press®

Dedicated to all who care about children.

Washington, D.C.

~ ~ ~

October, 2008

*Except for recognizable celebrities,
landmarks and history, all of the characters in this story
and all of their activities are fictional.*

~ One ~

Eliza Osborn's pulse quickened as the realtor approached the intersection. There was so little chance that the apartment would have the right view. She could barely contain her excitement when they pulled into the driveway at the end of the street.

Four windows faced their target perfectly, although a bouffant cherry tree in the front yard could make surveillance difficult. Maybe those windows weren't even part of the apartment. While the grand old homes in this neighborhood had mostly become two-family, some of the bigger ones had been divided into three units, and this house looked big enough to have a rear apartment.

Eliza started to think that maybe this wasn't even the right house as the agent's shaky hands fumbled with a ring of keys that didn't seem to work. She'd used her towering stature and grotesque scars to hustle an early showing, but she'd also made the realtor nervous. Maybe another agent had the right keys and would rent it right out from under them. She fretted that NEB just wasn't going to get this opportunity. Why should it get any breaks, she worried, when its methods were so devious? Was their cause really that just? She argued with herself as the realtor tried the last key. Just as she concluded their scheme was doomed, the latch clicked and they entered a foyer with a staircase.

"Now remember," the realtor scolded, "the previous tenant only just left, and we won't have a lockbox on the door or a cleaning crew here until next week. I've been told it's a mess up there and I'm only showing it to you because you were so insistent." Cobwebs in the creaky stairwell echoed the agent's warning, but once inside the apartment, the stench made both women gasp. What wasn't encrusted with splatter was veiled in smoke and dust. If not for the perfect view of the front door of the office of Doctors O'Ryan and Rourke across the street, Eliza would have run out holding her breath.

"Two thousand a month? In the condition this place is in?"

"Excuse me, Ms. Osborn. I told you this apartment wasn't ready to show, but you wouldn't hear it. The listing agent said an elderly widower lived here, and I'd guess he wasn't capable of taking care of himself, much less a three-bedroom apartment. He just got moved to a nursing home and the owner only called about the apartment yesterday. We barely got it into today's listings."

"Apologies. The reason I pressured for an early showing is that the family I'm renting this for has a very sickly child, and it's just so rare that an apartment this close to D.C. Memorial becomes available."

"Then I guess they'd be interested, but this intersection's awfully busy with sirens, day and night. Do you think they can stand the noise?"

"I do; but could you please contact the owners and ask them what they intend to do about the disgusting appliances. I'll leave a month's security now, and if it gets cleaned up well, I'll be back with another month's security and twenty percent of that as extra commission for you, if we can just work this out. Here's a list of references for the tenant. She's a very responsible person, and she'll appreciate the location, sirens and all."

The realtor returned to her car to call the owner while Eliza took some measurements. The doorways were just wide enough for Willie's wheelchair. The ideal apartment would have been on the first floor, but as she again looked out the window in the front bedroom, and clearly saw the face of a woman leaving the doctors' office, she knew Lydia would have no qualms about carrying Willie and his stuff in and out of the apartment for the year or two it might take for NEB to accomplish its mission.

Wondering what was taking the agent so long, Eliza decided to check on her. As she exited to the stair landing, she realized that a window above the stairwell faced the parking area on the side of the doctors' office, and she spotted the woman who had just exited the doctors' front door, getting into an old van with a baby-faced driver. She'd thought the woman was an adult, but the guy looked like a high school kid. She guessed the couple were the beneficiaries of the notorious physicians. Just as Eliza seized a bird's eye view of another patient leaving the doctors' office, the realtor returned with papers.

"Sorry it took so long. I had to get pretty descriptive before the landlady understood that more than a basic cleaning is needed. Her husband told her it was dirty, but he didn't give her the filthy details. She seemed sympathetic when I explained that the tenants need to be close to the hospital for their sick child. She said her brother's son has terrible asthma and the family almost lives at the children's hospital in Philadelphia. I didn't mince words describing the kitchen and bathroom. Maybe I even talked her into new appliances and I do have a rental agreement here if you'd like to take it to the family to sign."

Eliza wanted to kiss the realtor. The location of the apartment couldn't have been more perfect, and she would have taken it even if the rent was higher and nothing was going to be replaced. A good landlord was a bonus. She paid cash for the security, and hurried home to tell the others about NEB's remarkable acquisition.

~ Two ~

It was insanely busy in the labor and delivery ward of D.C. Memorial Hospital on Monday morning. Two scheduled C-sections, two normal deliveries, and an emergency C-section were all happening simultaneously, while Doctor Rourke was dealing with a forty-year-old first-timer who was laboring too long and refusing a C-section. Meanwhile, a foreign diplomat's wife with a history of multiple miscarriages was expected to arrive momentarily, in premature labor.

Just when it seemed there were no nurses to be rounded up from anywhere else in the hospital, Doctor Fox's office called to announce they were transferring a patient for emergency delivery of an extremely premature baby. Eliza Osborn was about to scrub in on the case herself when an exotic looking young woman in purple scrubs appeared. Her nametag read Karida Robbins RN. "Are you the float they promised me an hour ago?" Eliza looked down at the unfamiliar woman, who was as tiny as she herself was tall.

Karida sensed Eliza's urgency. "Got here as soon they freed me up from a surgery, complicated by a resuscitation. Ninety years old; she didn't make it."

"Sorry about your bad day. Have any perinatal experience?"

"I did six weeks in labor and delivery during training. Last year, I floated in Boston Medical Center and attended some high-risk deliveries. I was hoping to become full-time obstetrics there, but my husband's firm just transferred us to D.C. We've only been here a week and today's my first day in this hospital."

Her experience wasn't ideal, but her interest in obstetrics was a plus. Moreover, little Karida Robbins seemed rather self-assured in brand new surroundings. For lack of a better alternative, Eliza decided to send her in on Doctor Fox's case. Her only other available nurse had outright refused to attend.

"Let's get set up," she commanded as she headed towards the one delivery room that wasn't already in action. Karida had to run to match her stride. Exposing her disfigured arm as she rolled up her sleeves to scrub, Eliza was caught off guard by Karida touching the scars and locking eyes with her for an awkward few seconds. Nobody had ever responded like that in an initial encounter. She needed to feel this young nurse out.

"This delivery we're setting up for; it could be for a fetus with no chance of survival. The obstetrician is the Capitol abortionist."

Karida proceeded to check the oxygen gauge without so much as a raised eyebrow. Eliza decided to be more blunt. "If a senator's mistress is dealing with an unintended pregnancy, Doctor Fox is the obstetrician of choice. He'll treat her so-called menstrual irregularity with a little 'cleaning' of the uterus, in his office of posh private suites."

Karida went about checking the wall suction as if she'd just been told the sky is blue. Eliza wondered about her detached reaction. There was still time to send her to another case, but if Dr. Fox's delivery happened to produce a viable baby, two nurses might be needed to assist two patients and two doctors. She sat on a stool so she could get eye to eye with the petite Nurse Robbins.

"Sometimes though, our discreet abortionist gets caught off-guard when a woman misrepresents the duration of her pregnancy."

Karida tilted her head in curiosity.

"Twice in the past, Dr. Fox's 'D&Cs' for 'irregular menstrual bleeding' produced five-month-old fetuses, and on one occasion, we had a baby who survived two days in the NICU before extreme prematurity ravaged his little self. Some of my nurses won't attend Dr. Fox's deliveries."

Karida put her hand on Eliza's shoulder and was about to say something when an ambulance crew burst through the doors with an alarmingly skinny and hysterical girl on a stretcher. Doctor Roland Fox plodded behind with beads of perspiration on his upper lip, in spite of the cool autumn weather. "Glad you're here, Eliza," he said as he gowned. "I need a neonatologist for this one." While donning a cap and mask, he followed Eliza to the intercom. Before she could push the speaker button, he whispered, "Eliza, this is Congressman Mark Wagner's fourteen-year-old daughter. I don't know the other nurse in this room today, but this has got to stay confidential."

Eliza rolled her eyes. "That's really wishful thinking, Roland," she whispered back. "Of the twenty-eight full-time and nineteen part-time nurses that keep this obstetric unit staffed twenty-four, three sixty-five, I have eleven nurses who refuse to work with you, and two of them are working this shift. Now, the neonatal department will also be speculating about your case."

Defeated, Roland returned to the scrub sink as Eliza spoke into the intercom. "Neonatal attending to Delivery Room Seven ASAP. Interns and medical students need not attend."

As the ambulance crew departed, Eliza and Dr. Fox observed Nurse Robbins consoling the teenager and trying to listen for a fetal heartbeat.

"I can't hear the heart. How far along is she?" Karida asked as the physician joined her at the bedside and took his patient's bony hand into both of his own. "Pamela" he said gently, "Please think. It could not have been two months ago that you had a real menstrual period. We can't do our best if we don't have a better idea of when you actually became pregnant."

Pamela put her face in her hands and sobbed inconsolably.

The physician turned to Karida. "She initially reported a period mid-July, so I thought she might be twelve weeks when she first consulted me, just last Wednesday. On an ultrasound we did on Saturday, it looked like she might be closer to seventeen weeks. Now I'm worried that the fetus could be older and very small for age, since it looks like this young lady has been starving herself. Today, right after I dilated her, she said she felt fetal movement. That's when I got worried that she could be farther along than the ultrasound suggested. Then she went into labor, so I decided to transfer her here in case we have a viable baby. I don't intentionally perform late stage abortions."

Pamela's sobbing suddenly turned to screams. Karida propped her up and tried to get her to push, but Pamela used her whole being just to shriek. As Doctor Fox scrubbed, Eliza got paged out of the room. Then another woman in a yellow gown, cap and mask appeared. Doctor Lois Dubroff had only been on the staff of D.C. Memorial for a few months, but she'd been a neonatologist for eight years. She'd met Roland Fox at a staff meeting, and she'd heard the gossip about the abortions that turned out to be live births. "Hello, Doctor Fox. So what's going on here that you needed to pull an attending from the NICU?"

Roland was about to explain when Pamela's cries drowned him out. The physicians observed a tiny head crowning, but it receded back into the uterus. Unable to hear a fetal heartbeat through Pamela's skinny belly, they prepared an electronic lead to attach to the fetal scalp. As they waited for the next contraction and the head to re-emerge, Roland presented his case.

"Sorry to tell you we're dealing with a major unknown here. This mom consulted me five days ago, claiming she missed two periods. An ultrasound suggested the fetus could be about seventeen weeks, but now I'm worried it's older and small for its age. I think this young woman has been trying to conceal or terminate her pregnancy by starving herself. She lost two pounds since I first saw her, just five days ago.

"We gave a sedative in prep for an office D&C, before I noticed her weight loss and started to question fetal age. She seemed almost sedated up until the moment I told her we needed to transfer her to the hospital because her baby's age could be miscalculated. She's been agitated and hysterical ever since. Contractions have been irregular but as frequent as every…"

Pamela shrieked again and made an unsuccessful effort to push. The head appeared just enough for Doctor Dubroff to be able to attach an electrode before returning to the womb. Pamela's screams subsided. Nurse Robbins wiped her tears and spoke softly to her while Dr. Dubroff calibrated the heart monitor.

"The pain will end sooner if you push harder next time," Karida instructed. As the nurse cradled Pamela's shoulders and whispered to her, the doctors observed electronic evidence of a slow, irregular heart rhythm with ominous pauses. The fetus was in grave distress and both physicians knew their decisions in the next few minutes would have enormous impact on multiple lives.

The neonatologist would have a few seconds to assess the newborn's chances for survival, and decide about giving or withholding life support. If features were consistent with a fetal age of twenty-one weeks or younger, there was no chance of survival. If the newborn appeared to be as mature as twenty-four weeks, it was customary to attempt full resuscitation, even with less than a fifty percent chance of a good outcome. Dr. Dubroff's dilemma would be greatest if the fetus appeared to be twenty-two or three weeks old. Most survivors of that age would spend months in intensive care, only to die later or live with overwhelming health problems and families with broken hearts and financial ruin.

During her career, Lois Dubroff had been sued both for resuscitating and not resuscitating fetuses of questionable viability. As she worried about the split-second decision she'd have to make now, she wondered about the teenager who was laboring. The young girl appeared to be extremely distressed, alone, and not at all ready to be the parent of a critically ill child.

Seeing the deteriorating fetal heart rhythm, Doctor Roland Fox's own heart rate accelerated. If this were a wanted child, he would have already rescued it by C-Section. Now, in all probability, there would be severe brain damage if it did survive, and a C-section would leave the teenager with a scar on her belly to remind her of either her dead baby or a chronically ill one.

When Pamela and Mrs. Wagner had presented to his office late last Wednesday afternoon, he had implicitly advised them of all of the potential complications of today's procedure. Now it was evident that neither of them had been able to get past their denial. For the few minutes that he and his nurse had been alone with Pamela, she insisted that she could only be two months pregnant. When they had met with Mrs. Wagner alone, she didn't seem to digest the information that Pamela's irregular periods could be due to pregnancy. She signed the consent form without even pretending to read it.

This morning, when his nurse informed Mrs. Wagner that the possible complication of a live birth had presented, the woman became so distraught that she asked for a sedative. While Pamela was rushed to the hospital, would-be-Grandma Wagner was back in his office, stupefied by her duress.

Roland Fox hoped the neonatologist could make a more objective decision about resuscitation if she didn't know the politics of the situation, but he didn't know her well enough to guess how she'd react to not being told, and he was bothered by Eliza's absence. Nurse Robbins was giving excellent care and had managed to calm Pamela down to the extent that she might be able to work with him, but Eliza would know what to do about revealing the politics to the neonatologist. Eliza had incredibly good intuition about people. He was about to page her when another contraction started Pamela screaming.

"Push, Pamela, push!" Karida commanded as she propped her patient up and hugged her firmly. "You can do this! This pain will end if you just push really hard next time." Pamela cried out but made a successful effort. Doctors Fox and Dubroff watched the tiny head come further into the birth canal before returning to the womb. Birth was imminent now. Each of the physicians wallowed in their distress while watching Nurse Robbins enlist Pamela's cooperation.

Doctor Dubroff prepared for a full resuscitation. She checked the light on the scope that would facilitate placing a tube in the baby's airway to deliver oxygen by a ventilator. She drew up a syringe of a teensy dose of adrenalin she might need to jump-start the heart. She prepared a catheter to be inserted into the baby's umbilical cord vein to administer medicine and nutrition. She checked the heater on the warming table to be sure it was the right temperature. She calibrated the scale to weigh the newborn.

Lois Dubroff was wishing Eliza Osborn could be there too. Although the nursing supervisor never told a physician what to do, she had a way of looking at you that made you rethink your options. Having assisted dozens of doctors perform thousands of deliveries for more than three decades; Eliza had more experience than any of them. She smiled behind her facemask when Eliza re-entered the room and started scrubbing.

Roland Fox got into position as Pamela started shrieking again. Karida propped her up and got her to squeeze her pelvic muscles. Just as her cries crescendoed, a tiny figure slid into the waiting hands of the obstetrician.

"It's a boy," Roland Fox said reflexively as he suctioned amniotic fluid from the little nose and mouth. He clamped and cut the umbilical cord and handed the carrot-sized being to the neonatologist, who dried him with a blanket and placed him on the warmer. Eliza stood by, poised to assist in resuscitation, but in an instant, both women knew the monstrous decision was already made. Baby Boy Wagner weighed less than nine ounces. His immature features suggested he was barely twenty weeks old and too small for his age. He made only a feeble attempt to breathe. Mercifully, the monitor showed that his laboring heart stopped beating within four minutes. All that the neonatologist could do was hug him and let nature take its course. Lois sighed deeply as she cleaned the residual fluids from the still little body. Roland stopped sweating. Eliza looked at the clock to record the time of death. Feelings of relief washed over them briefly, before turning to sadness.

Pamela cried out once more as the obstetrician delivered the placenta. Lois documented the events on a computer as she waited for the young woman to calm down enough to be told of her fetus's death. When it appeared that she was able to listen, the neonatologist approached her with the blanketed bundle in her arms. "Pamela," she said, searching the girl's face for a sign of interest, "I'm terribly sorry to have to tell you that your baby was too young to survive." She paused, trying to discern what this might mean to the teen, but there was no change in Pamela's general state of despair. She continued, "He's perfectly formed. With more time, he would have been a healthy baby."

The teenager's expression turned to one of interest. The neonatologist held the little bundle forward. "Would you like to see him?"

Pamela's eyes widened. She started to shake her head no but then she bit her lip and nodded yes.

Doctor Dubroff cautioned. "Please understand he's very premature, so he's very tiny and his skin is very thin with fuzzy hair. His facial features are not yet fully formed and his color is bad, but he's perfect in every other way."

Pamela extended her arms to receive him. She stared at his face for a minute and then tenderly unwrapped him. For another minute she looked him over, but then she suddenly rewrapped him, cradled him to her chest, and once more, began to cry inconsolably. "I'm so sorry," she said repeatedly as she rocked herself back and forth, clutching the bundle. With tears streaming down her own cheeks, Karida Robbins hugged them both until Pamela was able to settle enough to let them take the fetus.

While Dr. Lois Dubroff and Nurse Eliza Osborn attended to documentation, they watched Pamela cry on the shoulder of Karida Robbins. Dr. Roland Fox slipped out of the room to phone his office to check on Pamela's mother. He looked distracted when Eliza intercepted him in the hallway to suggest that Pamela might need sedation in order to get some rest. Roland wrote the order and contacted the hospital social worker to arrange a meeting of relevant parties. The issue of a live birth would be another source of anguish for this traumatized teen and her family.

As Pamela drifted off to sleep, Doctor Fox asked Karida Robbins if she'd like to join him in the cafeteria for a cup of coffee. He needed to know what this newcomer to the obstetrics ward felt about what she had just witnessed, far more than he needed a snack, and Karida's especially soothing way with his patient had caught his attention.

~ Three ~

Vivian Evans was flabbergasted when the pregnancy test turned positive, though her period was already a week late. She was one hundred per cent certain that she'd never missed a pill. She went straight from school to the pharmacy and bought another test brand. She couldn't sleep just waiting to check Tuesday morning's first urine. When it was also positive, she was devastated. An Internet search said that the home tests weren't always accurate. Blood tests done by a lab were more reliable. She was able to get an appointment with Doctor Rourke the following week.

Greg wouldn't be home until the weekend. Although they talked by phone nightly, she couldn't bring herself to tell him. Not yet, anyway. Maybe the tests were wrong. She was bloated and her breasts hurt and it felt like her period would start any moment. Besides, she had no idea how Greg would react. Since he'd started college, she felt like their relationship was going south.

Her mother had warned her that might happen. "Most eighteen-year-old boys aren't ready to make a life-time commitment," Amelia Evans had said. "When he looks around at all the pretty girls on campus, the temptation to sample will be very strong. Even if he truly loves you, there'll be flirtatious girls who will tempt him to stray; just a function of his age and gender, Vivian. You have to be prepared for the possibility that he might want to play the field. He's a great catch, Honey, and he'll be meeting some very seductive women."

Vivian knew her mother just wanted for her to not get hurt, but her mother really didn't understand how strong their love was. The very first time they met, it was like the earth tilted on its axis. She had a crush on another boy in eighth grade, but by ninth grade, she'd decided he was a jerk. She'd met Greg Thatcher at a party at the end of ninth grade when he was a sophomore, and for more than two years they'd been in love. They both cried on the night before he left to start his economics studies at the University of Delaware. Their plan was for him to come home every other weekend, and for her to visit him on campus on the alternate weekends. She stayed in a sorority guesthouse when she'd visited two weekends ago, but he hadn't come home this past weekend, because he had to write a paper. Except for family stuff, it was the first time they hadn't seen each other on the weekend. He promised he'd be home this Friday night.

Vivian rehearsed over and over again how she'd tell Greg if she was pregnant. She had no doubt they would marry. She knew her parents would help them until she finished high school and he finished college. She'd defer her own education until Greg graduated, and their child was old enough to be in daycare. She'd always thought she wanted to be a doctor like her mother; not a psychiatrist like her mother, but maybe a cancer doctor like her grandfather. One of her childhood friends had been diagnosed with and cured of leukemia when they were in second grade, only to have to fight another cancer when they were in seventh grade. Psychiatrists just talked to crazy people, but her grandfather was out there saving lives.

She just hoped Greg wouldn't pursue a career in politics like her father. For all the status her dad's ascendancy to Congress had brought, she hated being in the public eye. Greg hated it too. Whatever happened in their lives had to be considered in terms of the scrutiny that her father's political career imposed. Yet Greg sometimes talked about getting a law degree and becoming a politician, when he wasn't talking about getting an MBA and becoming a corporate executive. He was so smart, he could be anything he wanted.

Not telling Greg about the possible pregnancy was getting harder and harder, but lately he seemed stressed by his coursework, which just wasn't like him. All through high school he feasted on academic competition, even though their school was full of academically gifted, competitive kids. She presumed college was much harder and she didn't want to add to any anxiety he might be experiencing. Maybe she wasn't pregnant.

Greg was supposed to pick her up at seven on Friday. His last class ended at four-thirty and the drive home could take a few hours. They planned to grab some fast food and go to a movie, but she'd spent hours trying to figure out if her outfit should look light and happy or more serious. She ended up in a short jeans skirt and a petal pink sweater. Blue suede boots reached up her long legs to her knees. A rose pink ribbon and dangly blue earrings adorned her cinnamon colored curls and accentuated her deep blue eyes. It was a much more playful outfit then her usual, more elegant style. She wondered if pregnancy hormones made you think of pink and blue. Her cheeks seemed especially rosy.

Greg called at six-thirty to say he wasn't going to make it until Saturday. His economics professor had divided the class into groups to tackle an assignment, and his group had decided to meet at a local diner right after class to start working on it. They probably wouldn't be done until around eight, and then it would be too late to drive home. Economics was his major so it was important that he go with the group.

Vivian couldn't decide what was upsetting her more: the feeling that she was no longer the most important thing in his life, or her anxiety that an unintended pregnancy could spoil both their lives. If he knew he wasn't coming home two hours ago, why had he waited so long to let her know? She'd spent all that time getting ready. Why was he being so inconsiderate? Then she started wondering what she'd do if she was pregnant and Greg didn't want to get married. That was unthinkable.

Never had she considered becoming a single, unwed mother. Now the possibility was gnawing at her. She cried for a few minutes. Then she went on-line and read about pregnancy for the umpteenth time, but this time, she started reading about abortion. Abortion was not an option of course; not the way she had been brought up. Yet, she wondered why so many people considered it an acceptable way to deal with an accidental pregnancy. The more she read, the more upset she became.

She had a burning desire to talk to her mother, but her parents would be at some campaign function until late. She tried to call her friend Glenna, but concluded she was probably at the movies and wasn't responding to texts. There wasn't anyone else she felt she could confide in. For about an hour, she just laid on the couch, cried, and cuddled with her cat, Nutmeg. She tried to practice her piano piece several times. It was the same concerto for which she had won two competitions, but she couldn't feel the music. Finally, she cried herself to sleep.

Greg had said he'd call her first thing Saturday morning but she didn't hear from him until ten-thirty. He said he needed to go to the library for a few hours but he was sure he'd be home by five and they'd go back to their Friday night plans, only they'd go somewhere nice for dinner.

Vivian tried to tell herself she needed to respect that he was dealing with many demands and she shouldn't assume that his unapologetic manners meant he no longer loved her. She gave herself a good pep talk and tried to bury herself in schoolwork. An hour later she found herself crying on her calculus notes, and she couldn't remember what she'd read. It was only two o'clock.

She heard her mother come home and went to greet her. She felt compelled to talk to her mother though she wasn't at all ready to tell her about the pregnancy. Her entire life had been a lesson in how not to wear her feelings on her sleeve. The psychiatrist in her mother was just too good at picking up on her moods and secrets, and she had thought it was a supreme accomplishment that her intimacy with Greg hadn't been revealed. Although her mother was acutely aware that premarital sex was the norm for her generation, both of her parents held her to a higher standard, and she did not want to disappoint them. Even if her mother was sympathetic, her father would be outraged.

"So how was the movie last night?" her mother asked.

"Actually, Greg didn't make it home last night, so we're going tonight. He had some coursework he had to coordinate with classmates." Vivian tried to sound nonchalant and cheerful. It didn't work.

"Is everything okay with you two?" Amelia Evans asked.

"I'd like to think so, Mom, but you sure were right about long-distance romance being hard. I really miss him."

"So what did *you* do last night?"

"Oh nothing much, some piano practice and schoolwork. I played with Nutmeg and her mousy toy and went to bed early."

Amelia gave her daughter one of those looks that said she knew there was more to tell, and Vivian knew she'd let it all out if she didn't escape. She turned away quickly with the excuse that she had to shower and get dressed. She wondered if her mother had already guessed what was going on. At that moment, a call from her friend Glenna saved her from her need to cry to her mother for help.

~ Four ~

Lorraine Wagner sat restlessly at the bedside of her sedated daughter. She couldn't believe she hadn't noticed how skinny Pamela was. Although this child had seemingly been watching her weight since age ten, along with her older sisters, Lorraine couldn't remember ever thinking she was too thin. Now, the hollow cheeks and protruding collarbones disturbed her.

Had she been *that* inattentive? For how long, she wondered, had she been so oblivious as to what was going on in the life of her youngest daughter, her baby, her *golden* child? Her three older kids all had Lorraine's brunette coloring and their father's stocky physique, but Pamela had somehow managed to inherit her father's pale blue eyes and golden blond hair, and her mother's fashion model figure. She had become a real head-turner by the time she turned thirteen. When had she become so thin? And when had she become so involved with a boy? How could this obedient, scholarly child, the one who had given her the fewest parenting challenges, wind up pregnant at fourteen, during an election no less?

As she stared at the gaunt face and scrawny arms, she wondered if she had been an absentee parent. At the time she had accidentally conceived Pamela, her other kids were thirteen, eleven and eight, and her career was soaring. She was scheduled to terminate this pregnancy when her husband's uncle unexpectedly died, and she had to postpone the appointment. Then her plans to abort were further waylaid by her husband's equally unexpected victory in a primary for the state legislature. Lorraine wound up spending the duration of her pregnancy helping Mark campaign, and she cried a lot.

Mark was elected a few weeks before Pamela was born, but his government salary was only a fraction of what he had earned as a prominent corporate attorney. So when Pamela was six months old, Lorraine resumed her career as a real estate agent, selling high-end properties. Her hours were long but her earnings were lucrative, and with a full-time nanny and three older siblings who loved to look after their baby sister, she never felt that Pamela was missing out on affection.

Pammy had just turned nine when they moved to Washington. Melissa, her oldest daughter, transferred to the University of Maryland so she could still be close to her little sister. Jackson was accepted into the prelaw program at Georgetown, and Lorraine marveled that even though he lived on campus, he still managed to visit his little sister often. Roberta, the least scholarly of the Wagner children, loved Pamela the most, and after completing high school, she attended business school, lived at home, and hovered over Pamela like a mother hen. She had married Edward and moved to Texas just fifteen months ago.

Lorraine had worried about how Pamela would respond to Roberta's departure. The sisters had been very close, but Pammy seemed to have no problems adjusting. She started spending more time with her friends, and until recently, she'd been riding her horse a few times a week. Lorraine's role as her husband's campaign partner had been demanding, and she'd spent little time with her daughter. Now it was apparent that Pamela didn't need her attention. She was getting plenty elsewhere.

Lorraine was lost in thought when Pamela awoke. She watched her mother for a few moments and then burst into tears. "Mommy, I'm so sorry." Her raspy voice was unrecognizable.

Lorraine reached out to hug her but felt too choked up to speak. They embraced and sobbed together for a few minutes.

"I need a drink, Mommy. Can you call the nurse for me?"

It was Eliza who brought the ice chips. "Your mouth must be parched from the sedative, Miss Wagner."

"It is." She sucked on the ice for a few seconds. "Thanks, that really helped. Is Nurse Karida here?"

"She was only here to help out when we were very busy and now she's helping out in another part of the hospital. Is there something I can do for you?"

"I just wanted to thank her; to tell her how much she helped me to not be a coward. I'm afraid I acted very immaturely."

Eliza had to suppress a smile. "Believe me, Miss Wagner, you were braver than many women going through their first delivery. I'll pass your thanks along to Nurse Karida when I see her." Eliza was reminded that she wanted to track that nurse down herself. There was something about Karida she felt drawn to.

With her mouth moister, Pamela took in a big breath and sighed. "Mommy, I know this was a big shock for you and I'm so, so sorry."

Lorraine lifted her daughter's drooping chin and looked at her inquisitively.

"Honest, I really did have a period in July. It wasn't maybe a normal period, but after skipping my period in June, I thought okay, now I'm back to normal. Then I missed it again in August, but since Jeremy and I didn't do anything in July, I didn't even think about pregnancy. How stupid of me. Then, when I missed my period in September, I did one of those home pregnancy tests and that's when I knew."

Lorraine bit her lower lip and stared at her daughter.

"Before I fell asleep, I was telling Nurse Karida why I thought I was only two months pregnant, but she said sometimes there can be some bleeding in the first month or two of pregnancy. That's probably what I had in July, only I thought it was a period. Honest, Mommy, if I had any idea that I was this much pregnant, I would never have done this, and now I've killed my baby."

Pamela's words turned into blubbering. Lorraine hugged her daughter, because it was easier than looking at her. "It's okay, Baby. It's all going to be okay," she lied over Pamela's bony shoulder. When Pamela finally stopped shuddering, Lorraine pulled away and asked "wouldn't you like to tell me about the baby's father?"

Pamela blew her nose and lifted her chin. Her mother hadn't asked her anything about any of her friends for a long time. She used to tell Roberta everything, but now she had to tell her over the phone. Her parents didn't notice how much she was on the phone because they were always on the phone or the computer. Once she told her father she was going out to get a tattoo, just to see if he was paying attention. He continued looking at the computer while saying "you have a good time and don't come home too late, Sweetheart."

"You've met Jeremy Barlow," Pamela began, realizing her mother didn't even recognize his name. "He's Edward's cousin. We met at Roberta and Ed's wedding. His older sister Jenny rents a horse at our stable, that pretty tan mare Honeydo, a few stalls down from Moon Flower's stall. We sometimes ride together and then she brings me home so Claire doesn't have to come get me."

Jeremy had met her parents a few times and she'd talked about him incessantly. Lorraine was nodding but Pamela suspected her mother had no idea who she was talking about. She worried that her mother's awareness and memory were becoming increasingly impaired. "Remember, Jeremy and Jenny came by with Edward and Roberta last Christmas Eve, and he gave me that blue cardigan that I always wear with jeans? He also came over last February when you and Daddy were entertaining the ambassador with the funny name."

Lorraine looked even more puzzled. "And how old is Jeremy?" she asked, mortified by her inability to recall anything about this very important person in her daughter's life.

"Almost sixteen."

"Oh! So way too young to marry!" Lorraine closed her eyes.

"Mommy, Mommy, listen! Jeremy would marry me if we thought it was the right thing. He's a really good person, Mommy, and he's very smart. His family is great too. His parents said they would support us if we wanted to get married, but we're not ready to get married and have kids."

Lorraine gulped at the thought of her daughter having taken this problem to others. Could Pamela think that little of her? What kind of people were these cousins of Edward's, her new son-in-law? "So, Pamela, why didn't you and your smart boyfriend protect yourselves from getting pregnant, let alone all those horrible diseases out there?"

"Well we did mostly use condoms, but just once in May, I thought it was safe, because it was right before my period. Neither of us ever did anything with anyone else, so we had no reason to worry about STIs. Sexually transmitted infections", she clarified for her mother. "And Mommy, I was really careful about keeping track of my cycle, for like six months, so I still don't understand how I got pregnant. I guess you have to be lucky to not get pregnant. I guess I had bad luck like you, Mommy, when you got pregnant with me. Roberta always said I was a fabulous accident."

Lorraine suppressed tears, thinking that her daughter felt unwanted, and that she was an unworthy parent. "Why didn't you tell me the real reason you wanted to see Dr. Fox, Pamela? Don't you think I would have helped you?"

"Because, Mommy, I didn't want you in trouble with Daddy. I thought that if I just had a problem with my periods, then that would be okay. Daddy always says: 'We're a political family. Discretion is the number one rule.' And, Roberta said that the best thing would be if neither you nor Daddy knew."

"Roberta said that?" Lorraine couldn't decide if the heat in her face was due to humiliation or a hot flash. Even her second youngest child perceived her as an incompetent parent, someone to be protected rather than included in a decision as critical as the one her little girl had made. She wondered if she would have done anything differently had she'd been in her daughter's place. The need to protect Mark's political career had dominated every aspect of their lives for the past fifteen years. She was trying to figure out some way to hide the hospital bills, when her thoughts were interrupted by the reappearance of the big, old, scarred nurse and a young, pretty little one bearing dinner trays.

"Well, Miss Wagner, you're looking a good deal better than earlier today," Eliza said. "I did find Nurse Karida for you. Her shift was supposed to have ended an hour ago but she got caught in up in a long surgery case and then she came back to Labor and Delivery, just to check on you."

Lorraine Wagner expressed her gratitude to both nurses and excused herself to make a phone call. Although Congress was expected to be in session late that night with lots of legislation to settle before recess, Lorraine needed to be sure that Mark wouldn't be alarmed if the house was empty when he finally got home. She left a message that Pamela was sleeping over at a friend's house and she'd be doing some late committee work for the Literacy Project. She made a few more calls and offered up a few more excuses regarding appointments. Even the luncheon with the vice presidential candidate on Friday would have to be cancelled if life wasn't back to normal by the end of the week.

Lorraine stepped back into Pamela's room to see her having a lively conversation with the young nurse with whom she seemed enamored. Pamela hadn't touched her food and Lorraine was about to cajole her into eating when Pamela announced that her boyfriend and his family were going to come at 7:30 to decide what to do about the baby.

Lorraine's brain froze. She hadn't given any thought to the baby and couldn't. She felt totally overcome by her need for a martini. "I guess I'll run home and freshen up a bit so I can come back and meet …."

"The Barlows, Mom", Pamela said, and then turned back to her conversation with Nurse Robbins, while Lorraine made a beeline for the door.

~ ~ ~

When she returned two hours later, Lorraine was stunned to find eight people in her daughter's room, and embarrassed to learn that the Barlows had gone to the hospital morgue to see their deceased grandson. Doctor Fox had suggested she might want to do the same when she'd first arrived at the hospital, and the big nurse had offered to accompany her while Pamela was zonked from the sedative, but she'd declined. She just couldn't face a dead baby.

The hospital social worker advised them that because the fetus was alive at birth, that his birth and death needed to be officially recorded, and that the family needed to consider what kind of services or burial arrangements they would want to have, if any. Before Lorraine even started to process that, Doctor Fox recommended she arrange some grief counseling for Pamela and he instructed her to bring her back for a physical exam by the end of the week.

The little nurse, Karida, came over to her and gently clasped her hands over Lorraine's. Her stare was penetrating. "Mrs. Wagner, when I was sixteen I had an experience like what Pamela went through today. Until I got some counseling, I suffered a lot. Please, I beg you, please don't let that happen to your daughter. It's so preventable with good counseling." She got up, gave Pamela a hug, and wrote 'call me' and her phone number on the napkin on Pamela's untouched dinner tray, before leaving the room.

As Eliza made the customary vital signs check and nursing notes, the other hospital personnel departed.

"You're working a terribly long day" Lorraine commented.

"When you're the head nurse," Eliza responded, "long days are routine." Sensing their need for privacy, she also left.

A minister had arrived before Lorraine and had obviously been briefed. "I know this is a big problem for you, Mrs. Wagner, but we may have a solution."

For the first time since they were together, Lorraine Wagner took a hard look at her daughter's boyfriend and his parents. At fifteen, Jeremy seemed physically and socially mature. He was ruggedly handsome but had soft brown eyes that looked lovingly at her daughter. His parents were introduced as John and Wendy. They were a beautiful couple, probably in their late forties. Wendy Barlow came across as warm and genuine, and Lorraine felt like an outsider as she observed her rapport with Pamela. No one mentioned that they had met at Roberta and Edward's wedding, since it was so obvious that Lorraine didn't remember them.

John Barlow said, "I'm so sorry we're seeing each other under these circumstances, Mrs. Wagner. My cousin Edward told us he was marrying into a fantastic family, but this is not the event anyone would have wanted to bring us together. I know this must be shocking for you, and as Pamela has explained, it puts you in a difficult situation with regard to your husband's campaign; but I think we might have a way to keep this secret. My family has a cemetery plot at Potomac Gardens. Reverend Taylor has agreed to conduct a service just for us. It would allow our baby boy to have a proper burial and it would give Pamela and Jeremy a meaningful way of dealing with this tragedy, without having to involve Representative Wagner. That is, depending on what you think."

Jeremy approached Lorraine with downcast eyes. "I'm so sorry, Mrs. Wagner. I know Pam's biggest fear through all of this was that it would embarrass her father. We would never have gone to Doctor Fox if we had known she was so far along. I'm really sorry, Mrs. Wagner."

Lorraine found herself speechless. She didn't know whether to hate these people for conspiring, or appreciate them for taking responsibility.

She did know that she'd do almost anything to conceal the mess from her husband.

"So we'll conduct a private graveside service for Walter Barlow Wagner at seven o'clock on Wednesday morning," the minister said.

Lorraine got a chill down her spine when she learned that Pamela and Jeremy had named their baby. She felt so frazzled she wasn't even sure if she could drive herself home.

~ ~ ~

Karida Robbins visited Pamela Wagner in her hospital room before starting her shift the next morning.

"Will you come to my baby's funeral? Pamela asked. "You are the only person in the world who kind of knew him."

Karida felt Pamela's overwhelming sense of loss. She'd try to follow up with this case to make sure this sweet young girl got appropriate help. She'd ask the head nurse Eliza to help her arrange the time off to attend.

~ Five ~

On Tuesday morning, the labor and delivery ward of D.C. Memorial Hospital was remarkably quiet, as peaceful as the previous day had been hectic. There were six new moms going home with healthy babies, an adorable young couple in a birthing room having an easy delivery, and only two admissions for premature labor.

Eliza Osborn was especially grateful for the calm. She was recovering from yesterday's double shift and she'd slept poorly. She'd spent the night fighting with her conscience about using the Wagner case for NEB's purposes. Her little cache of Pro-Choice activists referred to themselves as Nobody Else's Business, but "NEB" was committed to making it everybody's business if an associate of an Anti-Choice politician exercised choice. Pamela Wagner was the perfect case, except she hated to involve a girl as young and as sweet as Pamela.

She pondered what would be the worst outcome for the teenager; that in despair over ruining her father's career, she'd commit suicide? Eliza dismissed the idea. If Pamela was the suicidal type, she'd be just as likely to kill herself over having her abortion turn out to be a live, and then, a dead baby. Eliza perceived Pamela to be more of a survivor, and maybe even a fighter. You could tell a lot about a woman by how she got through her first delivery, especially one as unexpected and tragic as this one.

She'd cry no tears for Congressman Wagner's political death, should that occur. Eliza knew that if Mark Wagner had his way, tens of thousands of girls like Pamela would wind up deliberately or accidentally taking their own lives in despair over unintended pregnancies.

She'd watched too many women bleed to death and others suffer horrendous self-poisonings in her early years as an obstetric nurse, when the illegality of abortion had relegated it to the profiteering butchers in the back alleys.

Maybe a Pro-Life nut would kill Pamela. That was too scary an idea and she quickly supplanted it with thoughts of the potential benefits of exposing the case. Pamela might grow up to become a strong voice for choice. Maybe Mark Wagner would publicly compromise on the issue and turn his party in a new direction. Perhaps Lorraine Wagner would duck out of her husband's shadow and support Pamela's decision. Eliza hoped that somewhere within that troubled soul that Mrs. Wagner was displaying, there was a nurturing mother.

Eliza was still conflicted when Doctor Fox wrote a discharge order for Pamela early Tuesday morning. She was pushing Pamela down the hall on her mandatory wheelchair ride, when they passed a stretcher on which another very young, hysterical, and very pregnant girl was on her way to a delivery room. In the crowded elevator the nurse and her patient remained silent, but as Eliza pushed Pamela to the curb where her mother's car was waiting, the fourteen-year-old remarked, "I wonder who will be sadder: me, because I don't have my baby, or that girl on the stretcher who's about to have one?"

The young girl with the bursting belly was still on a stretcher in the hall when Eliza got back to her ward. While another nurse was fastening an ID bracelet to her wrist, Eliza read the transport note.

Fourteen-year-old Anya Linitsky broke water in eighth grade homeroom this morning, to the shock of her teacher and classmates. She reportedly lives with her older sister and the sister's boyfriend who work in a factory and couldn't be reached. The phone number the school had for her father was disconnected. The vice-principal signed the transport consent. She said Anya's only been a student there since September and her attendance has been poor. The school she transferred from reported that her grades feel off sharply in seventh grade when her parents separated and her mother moved back to Belarus. She was living with her father then, but it was her sister who enrolled her in this school.

Vital signs were stable during transport with contractions about every five minutes. From what little we could get her to say, she doesn't know when her last period was and she's had no prenatal care.

Upon returning the wheelchair to the unit desk, Eliza made extra noise placing Pamela Wagner's chart in the discharge rack. As she hoped, Cherise, the nosy desk clerk, quickly retrieved the chart to see who was so important a patient that the head nurse had been pushing a wheelchair. Cherise had proven herself to be a serious busybody within a week of arriving on Eliza's ward. She was also smart and efficient and she went out of her way to be helpful to nurses that would schmooze with her. If given really juicy tidbits about patients, she'd be extra helpful. Eliza had been fascinated by how quickly this manipulator had half her staff congregating at her desk and sharing cookie recipes. She also wondered if Cherise's insatiable appetite for gossip might prove useful to NEB.

In spite of federal legislation to promote patient privacy, it was almost impossible to suppress leaks about the health issues of prominent people. Even the most powerful Washingtonians, discreetly admitted to private facilities, could expect to see their gallbladder status make national headlines. Yet Cherise's penchant for gossip was excessive. Just last week, when one of the federal appeals court justice's wives was admitted for ovarian cancer, Eliza overheard Cherise blabbing about it on her cell phone. When an obstetric patient received a giant bouquet from a White House official, Cherise leaked it without saying the man was the expectant grandfather, and not a lover.

While documenting Anya's vital signs, Eliza covertly watched Cherise pour through Pamela's chart. As soon as the desk clerk thought she was out of earshot, Eliza heard her ask another nurse if she knew who Pamela Wagner was. The clerk might be worth putting up with as a cover.

Eliza checked out the schedule and with all still relatively quiet, except for poor shrieking Anya who was being examined by the chief resident, she took a rare out-of-the-hospital break. From the privacy of her car, she called Rita Rodriguez on a disposable phone. Although Rita could be on an out-of-town assignment, and they might have to feed another reporter, this story was so up Rita's alley that she'd probably catch the first plane back to Washington if they could just get the word to her.

Rita Rodriguez had become the hottest journalist in Washington since Woodward of Watergate. She had it all: pretty face, voluptuous figure, exceptional talent as a photographer, and a biting style of writing. She could get answers out of people who typically wouldn't give a reporter the time of day. Along with first-rate journalism training and a generous helping of political savvy, Rita's gifts enabled her to grab front-page bylines within a few months of attaining a position with the *Washington Chronicle*. She also exhibited a bold feminist perspective.

Luck was on NEB's side. Eliza was able to get through to Rita on the first try. She raised her husky voice an octave and traded in her Jamaican accent for a British one. "If you want to see the results of an abortion involving the family of Congressman and Pro-Life activist Mark Wagner, be at the Potomac Gardens Cemetery tomorrow morning at seven a.m. Look for a small group of people following a tiny coffin, and Ms. Rodriguez, it would be best if you could have some pretense for being there."

Eliza contemplated giving the same tip to journalist Fritz Anders of the *Baltimore Record*. Anders was pretty keen on stories like this and there was always the possibility that Rodriguez would have a conflicting assignment. Ultimately, Eliza concluded that more reporters might scare the funeral party away. Besides, Rita's story would likely be from a humanistic standpoint. Fritz was more apt to play politics to the extent that NEB's goals could get lost in the fireworks. Rita was going to get an exclusive.

Rita did have a conflict. Earlier that day, she'd received a tip about a planned protest in an exclusive private high school. Apparently, in attempt to ensure safety for the offspring of political bigwigs, the school had banned backpacks. Then the boys complained that they had to lug their books in their arms, while the girls were getting away with carrying theirs in large purses; so the administration said that only small purses could be used to carry essentials like sanitary napkins. That resulted in a security guard asking girls to show the contents of their purses, which prompted both boys and girls to start wearing necklaces made out of tampons, and the student who started that protest was suspended. Now the rest of the students were going to protest the suspension. As entertaining as the story was, it paled next to the tip she had just received. She decided to do a little pre-investigation and arrived at Potomac Gardens in the late afternoon.

Carrying flowers that she left on tombstones whenever someone looked her way, Rita located three grave diggings in progress, including a little one. She used binoculars to determine that the small grave was on a family plot. On the biggest headstone, it said "Martin Barlow, 1924-2002."

Then by sheer fortune, she observed a tombstone being set down by cemetery workers just a few plots away from Martin Barlow. Before it was draped, she was able to see the name: Harry Lyle Holmes, 1911-2008. Ninety-seven years old, she thought; this man had lived long enough for her to have a chance of finding something newsworthy about him. A quick smart phone search turned up a bonanza. Harry Lyle Holmes had been a university history professor from 1939 until 1990. He was practically an institution himself. His career and death could certainly justify a news piece and give her an excuse for being in the cemetery. There was no doubt in her mind which story she was going after. She passed the tip about the tampon demonstration to another reporter and started researching Martin Barlow. She found his obituary in the newspaper files and learned he had been a postal worker and was survived by two sons. There were no clues as to how the Barlows might be related to a congressman's dead baby. She hoped her photos would enable her to piece it all together.

Working into the night, Rita was able to reach a few older faculty members and learn enough about Harry Holmes to rough out a poignant piece about him and the role of American History in the college curriculum. She spent most of her night studying up on Congressman Mark Wagner. By ten p.m. she knew how he had voted on every piece of important legislation that had come across the House floor for the past six years. She had also cased out some information about his wife Lorraine and her work with the Literacy Project, and about the congressman's four children. Most conveniently, she had found a photo in his home state newspaper of his family attending the wedding of his daughter Roberta the previous summer.

Before heading for bed, Rita went to her garage to set up "Cameron," a blow up doll who sat in the passenger seat of her car, and whose head neatly concealed a video camera with a giant telephoto lens. Though not deceptive from close up, from a distance, Rita could secretly shoot reams of film.

~ ~ ~

Wednesday morning was blustery and cold. Wearing a gray trench coat, Rita arrived at the cemetery at six-thirty. Although a security guard had been advised to question any one attending the Barlow burial, he wasn't concerned that the pretty woman was early to attend the ceremony for Professor Holmes. With Cameron in the trunk, Rita explained that she had to pick up an elderly attendee, and she wanted to make sure she knew where the plot was in case she arrived late for the ceremony.

She parked and got Cameron and some still cameras set up, just as she saw cars approaching the Barlow plot. The previous afternoon she had located a great vantage point on a road that was higher up than the area where the small grave had been dug, and her silver car was somewhat concealed from below by a large tombstone.

Four cars pulled up near the small grave. Two men, one quite young, and a woman got out of a station wagon and the men took a little casket out of the back. A petite woman got out of an old hatchback with Massachusetts plates, and a man who got out of a jeep was dressed as a clergyman. From a luxury SUV exited two more people who Rita recognized from her research as Mark Wagner's wife and daughter. Representative Wagner was nowhere to be seen.

Rita took about ten minute's worth of video and several dozen snapshots as the clergyman spoke. Although the visuals were excellent, the voices were being blown away by the wind and Rita hoped the amplifier on the camcorder had picked them up. She could see through the telephoto that the women and the younger man were crying. The tiny casket was lowered into the ground and a bouquet was placed where the tombstone would eventually sit. It was a very brief ceremony.

While the attendees slowly drove away, Rita filmed their license plates and then quickly tossed her equipment into the back seat. She succeeded in tailing the SUV to one of the many D.C. private schools where the privileged offspring of the elite received their education, and where Lorraine Wagner dropped Pamela off. She then tailed Mrs. Wagner as she drove to her residence in an affluent suburb. She parked down the block and reviewed the photos she had taken with an old Polaroid. She selected the picture that best showed the Wagners' faces. On her professional letterhead she wrote:

Dear Mrs. Wagner,

As a reporter for the Washington Chronicle, *I happened to be at
the Potomac Gardens Cemetery this morning to do a story on the
recently deceased, esteemed American History professor, Harry Lyle
Homes, and I observed your graveside service. While I'm terribly sorry
that someone dear to you has suffered an untimely death, I'm also
hoping that you would be willing to speak with me about it to avoid
speculation. Please feel free to call me at the above number at your
convenience.*

Respectfully,
Rita Rodriguez

She put the note and photo in an envelope, addressed it, and slipped
it through the slot of the locked mailbox at the foot of the Wagner's
gated driveway. Then she took off to do more research on the Barlows,
contact the District's vital statistics office to see if a death certificate
had been filed, and seek counsel from her editor about this potentially
explosive story. She wanted to be absolutely certain she didn't mishan-
dle it, or put anyone on the newspaper's board, who might be a friend
of the congressman, in a compromised position.

~ Six ~

Gregory Thatcher wasn't relishing spending Saturday night with Vivian Evans. Though he thought he might still love her, he felt an overwhelming attraction to Colleen. She was just so hot with her delicate features, big turquoise eyes, ample curves and willowy limbs. Even in a simple white blouse and jeans she looked more seductive than all of the co-eds wearing sexier clothes. Vivian was a pretty girl too, but she didn't exude the sex appeal that emanated from Colleen.

Greg was blown away the very first Monday of the term when she walked into the classroom. When she sat down next to him, his heart fluttered. It took him a minute to collect his senses, and then he noticed just about every other guy in the room was staring at her. So were most of the girls. She acted like she wasn't aware of any of it, yet there was no doubt she knew she had that effect on people. He wondered what it must be like to have people ogling you like that all the time. The dude sitting on the other side of her had a slack jaw and was almost drooling. When the beauty gave him a dazzling smile, and asked him to plug in her laptop, Greg's whole body flushed. It took all of his energy to turn his attention to the professor when he introduced himself to the new freshmen. That night, Greg had to borrow his roommate's notes, because he missed most of the lecture. He could only think about Colleen.

He passed her in the hallway on Tuesday, and she smiled at him. He stopped and watched her walk away and observed others gawk.

He got to his economics class as early as he could on Wednesday. There were only three other students in the room when he tried to plot how to seat himself so that she might wind up next to him again. He opted to take the same seat as he had on Monday and he put his backpack on the seat next to him. There were at least a dozen empty seats when Colleen entered the room. He watched her look over the options and felt his heart race when she came towards him. "Is this taken," she asked. Her voice was surprisingly deep and melodic. He hadn't noticed that on Monday. He rushed to empty the chair while trying to look unfazed. "No. Please. Here, let me plug your laptop in." He was surprised by the sound of his own voice. He had unconsciously made it deeper.

The professor began speaking and Colleen started typing like a machine. Greg's fingers tripped and stumbled over his keyboard. He was desperately trying to follow the lecture, but the fact that this gorgeous girl had chosen to sit next to him, twice, kept hijacking his brain. He found himself looking critically at the other guys in the room and thinking he might just be the best looking one there. Maybe he'd have a chance. His fantasies ran wild, and again he came away from the class hoping his roommate would share notes. He told his roomie, "She could get any guy on this campus she wants. I'm just lucky I already have a pretty girlfriend. I'd have to be crazy to even want to be with a girl like that. The jealousy would kill me. She'll probably wind up with some snooty upper classman anyway."

Colleen took a different seat on Friday and he was crushed, but it made it easier for him to pay attention in class, and then drive home to see Vivian. She was so much more real he told himself. She was his soul mate. Colleen was probably a stuck up bitch anyway. Vivian was pretty, super smart, and she sincerely loved him. It also didn't hurt that her father was a powerful senator, and could possibly be of great help to his future. Even if he could get it on with Colleen, she'd maybe go off with someone of greater status and break his heart. He needed to be content with Vivian.

The following week he chose different seats for each class and did his best to ignore Colleen, until she sat next to him again on a Friday. He wondered if ignoring her had piqued her interest. Before the professor required their attention, they chatted.

"So where are you from?" Colleen asked first.

"Silver Springs, Maryland. How about you?"

"New Jersey. Short Hills. What are you majoring in?"

"Economics for now, but I might switch to pre-law. And you?"

"Business administration. I used to want to be a lawyer, but I've come to the conclusion that law's too contentious. I'm more of a lover than a fighter."

Just as Colleen's innuendo gave him a rush, the professor began the lecture. Again, Greg found himself unable to pay attention. He so wanted to ask her for a date, but Vivian would be arriving that night for the weekend. Then it occurred to him that maybe it would be like playing hard-to-get if he didn't ask her out. She probably got asked out a dozen times a day, so maybe the guy who didn't ask her out would be more interesting. He'd never had to get into these kinds of strategies before. Having a steady girlfriend through high school had been satisfying, but now he felt unprepared for the dating game. He hoped Colleen might even see him parading Vivian around campus.

The following Monday he saw Colleen walking with a guy who had to be on the football team. The man's neck was as thick as Greg's chest. He found a program for the U of Delaware's Fightin' Blue Hens, and sure enough, the dude was pictured as a junior and an offensive lineman. That made it a whole lot easier for Greg to enjoy Vivian's companionship for the next two weekends. His fantasies had been squelched.

Then, it seemed that Colleen was making an effort to sit next to him again, and each day that she did, she seemed friendlier. When he asked her after a Friday class to go to dinner, he was totally ready to be rejected and thunderstruck when she said yes. Next, they went to the football game on Saturday afternoon, followed by a study date on Sunday. He felt horrible about lying to Vivian about having to stay on campus to write a paper, but the guilt wasn't preoccupying him nearly as much as the pride and joy he felt walking around campus with Colleen.

He was all set to tell Vivian that he needed to break it off, when he again saw Colleen walking with another football type. It nearly killed him. How could he throw away the good relationship he already had for the tiny chance that he might wind up with this heartbreaker? He'd probably hate himself if he broke up with Vivian, Colleen didn't work out, and then Vivian found someone else. He had to give up on Colleen. It wasn't worth the agony she was causing him. He made up his mind to forget about her. Then, his economics professor put both of them into a study group on the Friday afternoon he was supposed to go home to see Vivian, and he got those vibes from Colleen that maybe she was interested. They did another study date on Saturday. It took every fiber of his being to pull himself away and drive home to spend the evening with Vivian, but it also felt like it fit into his hard-to-get strategy when he told Colleen he had a prior commitment for that night. He just hoped that she didn't too.

He wrestled with himself the entire time he was in the car. He hated himself for being unfaithful to Vivian, but he also felt that even if he didn't wind up in a relationship with Colleen, he really didn't want to be tied down anymore. If Colleen vanished tomorrow, he'd still like to be free, not only to date, but just to have more time to concentrate on his schoolwork. These weekend commitments were hamstringing him in too many ways. It wasn't fair to Vivian he rationalized. They were just too young when they fell in love. There was so much more of the world to experience. It didn't make sense for either of them to be so locked in at this stage of life. By the time he got to her house, he was resigned to tell her it was over.

~ Seven ~

Immediately after the burial, Karida Robbins reported to work. She was sent to surgical services, where a total hip replacement was getting underway. Karida didn't really like joint surgeries. Orthopedists worked with saws, drills, glues and screws, and she felt more like a carpenter than a nurse. Although this poor limping person would be able to walk well again, Karida wanted to be a nurse where life begins, on the obstetrics ward of D.C. Memorial, working with a wise old pro like Eliza Osborn. She didn't think she'd really like nursing in a doctor's office, but Doctor Roland Fox had invited her to accompany him to the cafeteria after the Pamela Wagner case, and before their time together ended, he had made her a very lucrative offer to work in his private practice.

Like most health professionals, Karida had trained in hospitals and she was under the impression that office practice would be boring. Prior to this offer, she'd never even thought about working in a doctor's office, and she felt conflicted. When the hip procedure ended early, she had an hour break before she'd have to scrub in on a knee case. Karida seized the opportunity to return to labor and delivery with the hopes she could speak to Eliza. She had a feeling that the nursing supervisor there would give her honest advice. It was nice to be wanted in more than one place, but she wasn't sure where she belonged.

According to the clerk at the desk, Eliza was attending a C-section, but she'd be done shortly. While waiting, Karida found herself eavesdropping on the clerk's end of a phone conversation that stunned her, because it was obviously about Pamela Wagner. The clerk was telling someone that Miss Wagner had been transferred by ambulance from Doctor Fox's office, that no one was with her, and that she delivered a very premature baby who died shortly after birth. The clerk then said "I don't know" a few times before hanging up.

Karida identified herself to the clerk as the nurse who had assisted in the Wagner case, and trying to seem just curious, she asked who was inquiring about this patient.

"That was Rita Rodriguez from the *Washington Chronicle.*" Cherise couldn't conceal her excitement. "She said she came across the baby's death certificate at the D.C. Health Department this morning, and it said the baby was born and died here, so she was just checking the facts. Did you know that the mother is the daughter of a congressman?" Cherise said, as though she was an authority on the subject.

"I certainly did," Karida responded without any attempt to mask her anger. "Don't you know that you have absolutely no business giving that kind of information out to anyone?"

Cherise looked indignant. "I didn't think someone from the *Washington Chronicle* is just anyone. The reporter already knew the baby died. She even knew his name. I thought it was the responsible thing to do to give her the actual facts. You do know who Rita Rodriguez is, don't you?"

Karida didn't, and she was about to chastise the clerk some more when Eliza approached the desk. Surprised to see Karida, Eliza was delighted for the opportunity to find out how the burial of the Wagner baby had gone. She was also intrigued as to what was the source of friction between the nurse and the desk clerk, having observed their less than cordial interaction.

"How nice to see you again, Nurse Robbins," Eliza greeted her. "I wanted to thank you for how well you handled that case you got called in on here on Monday. If you have a minute, I'd like to speak with you in my office."

Karida was glaring so fiercely at Cherise that the desk clerk was relieved when the two nurses headed for the tiny cubicle in the back of the nursing station that served as Eliza's sanctuary. Once a storage closet, it was windowless with minimal furnishings. Still, Eliza was grateful to have any private space in the old, overcrowded building.

"What was that about?" she asked, nodding towards the reception desk as soon as she closed the door.

Karida quickly composed herself. "Well, I came to see you because I wanted to ask your opinion about a job offer I received from Doctor Fox, but first, I have to tell you: that woman at the desk just gave some newspaper reporter details about Pamela Wagner's delivery."

"She did what?" Eliza did her best to look horrified.

Karida relayed as much of the telephone conversation as she could.

"Are you sure it was Rodriguez of the *Chronicle?*"

"I'm pretty sure that's who she said. Who's Rodriguez anyway?"

Eliza quickly summarized the smashing success of the young reporter and then asked Karida if she had noticed anyone else at the baby's burial. Karida said she hadn't, but then realized that she hadn't looked around. The cemetery was very quiet and it hadn't occurred to her that someone might be there to spy.

Eliza asked Karida if she had told anyone about attending the burial.

"Well my husband Peter knew, but he's an attorney and he certainly understands patient confidentiality. He also knows I'm worried about Pamela Wagner. He'd never go blabbing to a reporter about something like this."

"Are you certain he didn't tell a coworker?"

Karida's expression turned to one of concern. She wasn't certain of what he might have said to another lawyer. Eliza seemed determined to find out how a reporter could be onto this story. She explained how much trouble the desk clerk had been in her short time on the job and advised Karida that the confidentiality violation could not go unreported. The clerk was a shameless gossip who had no business working in this setting. She asked Karida to document what she had heard and submit it to the Clerical Services Supervisor.

Karida looked dismayed, and Eliza realized that as a brand new employee, it would be awkward for her to file such a report. "I'm sure this is very uncomfortable for you, Karida, but did you know that Pamela Wagner's father is a prominent Anti-Choice politician, and if Pamela's choice got publicized, it could be disastrous for her and her family? I'd report Cherise myself but I wasn't present to hear her talking to the reporter, so I have to leave that up to you."

"Poor Pamela!" Karida responded, looking genuinely upset. "I knew her father was a congressman, but I had no idea he was Anti-Choice. It sounds like her situation is much more complicated than I realized."

"Very much so," Eliza confirmed. She said she was more than willing to discuss Doctor Fox's job offer, but as time was running out on Karida's break, the two women agreed to meet for dinner. Eliza learned that Karida's husband Peter would be leaving for Europe that evening for an international law case. Karida learned that Eliza was a widow who lived alone in an apartment near the hospital. Her husband, a career army physician, was killed in the Gulf War in 1990. They would meet at Eliza's after their shifts.

As usual, Eliza didn't get off work when her shift ended. She had no time to cook, but picked up some takeout on her way home. Karida showed up with a bottle of wine. It would have been difficult to say which of them was more anxious to speak with the other. Karida had a feeling that Eliza was the wise and sympathetic mother she always wished she had. Eliza had a strong premonition that Karida, and the offer from Roland Fox, would be the best break NEB was ever going to get. They talked late into the evening.

"I have to ask you, Karida, what's your ethnic background? I'm usually good at figuring these things out, but with you, I can't even venture a guess."

Karida laughed. "That's me, Ms. Ethnic Mystery. No one can figure it out because I'm the ultimate mutt. My father's mother is a blue-eyed blond from Denmark and his father is Persian. We stopped saying we were Iranian right after nine-eleven. Before I married Peter, my last name was Hassein, and I have to admit, my life's been easier since I became Karida Robbins. My mother's mother was half Cherokee and half Irish, and my mother's father was Korean. I never met them. They both died before I was born. My mother looks more Asian than I do, and it's super weird how none of the kids in my family look alike. We're all different colors with different shaped eyes and hair textures. My little sister looks like a Persian version of my Danish grandmother."

"You kind of look like someone I've seen, but I can't figure out who."

"Alyssa Ogawa, I've been told."

Eliza shrugged. "Who?"

"The nurse from TNG."

"Pardon my ignorance, Karida, but what's TNG?"

"*Star Trek: The Next Generation*. Ever watch it?"

"Sorry! I have to admit I stopped watching *Star Trek* after they retired Captain Kirk and Mr. Spock. What were all those other Star Trek shows?"

"I grew up watching TNG which ran from '87 to '94. It was the character of Alyssa Ogawa that first influenced me to be a nurse. Then there was *Deep Space Nine* until '99. Then *Star Trek: Enterprise* from 2001 to 2005."

Eliza interrupted. "Okay, are you what they call a Trekkie?"

"Totally! My husband too! We even scheduled our move to Washington so we could go to the Trek Trak convention in Atlanta before we came here. Did you know Senator Obama is a Trekkie? So are Colin Powell, Al Gore, Arnold Schwarzenegger, Tom Hanks, and Angelina Jolie, just to name a few. We saw Ben Stiller at the convention."

"Wow! I must say that's all news to me. But if I never saw the nurse Alyssa on *Star Trek*, why is it that you remind me of her?"

"Oh, maybe because the actress that played her, Patti Yasutake, shows up on TV shows like *ER, Gray's Anatomy, Bones,* and some others. I don't think I look like her now, but maybe a little when she was younger.

"Anyway, what I really want to ask you is if there's any possibility of a position on your ward. I've worked just about every service, and obstetrics is what I like best."

Eliza responded that she would have loved to offer Karida a position but couldn't see that any of the current staff was leaving anytime soon, and there were already some nurses with seniority waiting to transfer to Eliza's ward if a position opened up. Also, the birth rate had trended downward in the past two years, so it was unlikely that new obstetric positions would be created at D.C. Memorial or other Capitol hospitals.

Eliza was curious as to how Roland Fox had approached her and Karida explained that when she and the physician left Pamela Wagner's room after her mother arrived, Doctor Fox had invited her to grab a snack in the cafeteria with him. He complimented her on the way she had handled the case, and told her he was looking for someone to take the place of one of his long time staff who was retiring. He told her about the abortions he performed, and offered her an extremely competitive salary. What Karida wanted to know from Eliza was more about Doctor Fox's reputation and character.

Eliza had known Roland Fox since he was a resident training at D.C. Memorial. She praised him as being very competent and caring. However he was widely known as an abortionist and on several occasions, violent right-to-lifers had victimized him. Someone had thrown Molotov cocktails into his office twice, and he and some of his staff had lived with death threats during the 1980's. He was however, totally committed to the Pro-Choice movement. Every hospital social worker in Washington knew that if a poor rape victim needed his brand of help, they could call him.

Eliza went on to explain that the reason Roland Fox was so committed to the Pro-Choice movement was because his sister had died at the hands of an illegal abortionist when he was a college student in 1970, three years before *Roe v. Wade* gave American women the right to choose.

"Roland's sister carried the gene for hemophilia which affected her first-born son. Her little boy suffered a serious brain bleed from bumping his head at age two. When she inadvertently became pregnant again, she and her husband decided they couldn't deal with the possibility of having another child with hemophilia. They were spending every penny they had to care for their little boy who was very disabled, and they were emotionally and financially exhausted. The abortionist she was able to find caused her to suffer a fatal blood clot. Roland and his wife took over the care of her brain-injured son, who bled to death a year later when he cut his knee.

"As soon as *Roe v. Wade* got through the court, Roland Fox made the decision to prevent other families from suffering the tragedy that his had. Ironically, it was also about this time that the clotting factor that could prevent a hemophiliac from bleeding to death from a minor injury became widely available, but it was too late for Roland's family."

Eliza was dramatically frank as she informed Karida that Roland Fox was a controversial figure in D.C. and that taking a position in his practice could be dangerous; but Karida didn't seem frightened by the warning. She said she knew that working in his office could make her a target, but just living in D.C. could also make her the victim of violence. Before she and Peter moved, they learned that the nation's capitol had one of the highest crime rates in the country, but they were determined to not live in fear.

Karida said she had great respect for doctors like Roland Fox who put their own safety on the line to protect the rights of others, and that she had a strong commitment to preserving the right to choose. She went on to confide in Eliza that she was really bothered by what she'd learned about Pamela Wagner's situation. She found out from a web search that Pamela's father was one of the politicians who wanted to reverse *Roe v. Wade.* This had made her feel an even stronger bond to the teenager who had exercised her rights. However, Karida was just as bothered by the fact that this privileged young girl had the means to seek an abortion, while many other troubled teens didn't have the resources to jump through the hoops that politicians like Mark Wagner kept putting in their way. While she didn't want to see Pamela hurt anymore than she already was, she said she felt a sense of satisfaction that a reporter had found out about it, and that Pamela's father's politics would be challenged. "I read that this Election Day, there are states with propositions that will make it really hard for a woman to obtain an abortion. What does that do to a woman who has already anguished over the realization that she is unable to provide for a child?"

Eliza was feeling enormously gratified that she had pursued a connection to Karida Robbins. She was pretty certain that NEB was going to get a huge boost from the association, but she needed to test the potential recruit further.

"You know, Karida, working for Roland Fox might someday give you the opportunity to expose a politician who has different standards for his own wife and daughter than for other people's families. What would you do if you had the chance to help the Pro-Choice movement by exposing a case like Pamela's?"

Karida's placid demeanor evaporated. She furrowed her brow and seemed to squirm in her chair. "Oh boy! I don't know what I would do in that situation. It would be horribly unfair to the poor woman who came to her doctor trusting in confidentiality. Then again, it might be foolish to not seize the opportunity, especially if it was a case like the

Wagner's, where the politician was actively trying to take away the right to choose. I'd like to be able to say I would never do such a thing, but the Wagner case would be very tempting. I don't really know what I'd do. What would you do, Eliza?"

"Well, Karida, I'm not the one who's looking at a potential job in the office practice of an abortionist. It's a lot more private than a hospital and no political relative ever voluntarily shows up in a hospital to terminate her pregnancy. The Wagner case is a very rare exception." Eliza wondered if Karida suspected that she had something to do with exposing Pamela's story. "Oh, the Wagner case was tempting all right. I might have considered leaking it, if the hospital blabbermouths hadn't already done so. It's rare that the grapevine doesn't expose secrets of VIPs. One staff member tells their spouse who tells a coworker, and so it goes. That's why people go to doctors like Roland Fox. If he didn't have a reputation for protecting their privacy, they'd go out of town.

"Your situation there will be very different from mine in the hospital. The dilemma would come up with greater frequency and you, as the source of an information leak, would be easier to identify than the hospital grapevine. You'd not only be at risk for losing your job, but also your nursing license. You could get sued for personal damages and it's even possible that a really unscrupulous politician would take you out. A lot of these Anti-Choice radicals, who wouldn't dream of allowing an embryo to perish, have no problem killing fully developed humans for their cause. Who knows what even Mark Wagner is capable of? Politicians sometimes make pregnant girlfriends disappear. Do you think it would be worth the risks?"

Eliza studied Karida's face as she delivered her warnings. Karida didn't look as frightened by the notion that an Anti-Choice nut might try to kill her as she looked guilty when Eliza mentioned that a hospital worker might give a secret away to a spouse. After a minute of appearing turned off by the conversation, she tilted her head in a way that made Eliza think she hadn't yet completely closed the door on the subject.

"You've really challenged me, Eliza. I took an ethics course in nursing school but no one ever asked me a question like that, and I have some soul searching to do. I do really have very strong feelings about the right to choose, and about people who try to force their beliefs on others."

Eliza ventured, "May I ask you about the experience you had that you told Mrs. Wagner was similar to Pamela's. You said it's why she needs counseling."

A sad expression came over Karida's face and tears welled up in her eyes. Eliza grabbed a box of tissues as her new friend composed herself to talk about her personal history with abortion. Karida was the oldest of three children. Her parents both grew up poor and had worked extremely hard to climb into the ranks of the middle class. She hardly knew her father because he had worked two full-time jobs ever since she could remember. As soon as Karida was deemed mature enough, at age eleven, to baby sit for her siblings, her mother took on a job as a delicatessen clerk daytime, and in the evening, she worked in a hospital laundry. The children were all good students and her parents were determined to be able to give them a chance to go to college.

Karida spent all of her adolescence trapped at home as the babysitter. Then, when she was fourteen, the family of Peter Robbins moved into the house next door, and she and Peter became inseparable companions. Although he was two years ahead of her in school, they connected when they realized they were both fanatical *Star Trek* fans. They studied together every night, when they weren't watching current and rerun *Star Trek* episodes with Karida's little sister and brother. When they ultimately became intimate, they depended on condoms. Because Karida had always had irregular periods, they never took a chance, so she didn't even think about pregnancy when her period was a no-show for two months. Her mother's gynecologist treated the so-called menstrual irregularity with birth control pills. At that point Karida had thought that her bloating and breast tenderness were due to the pills. Because she and Peter had been so careful, she had no idea that she had conceived. When she still didn't get a period after two cycles on the pill, her pregnancy was diagnosed and her parents and the gynecologist were furious that she hadn't admitted to being sexually active in the first place. She was told if she wasn't going to go through with the pregnancy, she needed to decide immediately before the fetus got any older.

The decision to terminate was agonizing for Karida and Peter. Neither of them wanted to quit school and end up on public assistance. They had both studied too hard to give up their goals. Karida had already spent a third of her short life tending to her siblings and she absolutely did not want to become a parent at sixteen. She also worried that adoptive families wouldn't want her mixed race baby. Her parents were furious with her and told her she would be on her own if she decided to have the baby. They hadn't killed themselves working multiple jobs so they could raise more kids; they'd done it so they could send their own kids to college. Her father forbade Peter from coming to their home or even calling. Peter's parents also refused to help them. Karida spent a week crying while waiting to get on the schedule of a local abortion clinic.

On the day she went for her procedure, an Anti-Choice demonstration had been staged outside the clinic. People were screaming "murderer" and "baby killer" as a security guard helped her get past the crowd. She was pelted with eggs and sprayed with red paint. Just as they got to the door, a man with a shaved head shoved a poster of a late stage abortion in her face. By the time she got into the clinic she was devastated and ready to change her mind. An older patient comforted her and encouraged her to not let a bunch of crazy people, who had nothing to do with her life, make her decision for her.

Then, as in Pamela Wagner's case, the fetus was older than suspected but stillborn. Once the placenta was delivered, Karida observed the fetus being carted away with the placenta. No one asked if she wanted to see it. No one assured her that it was not deformed, and that she could worry less about her reproductive potential in the future. No one suggested a funeral or a burial. She wasn't offered counseling. When her mother came to pick her up at the end of her tragic day, she again had to walk past the taunting demonstrators.

Her parents offered her no sympathy or psychological support. For three years after the experience, she suffered depression and nightmares, always seeing the faces of the demonstrators and herself in her tan coat splattered with red paint. She was frequently ill and she lost a year between high school and nursing school due to a protracted case of mono. Her relationship with her parents became cold and distant. It was only her clandestine relationship with Peter that kept her from killing herself.

Finally, in her first year of nursing school, a perceptive instructor picked up on her depression and assisted in getting her help. It took another year of intense counseling before she stopped punishing herself for unintentionally getting pregnant, and not knowing how advanced her pregnancy was. A year later, she and Peter married and she worked a retail job evenings and weekends while he finished law school and she finished her nursing degree. After Peter graduated, he accepted a low paying job with a Washington firm that specialized in international law. It would take a few years for him to have enough earnings for Karida to stop working and start a family. In the meantime, she wanted to use her own experience to help other women. That was the other reason she felt she really had to consider Doctor Fox's offer.

"No wonder you felt compelled to reach out to the Wagner girl. It must have been a déjà vu for you. I hope I didn't open up old wounds by having you attend that delivery," Eliza offered.

"No apology needed, Eliza. It was that experience that motivated me to become a nurse and to work in obstetrics. It's what makes me want to help Pamela Wagner. I don't want her to have to go through what I did."

"That's the best way to turn a bad experience into something positive. Say! Why don't we take a break and watch some news? I've been working double shifts this week and I feel disconnected."

They tuned in just as an anchorman announced, "And now from the campaign trail: a huge crowd attended a rally today where the vice presidential candidate announced that the top party priority is to seek a constitutional amendment to outlaw abortion, even in cases of incest and rape."

Karida became very animated. "That's just unbelievable. I think that gives me the answer to that question you asked before. If it were that politician's daughter who was having a closet abortion, I'd blow the whistle loud and clear. It's absolutely beyond my comprehension that anyone would want their own daughter to give birth to a rapist's baby."

Karida noticed that Eliza was scowling. "It looks like that upsets you as much as it upsets me, Eliza."

Eliza gave a deep sigh and turned the TV down. "It certainly does. A rapist's baby killed my whole family, Karida. I grew up in Jamaica. My parents were as fertile as they were poor. My father worked as a fisherman and when his catch was good and my mother had the money for ingredients, she used to bake little cakes that my older siblings would sell to sailors docked in Kingston harbor. My oldest sister was fifteen and I was six when she was gang raped by four, maybe five sailors, and impregnated. Abortion wasn't an option for my Catholic family. The little boy Francesca gave birth to grew up to be a psychotic monster, extremely irritable as an infant and increasingly violent every year. That little psychopath, for whom my family sacrificed so much, was ten years old when he burned down our house while my parents and siblings slept. I was the survivor because he started the fire in the back of the house and I slept on a couch right next to the front door."

"Oh my God, that's horrible! I'm so sorry, Eliza. Your experience is much more devastating than mine. Those are burn scars, aren't they?"

"My nightgown caught on fire as I ran out. Burn care wasn't very good then. I'm pretty lucky to have survived."

Karida became still and pensive. "I think that news about the VP candidate has prompted me to make up my mind. I think I will accept Doctor Fox's offer."

Eliza suppressed her joy. "I think that job could just be your destiny, Karida. You will be able to help some very distraught women in that position. Thank you for confiding in me. I think we share some goals and interests and I'd like us to stay in touch. I have some friends who are very involved in the Pro-Choice movement who I'd like you to meet. Let's try to get together again soon. I'll give you a call if you don't float back to labor and delivery."

~ Eight ~

Vivian looked gorgeous and she seemed overjoyed to see him. When they got into the car and she gestured to kiss him, Greg kissed her back as passionately as he could. He wondered if she could tell that his heart wasn't in it anymore, but if she did, she didn't show it. Vivian was really good at keeping her emotions in check. Having a psychiatrist for a mother had made her an expert at hiding her feelings, although he believed that she had always been honest with him. She smiled, snuggled up against him, squeezed his arm and told him how much she missed him. Letting her know that the relationship was over was going to be a real bummer, but he needed to be honest too.

"So what would you like to have for dinner?" he asked. "Sushi? Mexican? Italian? It's still pretty early, so hopefully we won't hit the crowds and we can get to the theater by 7:00."

"How about The Crockpot? We haven't been there for a while and I'm craving their French onion soup. And, it's close to the cinema, so no traffic."

"The Crockpot it is." As they drove, Greg resigned himself to try to have a good time and wait until tomorrow to tell her. After standing her up on Friday, he at least owed her a nice Saturday. Then he thought maybe he should tell her at the end of the evening and then he would be free on Sunday. He could drive back to campus and study, or maybe, somehow, catch up with Colleen.

Even at 5:30, there was a line to get a table at the popular family restaurant. As they sat in the foyer waiting, Vivian found herself observing the baby in the arms of a young woman, while the man she sat next to was trying to restrain a rambunctious toddler. She had never previously paid much attention to babies, but now she was totally absorbed in watching this one. It was sucking on a pacifier, drooling, and squirming in its mother's lap. Dressed in yellow and almost bald, she couldn't tell if it was a boy or girl.

Even with the father holding onto the toddler, he was bouncing about, peering under the seats, and trying to put dust-bunnies in his mouth. The mother pulled a little penguin toy out of a diaper bag to distract him. He pushed the buttons on its belly to make it emit noises and lights for about a minute, and then tossed it on the floor. When his father let go of him to retrieve the toy, the toddler went scurrying off and almost got to the exit before his father caught him and carried him back to the bench. When he sat the child on his lap, the little guy started to kick and scream and then the baby started crying.

"Geez, I sure hope we don't wind up sitting next to them," Greg remarked.

To Vivian, his comment felt like a kick in the gut, but they were both relieved when the young family got ushered to a table in the back of the restaurant while a hostess escorted them to the front. Vivian wanted to know all about Greg's classes. They gossiped about kids they knew from high school. Just as the soup arrived, another young family was seated at the table next to them. Again, Vivian found herself watching.

A highchair was brought to the table and a baby in pink was strapped in. The mother put a bib on her and gave her a biscuit that she promptly mashed into the seat. Then, a little girl complained that her brother was kicking her under the table. The little boy was reprimanded and the mother took out coloring books and crayons for both of them. A minute later, the little boy was standing on the seat and crying that he had to pee. The father got up to take him.

"Nice peaceful dinner out," Greg commented. "Makes you want to never have kids."

Vivian almost choked on her soup. She already had this gnawing feeling that the relationship was fizzling, and now Greg's reactions to these kids made it obvious that he wasn't going to want to hear she was pregnant. Suddenly she felt physically ill, like her chest was being squeezed. She pushed her soup away and excused herself to the ladies room.

Still, no period. "Please God," she prayed in the privacy of the stall. "Help me to know what to do. I don't want to lose this relationship and I definitely don't want to have this baby by myself." She cried for a few minutes and then stared at herself in the mirror, losing track of time until a woman tapped her on the shoulder and asked if she was Vivian. "There's a young man out there who's worried about you and asked me to see if you're okay."

She splashed cold water on her face and returned to the table. "Sorry I upset you. I thought I was going to be sick there for a minute, but it passed."

"Well I'm glad you're alright. I hope you don't mind that I finished your soup. You missed quite a show out here. The baby at that table threw up and then the little boy threw up. They left even before the waiter brought water, and left the mess all over. Hope you don't have whatever they have. I can't believe what a pain in the butt kids are. It's a miracle anyone wants to have a family."

Vivian heard Greg's words but they sounded as though he was very far away. Even the lights seemed dim. Her heart was beating funny and her face and fingers were tingly. She felt as though she couldn't catch her breath and a wave of nausea and dizziness overcame her.

"Maybe I do have what they have," she mumbled. "Suddenly I don't feel very well. I'm sorry; I think I need to go home."

"Yeah, puke makes me sick too. Let's get out of here. I'll tell the waiter we have to cancel the meals after those kids ruined our dinner. Let's get you home. You don't look so good."

They drove away in silence. Cold as it was, Vivian rolled down the car window. The chilly air gave her some relief from her physical distress. The emotional pain was still consuming her.

Greg was relieved the night would end early. As much as he wanted to break up, he hadn't yet figured out how to tell her. He certainly wasn't going to lay it on her when she was sick. Now he'd have another day to think about it. What a waste this weekend was turning out to be. He so wished he was back on campus, but even more, he yearned to be with Colleen. He hoped he could use the night to at least study. Pursuing one girl and trying to dump another had preoccupied him to the extent that he wasn't keeping up with his courses.

He walked Vivian to the door and was relieved when she didn't invite him in. "Hope you feel better, Viv. I'll call you in the morning to see how you're doing. Maybe we can catch a matinee. It's supposed to be a really funny movie."

~ Nine ~

After the burial, Lorraine Wagner dropped Pamela off at school with the hopes that life could return to normal. She desperately wanted to put the events of the week behind her. As soon as she got home she called her manicurist. She'd fought the compulsion to bite her nails her entire life, but the stress of Pamela's ordeal had caused her to give in and her hands were a mess.

The manicurist couldn't come until two, but since Lorraine had cancelled her other appointments for the day, she decided to just relax for a little while after doing a long stint on the treadmill. She took a sauna and a leisurely bath and then tried to catch up with the news from the past two days. She selected her outfit for the luncheon with the vice presidential candidate on Friday and got some clothes ready for Claire, her housekeeper, to take to the dry cleaners. The chilly morning in the cemetery reminded her of her winter coats.

While she picked at the lunch that Claire prepared, a large bouquet was delivered, addressed to Pamela from the Barlows. Lorraine was touched by the kindness these people had shown her daughter, and she wrote herself a note to find some special gift to send them in return. By the time the manicurist arrived, Lorraine had treated herself to a martini and was finally feeling less anxious.

It was in the middle of her manicure that Claire announced that a Ms. Rodriguez from the *Washington Chronicle* was on the phone. Momentarily, Lorraine worried that their secret might have gotten out, but of course the reporter could be calling about the Literacy Project. It would be great if a journalist of Rodriguez's stature would give it some

•

attention; but her nails were wet, so she told Claire to tell the reporter she'd call her back in a half-hour.

Claire returned a moment later and interrupted again. "She wants to know if you got the envelope she put in the mailbox."

Lorraine hadn't bothered to look at the mail that Claire had left on her desk. There was always a huge pile and it was a pain to sort through it and read anything that wasn't junk. She just wasn't in the mood today, but she asked Claire to see if there was something from Rodriguez or the *Chronicle*. When Claire showed her an envelope with the newspaper's logo on it, Lorraine asked her to open it. A photo popped out and Claire spent a minute staring at it. "This looks like a burial." She held it up for Lorraine to see.

Lorraine's heart started to pound. She broke into a sweat and her hands started to tremble so badly that the manicurist couldn't finish. "Excuse me for a minute," she stammered. "I'm not feeling very well. I thought this menopause thing was winding down, but I'm having a really bad hot flash. Claire, could you please get me a magnifying glass? There should be one in my desk drawer."

Literally shaking, she tried to get a better look at the photo. It was pretty difficult to distinguish anyone's face from the distance it was taken, but if the reporter had been there to snap this picture, and knew who to send it to, then she knew a whole lot more.

"Is Ms. Rodriguez still holding?"

"No, Mrs. Wagner. She said she couldn't hold, but that you'd know how to reach her from her letter. Anything I can do for you?"

Lorraine read the letter twice but her mind was racing so fast she could barely comprehend what she was reading. Never in her life had she felt so unprepared to handle a crisis. She decided she just needed to calm down a little. She asked Claire to bring her another martini. "Please make it strong!"

As she sipped, she composed herself enough to enable the manicurist to finish. She had Claire pay the woman and then told the housekeeper to take a hundred dollars for herself and take the rest of the afternoon off. Claire was the best housekeeper she'd ever had and she'd long ago concluded that bonuses were the best way to ensure a worker's loyalty. She sipped her drink through a straw as she waited for her nails to dry, while trying to think of some way to handle her predicament. A half-hour later she had yet to come up with even a fragment of a solution to the problems she imagined befalling her, so she decided she should at least talk to the reporter to find out what she actually knew. None of the numbers in Rita's letter enabled her to get through. She tried multiple times, but could only leave a message.

Lorraine felt panicky. Pamela would be home from school soon and somehow, some way, before this day was over, they were going to have to tell Mark. She thought about calling her oldest daughter Melissa for advice, but then thought she'd only be burdening the young mother. Besides, Melissa wouldn't know what to do either. She tried to call her son Jackson but couldn't get through. Jack was in his final year of law school and was often clerking in court. Lorraine considered turning to her daughter Roberta, who apparently was the only member of the family who knew about Pamela's pregnancy, but she didn't perceive Roberta as someone who could offer good advice, especially since learning that Roberta had counseled Pamela to not even tell her about her pregnancy. She tried to reach one of her sisters without success.

Ultimately, she called her husband's oldest friend and chief aide, Phil Dreyer. Phil had been with Mark wherever he went throughout his political career. In the past, Phil's wife Judy had been Lorraine's best friend, but the Dreyers had divorced a few years ago, and Judy remarried and severed previous ties. When Phil's secretary said he wouldn't be available for at least an hour, Lorraine's sense of panic intensified. She mixed another drink to steady her nerves while she tried to think of a way to deal with the impending storm.

~ ~ ~

After the burial and the car pursuit of Lorraine Wagner, Rita Rodriguez's day just got busier. Her editor was inordinately impressed with her camera work. As soon as they had the pictures downloaded, he locked the photo cards in the *Chronicle's* security vault. He cautioned Rita to go slowly on this story and to make sure every single fact was double checked for accuracy, even if it took them a week to bring it to press. He agreed to publish her alibi piece on Professor Harry Holmes the next day.

For a few minutes the editor joked about not even publishing the Wagner story because it would be so hot, some bigger publication would steal Rita away. He was sure she would ultimately wind up as a star anchorwoman for a major network, but Rita insisted that wasn't her thing. She much preferred being an investigative reporter to being a talking head reading a teleprompter, and she told her boss "real journalists find and write the news. TV anchorwomen spend their days at the hairdresser."

The editor admired her idealism but still worried. This bonanza of a story, that she had so carefully sniffed out and captured, could be the one that parlayed her career well beyond what he could afford. It could also be the one that put her in grave danger. He reminded her about how cruel D.C. could be.

Rita raced out of his office in high gear. She obtained a copy of the birth and death certificates for Walter Barlow Wagner from the vital statistics desk of the health department. She squeezed juicy information out of a gabby clerk at D.C. Memorial Hospital where the baby was delivered. Her radiant smile motivated a dispatcher from the ambulance service to confirm that they had transferred a teen-aged girl in labor from Doctor Roland Fox's office to the obstetric service of D.C. Memorial.

Telephone calls to all of the Barlows in all the local phone books finally connected her to the family she suspected was present at the gravesite. She used the tactic of asking, "is this Mrs. Barlow who was at the Potomac Gardens Cemetery this morning?" All of the responders had said "what" or "excuse me" or "I think you have the wrong number," except for one woman who paused and then said, "who is this?" Rita identified herself and again waited through a long pause, until the woman said, "You must have the wrong number," and hung up.

Rita called again but no one answered. She was anxious to drive over and take a different approach with the Barlows, but she was much more intent on trying to talk with the Wagners. By mid afternoon, she had obtained Lorraine Wagner's phone numbers from another congressional wife by telling the woman that she was going to do a story about the Literacy Project. After having gotten through to a housekeeper, it seemed that either Lorraine Wagner hadn't yet received her letter or, was playing hard-to-get. What she could hear of some muffled conversation suggested Mrs. Wagner was home.

Rita continued her research by checking into the background of Doctor Roland Fox. She learned that he was an obstetrician who advocated for Pro-Choice causes. In addition to his private practice, he was on a medical advisory board for Planned Parenthood as well as a volunteer physician for the local chapter. Several contacts she made informed her that Doctor Fox was extremely generous with his time and expertise in helping disadvantaged rape victims. Rita also found old newspaper stories of the violence that Anti-Choice radicals had inflicted on the physician and his staff. She was so impressed with him that she decided to completely avoid entangling him in the Wagner story, while promising herself to do a story about him after the scandal passed.

It was almost five p.m. when Rita got around to playing back messages from the calls she had missed. Three of the messages were from Lorraine Wagner, returning her call and pleading with her to call back as soon as possible. Now there was no doubt the woman had received her letter and photo. She called but no one answered. She decided to have dinner and pursue them later.

~ ~ ~

Pamela Wagner had endured a hard day at school. She was still having cramps and some bleeding, and the burial had left her sick at heart. Not only was she exhausted, but also anxious about returning home. She decided she had to get class notes from the days she had missed, so she got off the bus at her friend Meghan Wright's house to try to do some catch-up. She called her mother to tell her that Mrs. Wright would drive her home in a little while, but neither Claire nor her mother answered the house or cell phone. She left a message and took her time in the company of her friend. She hated missing school and falling behind in assignments.

When she did get home at about five-thirty, the house seemed deserted. At least no one answered when she called out "Mom" or "Claire," and there were no lights on or noise coming from the kitchen. Pamela was accustomed to coming home to an empty house and heating up whatever Claire had left in the refrigerator, but she didn't feel like eating. She went to her room to call Jeremy.

The teenagers spoke every school night after Jeremy got home from soccer practice. This night they talked for a long time, sharing their relief and their grief. After Pamela hung up, she went back downstairs to see the bouquet that Jeremy said his mom sent. The flowers had been placed on the dining room table where she also noticed her mother's purse and car keys. It was unlike her mother to leave them there and that prompted her to find her mother's car parked in the garage, which sent her running back upstairs to see if her mother was in her sauna. When she didn't find her there, she went back downstairs and found her mother unconscious, face down in a pool of vomit, in the bathroom behind the little sitting room that Lorraine used as an office. She reeked of alcohol and Pamela was unable to arouse her.

Her first instinct was to call an ambulance, but when she went for the phone on her mother's desk, she found the letter from a newspaper person and the photo of the burial. Instantly, she understood what had motivated her mother to drink herself unconscious. Although she had been worried about her mother's drinking for several years, and on occasion, had seen her mother act a little ditzy, she'd never before seen her really intoxicated, let alone passed out.

She felt inordinately guilty and now she was horrified to think of how much worse things could get. It occurred to her that calling an ambulance would attract far more attention then her parents would want. She ran to the kitchen and got some ice cubes, wrapped them in a paper towel and put the cold pack on her mother's neck. After a half-minute Lorraine stirred and Pamela tried again to arouse her. For a few seconds Lorraine opened her eyes, but when Pamela tried to sit her up, she slumped back down and passed out again.

Pamela put the cold pack on her mother's forehead and went back to looking at the photo. Feeling like she had to run away, she was wondering where she could go, when the phone ringing interrupted her thoughts. She hesitated momentarily before answering it. "Hello."

"Mrs. Wagner?" an unfamiliar voice said.

Pamela tried to sound calm. "She can't come to the phone right now. May I take a message?"

"Is this her daughter Pamela?" the voice asked.

"Who's calling please?"

"This is Rita Rodriguez from the *Washington Chronicle*." Silence ensued until Rita said, "How are you feeling, Pamela? I know you've been through a terrible ordeal."

As much as Pamela wanted to hang up, she also wanted to find out what this newspaper person wanted. "Why are you calling, Ms. Rodriguez?"

Rita could hear fear in the girl's voice and didn't really want to upset her. "Well actually I was returning a call to your mother, but..."

Pamela interrupted her to say she had seen the letter and the picture, and she asked again why the reporter wanted to speak to her mother.

This time it was Rita who paused. She considered several responses but decided to be frank. "Well actually, Pamela, I was wondering if your father knows that you had an abortion."

"He doesn't," Pamela replied, choking on tears. "But I guess if you're going to write about it in the newspaper, he's going to find out. I know that because he's running for the Senate, that he's fair game for reporters, but what happened to me has nothing to do with him. And what's happened to me is awful enough. Please, I'm begging you. Please leave my family alone."

Rita was taken aback. She hadn't planned to deal directly with this youngster and now she was wishing she hadn't gotten involved with her; but she had, and she felt she had to capitalize on it. "I know this is a very bad time for you, Pamela, and I'm sorry to intrude, but I have to ask you why you would have an abortion when your father is so strongly against it?"

Through her sobs Pamela replied, "What would you do if you were fourteen, and in spite of everything you did to avoid getting pregnant, it happened anyway?"

"I'd do what you did, Pamela, but that's not why I'm interested in your story. The question I must ask is: what would you have done if abortion wasn't legal? Along with your father, there are some very powerful people trying to take away the option that you, I, and many other women would want to have if they found themselves in your situation. If this happened to you and abortion was illegal, what would you do?"

Pamela didn't hesitate. "I'd go somewhere where it was legal."

Rita began to think the conversation with Pamela might be even better than one she might have had with her mother, and she pushed on. "But Pamela, what if you didn't have the means to go somewhere else?"

"I know what you're saying, Ms. Rodriguez. I get it that if there was a law against abortion, it would be poor girls who would be most affected, and I don't think that's right or fair. I don't believe my father is right either, but I'm just a kid and I can't change my father. Right now, I wouldn't blame him if he disowned me. What I've done is going to cause him tremendous embarrassment…unless of course, you'd be nice enough to not write about it; because if you hadn't been there, he would never have known."

Rita found herself feeling sympathetic towards this girl. She was also impressed with the kid's maturity and candor and felt that on some level, Pamela would actually approve of the media blitz that was about to be aimed at her father. "Do you really think your father will disown you, Pamela?"

"I don't know what my father will do. My worst fear is that he'll take it out on my mother and my mother didn't really know anything about my situation until we realized that my pregnancy was farther along than we thought."

Pamela's voice started to get shaky. "I would never have done this if I had known there was going to be a live baby, I swear. I've made stupid, horrible mistakes and my parents are going to be so disappointed in me and I don't blame them. It's not their fault. I've done a terrible thing." She was crying to the point that she could no longer speak.

Rita tried to offer some words of comfort but realized she had exceeded the girl's tolerance. "Please, Pamela, listen to me. Please understand that there are millions of people in this country who would approve of the choice you made. I realize that's not going to help you resolve things with your family, but that's what you have to do Pamela. That is the most important thing you have to do. If I can help you to do that, I will."

Through her tears, Pamela mustered some polite anger. "What you can do to help me, Ms. Rodriguez, is not publish this. Please! I'm begging you. Please! Please tell me you won't!"

"I'm so sorry, Pamela. I can only promise that my story will be sensitive to your situation. That probably sounds ridiculous to you now, but I hope that someday, you'll see that going public with this may help hundreds of thousands of other girls and women. And Pamela, sincerely, if there's some other way that I can help you, please call me. I think you are a very brave and special person and I'm sorry for your loss. I'm also sorry that it's my job to write about your story, but talking to you has given me a better opportunity to do my job well. Oh, and Pamela, I'm still interested in talking to your mother before I write my story, if she would be willing to speak to me. Perhaps I can do my job even more sensitively if I know her feelings about this."

In spite of the realization that this woman was about to ruin her life, Pamela found herself kind of liking the reporter. "My mother's not here right now, Ms. Rodriguez, but I'll ask her to call you when she can."

Thinking about her mother made Pamela want to get off the phone, and she hung up with a final plea for the reporter to not write her story. She returned to the bathroom to find Lorraine still on the floor and snoring. While trying to think about where she could run away to, she cleaned up the vomit. It was six-thirty and she presumed her father wouldn't be home until nine or ten. She tried to call Karida Robbins. As a nurse, Karida would know if there was something else she could do for her mother, but Karida didn't answer her phone. She thought about calling her sisters, but Roberta was too far away and Melissa probably couldn't come because her husband was away and she had her baby to care for. She hoped she could reach her brother Jackson.

"We're having dinner now, Pam," her sister-in-law Alicia said. Can Jack call you back a little later?"

"It's really important," Pamela insisted. "I need to speak to him now."

Alicia got protective. "Jack's just walked in from a big court case, Pammy, and his dinner's getting cold. Can't it wait just a little while?"

Pamela had always felt that Alicia was jealous of how much Jackson cared for his baby sister and she was at the end of her emotional rope.

Her brother seemed like her only hope for help. "Listen, Alicia! I've just had an abortion that turned out to be a live baby that my father knows nothing about, but the baby died. Tomorrow it's going to be on the front page of the newspaper and my mother is passed out drunk in her own vomit. I really need to speak to Jackson."

Pamela heard Alicia call her brother to the phone and tell him "you're not going to believe this."

"Hi, Baby. What's up?"

Pamela couldn't remember ever feeling so glad to hear Jack's voice. In a few anguished sentences she told him of the events of the past few days and the upcoming storm.

"Do we need to get an ambulance for Mom?" was Jack's first response.

"I don't know, Jack. I checked to see if she bumped her head or something but I think she's just plain drunk."

"I'll be right there. Please don't talk to anyone else until I get there." Jack and Alicia lived on the other side of the Potomac, about a thirty-five-minute drive in normal traffic, but they arrived at the Wagner house in a half-hour. Jack was astounded to see how thin and tired Pamela looked. He tried to assess his mother's condition and at this point, she was arousable but incoherent. He was pretty sure she just needed to sleep it off and the three of them succeeded in moving her to the couch in her office where she resumed snoring. Pamela filled her brother in on the details and showed him the Rodriguez letter and photo.

Jack didn't know whether to send his little sister off for some badly needed food and rest or include her in the confrontation. He suggested that Pamela and Alicia go out for some food while he dealt with Dad. Pamela refused. She insisted that this was her problem and she had to face her father herself. Alicia went out for the food while Jack tried to page his father out of a congressional committee meeting. Even though he emphasized to the operator that this was a serious family emergency, he waited fifteen minutes for his father to come to the phone. Initially, Jack advised his father that Pamela was in the midst of a major adolescent crisis and that Lorraine had suddenly taken ill, to which his father responded that he'd be home in about two hours.

"You don't understand, Dad," Jack persisted. "Mom is semi-conscious and Pamela is dealing with a very serious problem here."

Mark Wagner responded that Jack should call Doctor Orton for his wife and maybe Melissa could help with some girl thing, if Jack couldn't.

"Listen really carefully, Dad! Pamela just had an abortion, Mom's passed out drunk, and Rita Rodriguez is going to write about it in tomorrow's *Washington Chronicle*."

~ Ten ~

Mark Wagner made it home in record time. Jack had convinced Pamela to let him try to soften things before she and Dad talked, so when Mark demanded to know where "the little whore" was, Jack responded that she was having some cramps and was upstairs with Alicia.

"Just great," Mark mumbled. "And where's her drunken mother?"

Jack brought his father back to his mother's office where she was still snoring on the couch. Mark reflexively felt for a pulse, then dropped her arm, turned away in disgust, and headed for his bar. Jack was about to interject that maybe someone ought to stay sober but thought better of it. He remained silent as he watched his father pour himself a huge glass of straight bourbon, take a long drink and seat himself, with his big belly lopping over his belt. He then seemed a little less furious, though his fair complexion remained a ruddy red.

Jack gave his father an overview of Pamela's relationship with Jeremy, her attempt to try to manage her pregnancy without involving them so she wouldn't cause embarrassment, her unexpected live birth, the burial, and her phone encounter with Rita Rodriguez.

As he listened, Mark kept staring at the picture of the burial, while sipping his bourbon. When Jack finished, Mark's initial comment was "You know what makes this Rodriguez so effective is her photos. Sometimes she has nothing at all to write about; but she snaps an awesome picture of some bum on the steps of the Lincoln Memorial and abracadabra, you read a story that would never have otherwise captured your attention." Mark threw the picture down and drained his glass. "I'll bet Ms. Rodriguez has some really good photos of this fiasco. I just wish she had photos of that poor dead baby though, because that's what the public should be seeing."

Jack wasn't surprised by his father's reaction. It was obvious his concerns centered on his political career, and not what was going on with his family. He realized that if he was going to be able to help his sister, he was first going to have to humor his father, who was now pouring himself another tall bourbon.

"Dad, I know you're going to have to do a lot of strategizing to be prepared to deal with the press tomorrow. How about calling Phil and having him round up a spin-doctor? He brought in someone really sharp back when that farm lobby caused you bad publicity. I don't remember the guy's name but he did some good damage control when Fritz Anders of the *Baltimore Record* was on your case."

Mark smiled. "You're a hundred per cent on the ball, Jackson, my boy." He poured another glass of bourbon, handed it to his son, and raised his glass. "You and me, Kid. A toast. If they vote my ass out of Congress, the two of us are going to have the loftiest law practice in town."

Jack gestured at taking a swig while Mark took a big one. Mark then called Phil, explained the problem, and asked him to get a hold of one of the PR wizards and anyone else Phil thought might be helpful. Father and son set down to eat the sandwiches that Alicia had brought.

Jack kept trying to act supportive, while Mark ranted about having Pamela talk to reporters. "We'll have her tell them that she's a great example of why abortion must be illegal. Gabe Mackey! He's the journalist we want her talking to. He'll give those Rodriguez readers something to think about. We're going to fight fire with fire," he fumed.

Jack was finding it harder and harder to humor him. "Dad, don't you think you ought to at least talk to Pamela yourself, first? She's been through an awful experience already. I know you need to protect your career but, please don't hurt your already traumatized child in the process."

"Well then let's get the little slut down here right now. It's high time we had a talk."

Jack could no longer contain himself. He grabbed and gripped his father's waving arm with enough force that his father was stunned. "Pamela is not a little slut. You have no idea what a really good kid Pamela is; do you, Dad?" Mark looked humble and Jack released his arm. "And, you have no idea how lonely she's been since Roberta left. She says she sometimes doesn't see you for weeks and it can even be days before she crosses paths with Mom. Even when she does see you, she says you're so absorbed in your own stuff that you don't pay attention to anything she says. She recently told me that she told you she was going to sleep over at Jeremy's house, just to see if you were listening and you said, 'that's nice, Dear.' I get the impression she rambles around this big old house just feeling lonely, while you two are out solving the world's problems. Meanwhile she goes to school, does her homework, rides that sassy white mare of hers, and bothers no one. I'm mad at myself for not telling you this stuff before this happened.

"Pamela told me she's introduced Jeremy to both you and Mom on several occasions, she talks to him on the phone every night, and she sees him just about every weekend. Yet when Mom met him in the hospital Monday night, Pamela thought Mom didn't know him from a hole in the wall."

"Well your mother certainly should have known," Mark countered.

"You both should have known your baby daughter had a boyfriend, Dad. Did you know that they've been steadily dating for over a year? Do you know anything about your daughter's friends or life, Dad? I'd be willing to bet you could still name some of my friends from when I was fourteen, but can you tell me anything about anyone who might be important to Pamela? Can you name even one of her friends, Dad?"

The look on Mark's face said Jack had hit a nerve. "So you know this boyfriend of hers, Jackson?"

"Yeah, Dad, I do. His father is a cousin of Edward's. Pamela met him at Roberta and Ed's wedding. He's a really nice kid, very bright and mature, and his parents seem like terrific people too. He and Pamela had dinner at our house in June and Alicia and I took them to the beach a few times this summer. I think you and Mom were at a meeting in New York one of those weekends. If you could ever take the time to get to know him, you'd like him."

Mark shook his head and started fidgeting with the Polaroid picture again.

"Really, Dad! Anyone who had open eyes at Roberta's wedding watched Pamela and Jeremy snap together like magnets. They had sparkles in their eyes and they danced together most of the night. It was a fantastic demonstration of the magic of young love. Can you remember your first love, Dad? Can you remember how powerful it was?"

Mark's expression changed from one of humility to anger. "Yes, Jackson, I can. In fact what I remember best was taking cold showers because in my day, you didn't just jump into bed with the first person that got you hot, especially if you were fourteen. If you had half a brain, you didn't risk becoming a parent before you were capable of making a living. These kids think they have all the answers and that they're much smarter than they are, and they act like animals."

"You're so wrong, Dad. Pamela and Jeremy are anything but animals. They're two mature young people who love one another. If the pill and access to abortion had been available when you were a kid, there would have been a lot more teenage intimacy back then too. I really don't believe for a minute that when you were a kid, people were so much more moral. What stopped kids back then was a lack of access to birth control. The passion was just as strong."

Mark looked like he was almost agreeing and Jack decided he'd better let his father confront his sister now, before his political interests fired him up again. "I'm going to go upstairs and see if Pamela is well enough to come down here and talk to you, and I just hope you can treat her with respect."

Jack headed upstairs with the intention of preparing Pamela for what their father was planning to do. He found his wife and sister with their ears to the vent in the floor of Roberta's old bedroom, and they confessed they had been able to hear most of the conversation downstairs. Roberta and Pamela had discovered this sound conduit a year after the Wagners moved into the house. Jackson was surprised. He'd always thought that the vent in his old room was the only eavesdropping station.

Pamela started to tell her brother that she couldn't believe her father intended to make a public example out of her and that she didn't want to lie about her own feelings about the right to choose. Jack encouraged her to tell it directly to Dad. He sensed that Pamela's own words might have greater impact on their father than anything he might coach her to say.

"Pammy, you just speak your mind and heart. I might try to make Dad think I'm his ally at some point, just to keep things from getting too crazy, but please believe me when I tell you; I'm one hundred per cent on your side."

"We both are." Alicia assured her sister-in-law. Jackson gave her a hug and the three of them went downstairs to face their father.

As had been the rest of the family, Mark Wagner was shocked at the appearance of his youngest child. She looked emaciated, pale, exhausted and depressed. She walked towards him with slumped posture, and when she did raise her chin, Mark saw her biting her lower lip as tears streamed down her cheeks. As their eyes met, a surge of paternal feelings overwhelmed him. He wrapped his arms around her and wailed, "What have they done to my baby?"

His much-unexpected embrace just made Pamela cry harder. "I'm sorry, Daddy, I wanted so much not to hurt you. I'm so, so sorry, Daddy," she sobbed repeatedly.

Mark continued to embrace Pamela until she cried herself out and started to pull away. He chugged down some more bourbon as his daughter dried her tears. As soon as she composed herself, she asked if Mommy was okay, and they all followed her back to the couch where Lorraine was still zonked. Mark watched silently as Pamela took her mother's hand and stroked her hair. "Can you hear me, Mommy?" she said softly and then a little louder. Lorraine seemed to stir and she opened her eyes. "Can I get you some hot tea, Mommy?" Lorraine just closed her eyes again.

Pamela turned to the three adults with a pained expression. "I'm really worried about her. This whole thing has been terrible for her, and it's all my fault." Again tears flowed, and it took another few minutes, this time in Jack's arms, before she could stop sobbing and shuddering.

Mark put his bourbon down. He had known for a long time that both he and Lorraine were drinking too much, but he had rationalized it was just their way of relieving the stress in their lives. Up until now, he had never perceived that it was causing them any problems. Suddenly, he wondered if Pamela's troubles weren't a direct result of Rainy's fondness for martinis and his own penchant for bourbon. His extreme anger at his daughter was starting to turn into guilt as he watched her attending to his wife. She probably was neglected and lonely. As she was simultaneously crying and trying to pull herself together, she suddenly looked much older than her fourteen years. The image erased his mental picture of her as a happy little girl. Here she was, the mother of a dead baby, trying to take care of her own mother, when it was she who desperately needed some care.

Mark wondered how long he had been so oblivious. He couldn't remember the last time he had even really looked at his daughter. During their embrace, he wondered when he had last hugged her. He couldn't remember having given her a kiss since mid childhood. Nor could he recall he and Rainy having discussed anything about her for years. Whenever they talked about anything other than their political world, it was about their grown children: Melissa's baby, Jack's law firm options, or how much Roberta disliked living in her husband's home state of Texas. The adolescence of their youngest child apparently hadn't been of much interest to either of them. What Jack had said was still ringing in his ears. All he really knew about Pamela was that she was a good student, and except for the expenses of her damn horse, she'd never caused them any trouble.

Mark took Pamela by the hand and gestured that she get up from the edge of the couch where she'd perched herself next to Lorraine. "Why don't we all have a cup of tea?" he suggested, as he wondered what to say next.

"I'll take care of it," Alicia offered, blocking Pamela's steps toward the kitchen. "You three go talk and I'll fix us some tea and a snack."

Mark picked up the Polaroid picture of the burial as they walked into the living room. "Who are all these people?" he asked as they sat down. Pamela explained about the Barlows, and her wonderful nurse, Karida.

"You never saw the person who took this picture?" Mark wanted to know. Pamela said she didn't see anyone else but the cemetery workers. She certainly didn't know if other reporters were hiding there.

"I know you must be exhausted, Pamela, but I have some important questions I have to ask. First, did your mother know you were pregnant?"

"No, Daddy. Mommy had no idea. About two weeks ago I told her my periods were messed up and that this doctor was highly recommended by the school counselor. Mrs. Spencer said he was especially good with adolescents. Mom said 'fine', she'd have Claire take me, but I told her she might have to sign some papers, so she went with me to an appointment a week ago. When we were there, she didn't go in with me to see the doctor, so she didn't hear anything about the pregnancy test. Then when the doctor had her come in and he started to explain things, she just said he should do whatever was necessary and she'd sign the consent. She thought I was going to have a D&C to get my periods under control."

"Why didn't you tell her, Pamela? I can understand why you didn't tell me, but your mother would have understood. Maybe she would have been able to help you so things wouldn't have worked out so badly."

"You're right, Daddy. I should have gone to Mom. It's just that I thought she'd be so upset and when she gets upset, she turns into a nervous wreck and drinks too much. I also thought I could just take care of things myself, and then neither of you would be upset. That's what I wanted the most, to not cause you a problem; but I failed, and now I've made a big mess. I'm so sorry, Daddy."

Once more the tears started to spill, and Mark had to wait a few minutes before Pamela could listen. "Pamela, didn't you consider having your baby and putting it up for adoption? Wouldn't that have worked out better all around? There are so many unfortunate couples out there, unable to have children of their own, who would give anything to have a baby from smart people like yourself and Jerry."

"His name is Jeremy, Daddy, and yes, we thought about adoption, except I didn't think my baby would be healthy. I had no idea I was pregnant the first two months because I thought I was still having periods. I also felt sick. I was so tired and sick to my stomach most of the time that I couldn't eat, and I could barely ride Moon Flower and I lost about ten pounds. I didn't even go for my riding lessons. And when I did eat, I didn't eat very well. When Claire was on vacation in August, and when Mom wasn't around to cook, I was mostly eating chips and stuff. I know better than that, but I was so tired, I couldn't even bother to make myself a sandwich.

"Then, when I went back to school in September, I got the flu, and for about a week I was taking aspirin and cold medicines and I lost more weight. It was right after that that I realized I was pregnant. I read that it's very unhealthy to lose that much weight during pregnancy. Then I called a pharmacist who said the aspirin could hurt the baby's eyes and the cold medicine could also be a problem. So I was scared that I would have a baby with birth defects and no one would want to adopt it. I read that it's very hard for babies with birth defects to get adopted. They just live in foster homes and no one ever loves them."

Even the lawyer in Mark couldn't come up with an argument fast enough to interrupt.

"Another thing that scared us, Daddy, is my best friend Meghan Wright's little brother. He's adopted. After Meghan was born her mother couldn't have more children, so they did a private adoption and they got her brother James when he was a week old. He's nine now, and he's known he's adopted since about age seven, but for the last year or so, he keeps asking where his real parents are. The Wrights took him to a psychiatrist who told them it was probably just a phase he was going through, but she also said that some adopted kids spend their whole lives searching for their biologic parents.

"The same week I found out I was pregnant, I was over at Meghan's house and James was throwing a wicked tantrum because Mrs. Wright wouldn't let him have candy before dinner. He started screaming, 'you're not my real mother. My real mother would give me candy.' No matter what they did to calm him down, he just kept going crazy and Meghan says she and her mother are getting kind afraid of him.

"Then, when I was telling Jeremy and Mrs. Barlow about James, Mrs. Barlow told us that when she was a teenager, one of her friends had a baby that she put up for adoption, but her friend's never been at peace with herself, and she's spending the rest of her life looking for her child."

Mark still couldn't find the right words to dispute Pamela's reasoning, and she figured as long as he was listening so intently, she'd tell him the rest.

"Then one of my school friends told me that her older sister had a baby who was openly adopted by a nice couple who sent her pictures and reports. But then, when her child was four, the couple divorced and the mother got involved with a bad guy who was selling drugs and her little girl was taken away. They've lost contact with the adoptive mother and they don't know what's happened to the little girl."

Mark was astonished by Pamela's litany of negative stories about adoption. "Pamela, Pamela. Didn't you stop to think that your mother and I could have made arrangements for your baby to be adopted by very good people?"

"We did, Daddy, but Jeremy and I just didn't think we could turn our baby over to strangers and never see it again, or spend our lives worrying if it had a good life. I mean could you and Mommy have just given one of us kids to some stranger? Do you think you could have done that if you were in our situation?"

"You know, Pamela, I can't say for sure whether or not I could have handed any of you kids over to a stranger, but I'm one hundred per cent sure that I couldn't have killed any of you either. Do you really and truly believe, Pamela, that it was better to kill your baby than to give him up for adoption?"

Once more Pamela burst into tears. Mark tried to hug her but this only fueled her hysteria. Alicia chose the moment to join them with a tray of teacups and some stale pretzels. She was astounded by how little food there was in the Wagner's elaborate kitchen.

It took quite a bit of coaxing, but Pamela finally calmed down enough to accept a cup of tea. Mark took a cup but then got up to exchange the tea for the glass of bourbon he had put down earlier. Jack and Alicia sipped at their cups intently because it was much easier to do than to try to initiate conversation. The silence lasted an uncomfortably long time until Pamela broke it.

"I never intended to kill my baby, Daddy. If I had any idea that my pregnancy was as far along as it was, I would never have gone for an abortion. Whether I would have put him up for adoption, I don't know. I'm afraid that I would have found that too hard to do, but I don't think I would want to try to raise him either. A child shouldn't have to pay for its parents' mistakes. I made really stupid mistakes. I shouldn't have been having sex. I should have done a much better job of avoiding pregnancy. And, not realizing my irregular periods could be due to pregnancy was really lame. But, Daddy, I don't believe it's wrong for a woman to end a pregnancy that she never intended to happen. I believe that it's a woman's personal decision as to whether or not she will give life."

"And just who has been filling your head with such garbage, Pamela?"

She stood up and looked down at her father. "I do have a mind of my own, Daddy. I've read about abortion and I made my own decision. I'm just so sorry it worked out all wrong. I tried so hard to not cause you trouble, Daddy. It must be so disappointing when kids don't believe the same as their parents, but I don't believe the same as you. I'm really sorry."

Mark was almost amused as he watched his baby daughter argue her case like a good lawyer. Then he looked at the photo and his eyes narrowed. How was he going to undo the damage if this strong-headed kid wouldn't cooperate?

"Pamela, we will discuss this more at another time. Right now I've got to start to deal with the trouble you've caused around here. Go get some rest."

"I will, Daddy, but what about Mommy?"

"Jack and Alicia and I will take care of Mommy. Now please go upstairs and go to bed. And go eat something; you look like a cancer patient!"

Pamela was out of tears. Had she any left she would have cried with relief that the confrontation with her father hadn't been as terrible as she expected. She welcomed the opportunity to escape and headed upstairs to call Jeremy.

~ Eleven ~

Vivian Evans did her best to conceal her anguish from her parents. They came home shortly after she did, and her mother was surprised to find her home so early. "What's up, Viv? I thought you and Greg went to the movies."

"We were supposed to, but we went to The Crockpot for dinner and there was a family sitting next to us with little kids who barfed all over the table. It smelled gross and I got queasy and I asked Greg to bring me home."

"Yuck! Dad and I once had a similar experience in an elegant restaurant, bad for the appetite. How's Greg doing at school? Are you going to go back to campus next weekend?"

Vivian knew that her mother had probably figured out that there was a problem. "I'm not sure, Mom, but I think you were right that he doesn't want to be tied down anymore. He hasn't said as much, but I just sense it. I feel like my heart is going to break. Just a few weeks ago he was distressed that he had to leave me, and now it feels like he doesn't even want to be with me."

"Are you sure it isn't just the stress of college? He's a competitive kid and he's probably encountering stiffer competition than before. Maybe it's the time commitment of spending weekends with you that's weighing on him."

"Maybe, but I have this feeling in my gut that he doesn't love me anymore. I just don't know what to do. He said if I felt better we could go see the movie tomorrow. Should I go and act like nothing's wrong or confront him?"

"I know what I would do in your situation, Viv, but what do *you* think you should do? Some people say that when head and heart conflict; you should follow your heart. I believe that in matters of the heart, the head knows better."

"My head says confront him, but if he says he wants to break up, I think I'll have a heart attack. I can't even imagine my life without him."

"But you must, Vivian. Every one of us who loves someone has to be able to face life without that person. Not just because of loss of love, but an accident, or as you say, a heart attack, can take a loved one away from any of us at any time. Then we grieve and rebuild our lives. That is the burden of all mankind. You are a strong person, Vivian. You'll be sad for a while, but you have a great future ahead of you, with or without Greg, and you'll meet someone you'll love even more. That's probably hard for you to see right now, but I promise you, that's what's in store for you if you open yourself to it."

"So what would you do if you were me, Mom?"

"I'd break up with him. If he's ready to move on, you'll have done him a favor. It might even be a good experience for him to have his ego a little bruised. If you're misreading him and he still loves you, he'll want to reconcile. Either way, your pride won't be shattered, even if your heart aches. If he does want to break up, some time later he may have regrets and boomerang back. I wouldn't break if off with the hope that that will happen though, because it probably won't. I'd break it off because fast pain is better than slow pain, and I can see you're already in pain. Trust your instincts, Vivian. Without a crystal ball, instincts are the best thing you've got to go on."

"Thanks, Mom. My head knows you're right." She paused, aching to tell her mother of her other huge burden, but somehow, the possibility that maybe she wasn't pregnant, or that if she told Greg, everything would work out okay, made her decide to keep her secret.

~ ~ ~

While sitting in church with his mother, Greg ignored the sermon and rehearsed in his head what he would say. They were both too young to be tied down. College was more demanding than high school and he needed the weekends to study. They could just take a break for a while and see how they each felt. Maybe, come summer, they'd know for sure if they were better off apart or together. Once they knew where she was going to go to college, they could figure out if their relationship was still viable.

He'd tell her he still loved her, but he wasn't sure if he did. Even being friends might be an impediment to pursuing Colleen. Maybe if Colleen didn't pan out, he and Viv could get together when he came home for Christmas. He wasn't sure he wanted to close the door completely. Up until the day Colleen smiled at him, he thought he had a great girlfriend, and Vivian certainly hadn't changed. She was still a terrific girl.

If he broke up with her now, she wouldn't be limiting her college applications to just local schools. She could go to Yale or Stanford or anyplace she wanted with her math brain, or maybe Julliard for piano.

He was so lost in his internal arguments that his mother had to tap his shoulder when the church service ended.

~ ~ ~

"I'm fine today, but why don't you just come here for lunch?" Vivian said when Greg called. "Mom and Dad have a campaign event this afternoon, and they brought some great food home from the fundraiser they went to last night. We can still go to the movie later if we feel like it."

"Is your brother home?" Greg asked. If there were tears or a fight of some sort, he didn't want anyone else around.

"It's just me and Nutmeg. Chris hasn't come home on weekends this whole semester. Ever since the new girlfriend, he's stayed on campus. Dad had to beg him to make an appearance at his rally at the state capitol last month."

"What happened to Angie? I thought they were going to get engaged."

"I don't really know, except that Angie is history and now he's in love with Nadine. I feel sorry for anyone who falls in love with my brother; he's lovable, and loving, but he's as fickle as the wind."

Greg couldn't think of anything appropriate to say except that he'd be there in a little while. All the way to Vivian's house he lamented about what he intended to do. The word 'fickle' kept echoing in his head.

Vivian set a sumptuous table with the leftovers, but they both picked at the food with little enthusiasm. After some small talk, Greg said there was something important he needed to tell her.

"Well I have something really important to tell you too. I'm pregnant."

The color drained from Greg's face. He took in a huge breath of air through his nose and opened his mouth to speak, but couldn't produce a word.

"I'm a little more than two weeks late and I've done two different types of pregnancy tests; both positive. I have an appointment with Doctor Rourke on Thursday. I know it would be a huge imposition, Greg, but I was really hoping you'd take me there."

Greg remained speechless. He looked pale and his lips quivered. When he finally found his voice, the only word that came out was 'how?'

"*How* is the very first thing I asked? I swear I *never* missed a pill, but there is a failure rate of up to five percent with the pills I'm on. I calculated my dates and when you came home four weeks ago would probably have been around the time I ovulated and was most fertile."

"I can't believe this is happening. All those years we used condoms and the pullout, and finally you go on the pill and that fails. I thought that was safer."

After a long silence, Vivian said "Greg, I don't know why, but you and I never talked about what we'd do if this happened. I guess we were just so sure it wouldn't. But now that it has, I need to know what you're thinking."

Greg groaned. "Yeah! Stupid us. I never really gave it any thought. Are you sure you're pregnant?"

"Pretty sure. I've had periods for five years and I've never been late before, and I have all of the rest of the symptoms that go with pregnancy. Believe me, I've lost a lot of sleep just praying that I'm not, and that I'll wake up in the morning and my period will be there, full blast, but prayer isn't working."

Greg got up from the table, walked around in a circle and sat back down before he spoke again. "I don't know, Viv. I'm not prepared for this at all. The only thing I can tell you for sure is that I'm not ready to be a father at this stage of my life, especially after watching those kids in the restaurant yesterday. I'm sure I'll feel differently about it some day, but now, the mere thought of being a parent scares me to death. What are you planning to do?"

Vivian's eyes narrowed and she stood up. "What am *I* planning to do? I was thinking this is a '*we*', not an 'I' decision. This *our* baby, Greg."

Greg stood again. "Are you saying you're going to have it?"

"What do you think? You think I'm going to have an abortion?" Vivian turned her back to him, burst into tears and walked out of the room.

Greg ran after her and put his arm around her. "I'm sorry, Vivian. As much as I love you, I'm just not ready to get married and start a family. Are you?"

She pulled away and sat down on the bottom step of the thickly carpeted stair, burying her face in her hands. Greg sat down on the step beside her and tried to put an arm around her.

Vivian jumped up and started to pace. "You can't be serious. Just like that, you're ready to kill our baby. Maybe we don't know each other, Greg, but abortion isn't an option here. For me, the choices are try to raise this child or put it up for adoption. You have to know my father is a Pro-Life advocate. There is absolutely no way I'm having an abortion."

"Well I do know that's your father's political viewpoint, but, Viv, surely you can think for yourself. Are you really ready to raise a kid or give it away? Somehow, I can't imagine you want to do either."

"So you're saying if I'm pregnant, you're not willing to make it right? I really need to know, Greg, where you stand on us, on our relationship? If I did decide to terminate the pregnancy, is there still an us?"

Greg got up from the step and turned his back. He put his hands in his pockets and walked around in a circle again. He didn't have to say anything at that point. Vivian was certain that what she suspected was true.

"I don't know, Vivian. I just don't know. I need some time to process all of this. I'm really sorry that I can't give you an answer this minute. Obviously you've had some time to consider this. I haven't. I need to get in touch with my feelings about it. I need some time. I'm sorry I can't be more reassuring than that. I'm really sorry, Vivian."

"Will you at least come down Thursday and go with me to the doctor. I haven't told anyone else and I don't want to go alone. Please? The appointment's at eleven-thirty."

"Um…, sure. I'll go with you. Where should I pick you up?"

"I'm going to stay home from school on Thursday, so just come here. I'll call you if I get my period before then. Otherwise, see you Thursday."

Without another word, Greg got up and left.

~ Twelve ~

Mark turned to Jackson for his opinion about the encounter with Pamela. Jack was right: he really didn't know his youngest child.

"She's one tough little girl," Jack said. Then he corrected himself. "Young woman, I mean. I think if you're not too hard on her, she might even come around to agreeing with you that abortion is not the way. At her age, that sense of rebelliousness is very strong and if you totally discount her opinions, you'll just stoke the rebelliousness. I'm not so old that I can't relate to how that works."

"Probably good advice, Son. Did you really think I was hard on her? I thought I showed great restraint."

"You did, Dad. To be fair, you were actually pretty soft. I'm worried though, that the full impact of what's happened hasn't actually hit Pamela yet. These are major events in anyone's life, let alone a kid. It's going to take her some time to process all of this."

"Well hopefully she doesn't wind up with post-abortion syndrome."

"Actually, Dad, in my law course they said that there really isn't such a syndrome. In fact, in 1988, President Reagan authorized his Surgeon General, Everett Koop, to study the issue, and the report came back that there was no evidence that abortion causes mental illness, unless others torment a woman for making that decision."

"That's interesting," Mark replied. "Do you know who's the bastard that did Pamela's abortion?"

"Roland Fox. Why?"

"Roland Fox. Why does that name sound familiar?"

"He's a prominent obstetrician, known throughout the District for providing abortion services for rich and poor. Law firm gossip says he's such a magnanimous hero kind of doctor that you never want to oppose him in court. But to change the subject, Dad, how are we going to protect Pamela?"

Mark finished his glass of bourbon. He tossed the Polaroid picture he was still fiddling with onto the coffee table and went to refill his glass. His son was aghast at his tolerance. "Jackson, you're so on the ball. I appreciate you. I need you to help me get this right. I especially need you to help me deal with Pamela. She really looks up to you. But right now, I need you here with me tonight. You have great political instincts, Son. I think you were born to it. Send Alicia home and stay with me to try and get this mess cleaned up."

Jackson went to check on Pamela and arrange a taxi for Alicia. He actually would have preferred to have Alicia stay. She was not only a Pro-Choice voice, but also, her experience as a paralegal might have added perspective to Mark's preparation for dealing with the press. Alicia however, didn't like exposing her political views to her father-in-law and was relieved to be able to leave.

Mark went to check on Lorraine. Explaining his daughter's non-compliance with the party platform was humiliating enough; his wife's drunkenness was another matter. To his surprise, she was no longer on the couch. He found her emerging from the bathroom with a mostly empty martini glass. She looked worse than Pamela, also too thin. He took the martini glass from her hand and tasted the liquid to find it was just water.

"Want a drink?" he said sarcastically, holding his glass of bourbon to her lips. "You don't look quite shit-faced enough. How about a toast to the end of my career?" He raised both glasses up as Lorraine slumped back onto the couch. "I know, even more apropos: How about a toast to our dead grandson?"

Lorraine closed her eyes. The room was spinning and her innards were rumbling. Somewhere in the distant reaches of her consciousness, she could hear Mark piling on the accusations. The nausea peaked and she went stumbling back to the bathroom. When she was done, she felt more alert and could hear Mark still ranting about what a slut his daughter was because his wife was a drunken idiot. She tried to ignore his tirade as she sat on the cold tile floor hugging the toilet. When it seemed he was finally finished, she dragged herself back to the couch.

"I accept any blame you want to lay on me, Mark. I've come to many realizations over the past few days. Chief amongst them is that I've been a negligent parent to Pamela her whole life. Roberta actually raised her. I was too busy and too intoxicated most of the time. Did you know any of that, Mark? I was a pretty good parent for our older kids, but I passed the buck on Pamela. I failed her miserably." Tears came streaming down Lorraine's face. She bit her lower lip, the same way that Pamela did.

Mark had to admit to himself that he hadn't noticed. He had been too busy, too indifferent, and too indulgent of himself to notice much of anything going on his home, let alone something going wrong. When he remained silent, Lorraine took the opportunity to head to the kitchen to make some coffee. Mark followed her and put his bourbon glass in the sink.

"Make a big pot, Rainy. Phil and some other people are coming here tonight to plan a strategy for dealing with the media. Jackson is going to stay and help. I think he understands how to deal with Pamela better than I do. By the way, did you ever get to speak with Rita Rodriguez? Do you know that Pamela spoke to her? Goddam, this is a nightmare."

"I didn't know. I tried to reach her several times after I got the picture with her letter, but I couldn't get through. Maybe we can reach her now. Look, it's only eight thirty. Her numbers are in the letter. Try to call her while I go clean myself up. She plugged in the coffee maker and took two pills from a Tylenol bottle. "My head is just pounding."

"Not good, Rainy." Mark clucked after her as she started upstairs. "You're going to have to fill these people in on details if we're going to be ready to control the press. I need you sharp and fast."

Mark felt like he needed something else in his stomach and returned to the kitchen, only to encounter the same empty fridge and pantry that Alicia had struggled with. Forgetting about calling the journalist, he picked up his glass of bourbon and went to yell at Lorraine about nothing in the house to eat.

She yelled back that with hospitalizations and burials, she hadn't gotten around to giving Claire a shopping list.

"No wonder our daughter's emaciated," Mark shouted. He ranted some more to the bathroom door as he changed from his congressional suit to a sweater. He was gargling with mouthwash when Jack came to the bedroom to say that Phil Dryer and others had arrived.

~ ~ ~

Mark shook hands with two people he didn't know. Nora Sutton was a little old lady in a jogging suit and sneakers. Her almost white hair was pulled back in a ponytail and she wore Ben Franklin eyeglasses perched on the end of her nose. She was introduced as a legal expert on abortion issues. Phil's contact reported that she was exceedingly powerful in the courtroom, and she also happened to live in the neighborhood. With Nora came Aaron McGraf, a young, impeccably suited and groomed PR person, who Phil had recently recruited for Mark's campaign.

Mark took Phil aside while Jack hosted the others. "What do you know about this woman? Have you reviewed any cases she's handled? Who do we know that recommended her?"

"We don't know anything for certain, Mark. When you don't have time to verify, sometimes you have to trust. I checked her out with people from two Pro-Life organizations and they said she's a child welfare advocate and she knows both sides of the issue exceptionally well, and, she was available and willing to help. Under the circumstances, I doubt we could do much better."

Lorraine Wagner told the story. Nora Sutton and Phil Dreyer studied Rita's letter and the photograph. Aaron McGraf typed methodically on his laptop. An awkward silence ensued after the particulars were laid out. Mark poured himself another bourbon and offered a drink to his colleagues, but they all declined. It was Phil who finally spoke.

"The way I see it, Mark, you have two options. You could modify your position on abortion or let Pamela tell her story, and let the public see her tragic outcome as a reason for restricting on-demand abortion."

Nora Sutton remarked, "That would be a good idea, except, you might be skewering your daughter in the process. I doubt you want to risk that."

"What do you recommend as the core of our response, Ms. Sutton?" Mark asked. "What arguments actually change minds on this subject?"

"Currently, the issue of fetal pain and suffering is getting lots of attention. There's minimal controversy about relieving pain when the fetus has to live through its own murder."

"Or its own birth," Jackson countered. "Every baby has to live through the trauma and stress of birth."

Nora was surprised by Jack's remark, but moved right along as though that topic was finished. "One of the more difficult arguments you have to be prepared to tackle is the Pro-Choice position that if contraception was more accessible in the first place, there wouldn't be so many abortions. Teenagers in particular have been limited in their access to reliable methods of birth control, and now that the emergency contraceptive, PLAN B, is finally available in this country, its access by younger women has been seriously restricted. Youth are also being denied access to education about contraception."

Nora exhibited a sharp tongue and Mark could envision how difficult it might be to battle her in a courtroom. "Are you saying that no matter what we say in response to Rodriguez's article, it's going to help the Pro-Choice side?"

"I'm saying that if you focus on issues that have the most polarity, you'll boost the Pro-Choice agenda as well as the Pro-Life agenda. If you concentrate on less volatile issues, you may get sympathy from both sides."

"So besides fetal pain, what about abortion isn't controversial?"

"Probably nothing," Nora replied. "But some things are less controversial than others. For example, no one really supports elective late term abortions. Few would argue against saving the life of the mother, and the majority accepts that fetuses who are critically immature or have medical conditions that are incompatible with life, should not be kept alive by artificial means. A much more controversial issue would be parental consent."

"What's the parental consent law here?" the attorney in Mark wondered.

"I'm trying to tell you to avoid a controversy like that. Don't even think of going there with the press." Nora rebuked. "The other side will use that one against you big time, because so many pregnant teenagers don't have functioning parents. Statistics show that one out of four sexually abused girls deliberately gets pregnant by someone outside of the family in attempt to stop their fathers from molesting them, or their brothers, or their mothers' boyfriends. Too often, the abuser is someone the family is inclined to protect. In states that have strict parental consent laws, there's an increased risk of young pregnant girls killing themselves, rather than having to seek consent from parents who will blame *them* for seducing Uncle Al.

"Parental consent laws have done more harm than good in our fight against *Roe v. Wade*. In states that have such laws, the number of late stage abortions has increased and so has the number of unwanted children. If you bring up parental consent, you'll also be perceived as discriminating against youth who have the poorest access to effective birth control. Also, you'll unleash the issue of insurance plans not providing birth control coverage for sexually active young women, even though they're covering Viagra for sexually active old men."

"Have you got any helpful advice?" Mark asked. Nora Sutton was making him feel like his case was much harder than he thought it should be.

"Talk about adoption. There's nothing controversial about advocating for children. Neither side has a problem with adoption. That's my best advice, especially in view of this vice-presidential candidate who wants the party to take on a platform that says abortion is never acceptable, even in cases of rape and incest. That extreme position is only going to backfire and I'd recommend to anyone facing the voters now, even to someone who is not facing a personal conflict about abortion as you are, Congressman Wagner, to take a more moderate stance. You'll gain more politically then you'll lose."

"Dad, I think I see a tremendous opportunity for you here. Make our personal tragedy the breaking point from the party platform. Drop the abortion issue and become the party leader that champions children's welfare. It's time for someone in our political corner to do this. Seize this as a way to bring about a new direction for the party."

Mark looked exasperated. "Phil, you know where I stand on abortion. Tell me why I should let these people talk me into altering my position. I thought you brought this consultant here to help me."

Phil looked uncomfortable. "I don't know, Mark, but in cases of rape? I don't think anyone has the right to force a woman to give birth to a rapist's baby. I also disagree with this legislative push to allow medical personnel to deny a rape victim access to emergency contraception, and I have a major problem with the administration's plan to allow pharmacists and physicians to limit patient treatment options to those that conform to their personal beliefs."

Mark gave his chief aide a scolding look. It was Phil's job to agree with him. Phil returned the glare and looked defiant. "Mark, Old Buddy, my daughter Mandy maybe just missed being a rape victim. A few minutes after she parked her car in a campus lot and walked to her dorm this September, another student was jumped when exiting her car. The assailant cut her face, dragged her behind trees, raped, sodomized and left her naked and bleeding. They still haven't caught the guy. He's probably in some other college town stalking someone else's daughter. How can you support this notion that it's a physician or a pharmacist's prerogative to not offer PLAN B to a girl who was impregnated by a guy holding a knife to her throat? I know this has nothing to do with your daughter's situation, Mark, but our VP candidate's contention that abortion should be illegal, even for victims of rape and incest, is not what our party needs. Come on, Mark! Tell me you'd want your own wife or daughter to be forced to give birth to a rapist's baby."

Jack read 'gotcha' on his father's face. "Women's rights, Dad. It's every bit as important as the abortion issue. And a platform that improves the adoption process could be your key to political success. You heard Pamela's arguments about adoption. She's got this limited reference base about the things that go wrong. If she was better educated, she might be willing to promote adoption. Maybe she could become an advocate for a pro-adoption movement, so we can get away from this abstinence-only education agenda that's been infiltrating the schools. They could at least be teaching about adoption."

"Sex education *is* becoming a huge issue," Nora echoed. "Television bombards kids with sexuality based sitcoms, and data indicates that the more of these sitcoms kids watch, the higher the teen pregnancy rate. It's also a problem when unmarried celebrities, like the VP candidate's daughter, walk around with big bellies like it's something to be proud of. Surely you heard about that high school in New England where a group of girls thought it would be cool to all get pregnant simultaneously. Why aren't we teaching kids about the risks of teen pregnancy and what they need to know to avoid pregnancy? Why not become the party leader who attacks the folly of denying young people the knowledge they need to make informed choices?"

Mark's head was spinning, and he wasn't sure whether it was from too much bourbon, or because he was being counseled by everyone to do the daring thing and try to change the agenda of his political party in the heat of an election. He looked to Aaron McGraf, thinking somewhere there had to be another voice committed to the Pro-Life agenda. Then he looked away as he suddenly got a vibe from McGraf that the speechwriter was gay. He felt betrayed, even by his own son.

Seeing the congressman's frustration, Nora offered; "You could just stall for time with the simple statement that a very personal crisis has you re-evaluating your understanding of all sides of the abortion issue. That would at least buy you a few days to think about your options, while giving both sides a chance to show how they intend to play you in the press."

Phil Dreyer applauded Nora's idea and added, "playing up the personal crisis and stalling might even allow Rodriguez's story to grow cold."

Nora Sutton added. "Abortion is such a stinking quagmire that your best bet might be to glean personal sympathy for being in the stinking midst of it. You'll earn far more respect as a grieving grandfather trying to understand it all, than as a politician hitching his career to an extreme Anti-Choice platform."

"Roll over and play wounded" was the consensus. Step back to assist loved ones while studying the issues. This should take a week or so, leaving Mark enough time to make a public statement before Election Day. In the interim, he should tell reporters that his family, and especially his young daughter, needed to grieve in private as they coped with their loss.

Phil promised to grab the earliest edition of the *Washington Chronicle* and let Mark know how the Rodriguez story had been spun.

Jackson felt like he had accomplished multiple missions, giving his father support, battling for his sister's and women's rights, and maybe developing his own platform for a future career in politics.

Phil Dreyer knew his friend had been placated and he had played his cards as well as he could. It felt good to take a nip at the master's hand now and then. He really didn't personally believe that *Roe v. Wade* should be overturned anyway. In the morning he'd start to check out law firm openings, in case his meal ticket got voted out of Congress.

Nora Sutton hoped she'd accomplished her goals. She knew she had gotten under the politician's skin a little, but he'd also been given a temporary way out of his predicament. She hoped he would come to her again and maybe, play right into NEB's hands.

~ ~ ~

Mark Wagner's phone rang at six fifteen on Thursday morning. Phil had picked up a copy of the *Washington Chronicle* and searched it cover to cover, but there was no story about Pamela or Mark. The only article by Rita Rodriguez was about some dead history professor. Maybe they had another day to brainstorm.

Mark tried to return to sleep but was beckoned out of bed when he heard a phone ring in Pamela's room. He awakened Lorraine to tell her he wanted Pamela's phone cut off immediately. The last thing he needed was for her to go espousing her nonsense while he formulated his own position.

John Barlow had picked up a copy of the *Chronicle* and Pamela was relieved to hear from Jeremy that there was nothing in the newspaper about them. Now she could go to school like normal.

Lorraine barged in. "Who are you talking to?" she demanded to know, as Pamela hung up.

"Jeremy. We sometimes talk in the morning before school. He wanted to know how I was feeling, and he told me there's nothing in the newspaper about us. How are you feeling, Mom? Is everything okay with you and Daddy?"

"I'm much better today, Pammy. I'm so ashamed about yesterday. I handled things very badly. I'm sorry, Baby. How are you today?"

"That depends on how Daddy is."

"I think he's taking it very well so far, but this is a long way from being over. Until he's dealt with the political fallout, he doesn't want either of us talking to anyone. He asked me to take your phone away and you can't go to school."

"Mom! I have to go to school. I've already missed too much. I swear I won't tell anyone anything. Mom! Please! It's illegal to not go to school."

"I don't need another lawyer in this family." Lorraine snapped.

"Then how can I get my assignments if I can't even use the phone?"

At that moment, Pamela's phone rang and she answered it as her mother stood motionless. It was Karida Robbins. She apologized for not calling back last evening, but she was with a friend and didn't pick up messages until late.

Pamela no longer needed advice on what to do for her drunken mother, but before Lorraine could react, she told Karida about the newspaper reporter that took pictures of the burial, and that she didn't know if she'd be able to talk to Karida again; at which point Lorraine demanded that she hang up.

"And who was that?" Mark wanted to know as he came into her bedroom.

"That nurse, Karida, who helped me so much. I called her yesterday when I didn't know what to do for Mommy when she passed out. She was just returning my call. She's the one in the picture. She's so nice and I didn't know who else to call that would know what to do for Mom."

"You get her back on the phone. I want her here today before Rodriguez gets a hold of her." Mark was glowering and Pamela knew there was no sense in arguing. She called Karida back, but the nurse's phone was in her locker as she scrubbed up for a mastectomy at seven in the morning.

"Lorraine, you take her phone. She talks to no one without you present."

"Daddy, I have to talk to Jeremy. Please!"

"Only in your mother's presence. You've probably said way too much already to that Rita Rodriguez. There are a lot of people out there, Pamela, who will want to make an example of you. Radicals could even pose a danger to you. When you talk to reporters, Pamela, you leave yourself exposed to the world. You may not be going to school for a while. You may not be going anywhere for a long time."

~ Thirteen ~

Rita Rodriquez had her story roughed out by early Thursday afternoon but was still checking out final details. Her photos of the license plates had enabled her to verify the identity of the Barlows, Wagners, and Reverend Taylor, but the woman who left in the old car with a muddied license plate remained unidentified. Rita worried that the mystery woman was a key player and it frustrated her that her best photos weren't completely explained.

Before taking her story to her editor, she decided to try calling the Wagners one more time. The housekeeper said she'd convey the message. She got nowhere trying to call Congressman Wagner. She made a final attempt to speak with the Barlows and failed to get through to them as well. Rita was surprised. She thought the Wagners would want to speak with her, but as the day wore on and her calls went unreturned, she decided she should go with what she had, unless she could find a way to speak to the Barlow boy.

When she couldn't find out what school he attended, she parked herself near the Barlow home to see if she could catch him coming home from school. She was disappointed when he didn't get off of a school bus, but she decided to wait longer and was rewarded when she spotted him getting out of a private school van. He looked younger in school clothes than he did in the suit he wore to the burial. Rita intercepted him a few houses down from his address. Walking beside him she said, "Hi. My name's Rita. I've been speaking with your girlfriend, Pamela, and wondered if you have a minute to talk with me."

It took Jeremy an instant to realize that this beautiful woman was the person who was going to rain havoc on their lives.

"Are you that reporter who sent a picture to Pam's mother?"

Rita showed him a better picture she had taken with the telephoto lens. In it, he and Pam could clearly be seen behind the little casket. Seeing himself in the photo gave Jeremy a sick feeling. He could be ruined for life.

"I'm worried about Pamela," Rita continued. "I spoke with her yesterday and I'm afraid that she's in a very bad predicament with her father."

"She will be if you're going to publish that picture." Jeremy had been so concerned about how Pam was affected, that he hadn't stopped to consider his own fate. The picture made him fearful of public shame.

Rita sensed he was realizing he was about to be dragged through the mud. She flipped through her handful of photos and held up a different picture that showed the back of Jeremy and Pamela, but showed the faces of Mrs. Wagner and the unidentified woman. As Jeremy looked at the photo, Rita told him she was hoping not to focus her story on them, but she couldn't use these other pictures because she didn't know who that woman was.

"What do you want to know?" Jeremy thought that maybe the reporter was trying to be sensitive. Pam had said she was really nice. What could it hurt to tell her the truth if she was going to write about him anyway?

"There are a couple of things I'd like to ask you, Jeremy." She didn't know his name until she saw it on his gym bag. "Can I buy you a hamburger or something, or could we just sit and talk somewhere?"

Jeremy felt nervous. He thought his parents should be present if he was going to talk to this person. His father had counseled him to avoid reporters. He was pretty sure if he brought Rita home, his mother would politely decline to talk to her and he'd never get a chance to defend himself. If he talked to her without his parents present, then they couldn't be blamed for anything he said. Maybe he could convince her to leave them all alone. He had to try.

"There's a donut shop three blocks over from the end of this street. I'll put my books in the house and tell my mom I'm going over to a friend's. It'll be cool. It'll only take me about ten minutes to get there."

Rita took a table wondering if the kid was going to no-show or come with a parent. She was relieved when he walked in by himself. She went to get food while he tried to call Pamela. When Rita returned with hot chocolate and cookies, Jeremy looked troubled. "Problem?" she asked.

"Yeah. Pam's phone's been disconnected. I don't even know the number to her parents' house, but I've got to talk to her."

"I have the Wagner's number," Rita offered. Jeremy's expression said she wouldn't get much out of him because he was so upset. She pulled up the number and handed him her phone. He connected with voicemail.

"I'll bet they went out to dinner," Rita offered. "They really do need some family time. Do you know how Pamela's doing?"

"Family time? Since I've known Pam, I think the only thing they ever do as a family is make a guest appearance at church, once or twice a year. It's like my family is her family and she doesn't even have one of her own."

"I'll bet her family is one now. They're all in this together. So it was your family that made the burial arrangements?"

"My mother insisted that we have a proper burial."

"Did your parents know about the pregnancy before that?"

"At first, we wanted to spare our parents the embarrassment, and try to handle it ourselves. Then, we decided to tell my mom and she offered to help us. When we found out that it could be called a D&C for irregular periods, my mother was going to take Pam to the doctor. Then we learned that she wouldn't be able to sign the consent so that Pam could get her family insurance benefits.

"We had no idea Pam's pregnancy was so far along. It was only after my parents saw our baby in the hospital, that they thought we should have a burial. Why do you have to make a story out of our dead baby, Ms. Rodriguez? How'd you get those pictures anyway?"

"I didn't set out to hurt you, Jeremy. I was there to do a story about the people attending a service for a great professor," she lied. "Stories from cemeteries go well with the Halloween spirit of October. It was just a coincidence that I happened to see your burial service, and, it's just my nature to photograph every interesting thing I see, every single day."

"But how did you know who we were?"

"I recognized Lorraine Wagner. She's active in the Literacy Project that often seeks press coverage. I make my living taking pictures, Jeremy, and I carry cameras wherever I go. From my photos, I was able to identify the rest of you. Except I can't figure out who this is." Rita pointed to the mystery woman in the photo and Jeremy told her what he knew about the nurse Karida who befriended Pam. He didn't know her last name.

"I'm really sorry that what's important news to the rest of the country is bad news for a couple of nice kids like you and Pam. Unfortunately, the right to choose is at stake. I'd like to portray your side of the story as fairly as I can. Would you tell me if you thought about putting your baby up for adoption?"

"We talked about it a lot, but wanted more than anything to spare our parents the embarrassment of the pregnancy. Also, we weren't sure we could give our baby up after he was born. We both know of adoptions gone wrong. Pam's best friend has an adopted brother, a little brat who's always threatening to go find his real parents if he can't have his way. He's got their whole family terrorized. Then there's an adopted kid on my soccer team who doesn't get along with anyone. He's just obnoxious, spoiled. No one likes him."

"If we could go back in time, Jeremy, would you make the same decision?"

"Knowing what I know now, that the baby was close to five months, I don't know, but I don't think so."

"What if this happened a year from now and abortion was no longer legal? Then it would be your responsibility to raise the child or give it up for adoption. What do you think you would do then?"

"Even if he was sick or deformed and no one wanted to adopt him? Pam got sick before she knew she was pregnant and she took some medicine that could have hurt the baby. Then what happens?"

"It's so sad that people rarely choose to adopt an imperfect child," Rita concurred. "Do you support a woman's right to choose?"

Jeremy pursed his lips and shook his head yes.

"Jeremy, what if Pam wanted this baby and you didn't. Would you still support her right to choose?"

"Whew! I hate that question. I've been talking to my parents and sister about that. I have to answer that it's a woman's body, so the right to choose is hers. A man shouldn't make her have a baby she doesn't want, and he shouldn't make her get rid of a baby she does want. The right thing to do is for the man to help her support the child, but I sure can't do that yet. We made a horrible mistake. Couldn't you please not write about it, Ms. Rodriguez?"

"I'm so sorry, Jeremy, but this is really important news and I appreciate your talking to me. I'll be focusing my story on Pam's father and not you. Perhaps, someday you kids will be recognized as heroes in the fight for reproductive freedom. Here's my card. Please call me if there's something else you would like to say."

Rita spent some time trying to learn about the nurse from D.C. Memorial to understand why this woman was the only outsider at the burial. No one she contacted seemed to know anything about her and Rita concluded the nurse's connection was too unimportant to delay her story another day. She phoned her editor and promised she'd have her article ready for the Friday morning edition.

The front page headline read:

PRO-LIFE CONGRESSMAN'S DAUGHTER HAS LATE STAGE ABORTION.

A picture under the headline showed Lorraine Wagner and another woman along with the backs of a few people, watching a small casket being lowered into the ground. The caption read "Bereaved family and friends minus the Congressman." The story read:

Washington D.C.: The youngest daughter of Congressman and senatorial candidate Mark Wagner, was accompanied by her mother and boyfriend's family as she buried an aborted fetus at the Potomac Gardens Cemetery in the chilling winds of Wednesday morning. The young couple thought their fetus was three months younger than he actually was when they sought to terminate the pregnancy.

Medical personnel caring for Miss Wagner didn't anticipate a live birth, but made an emergency transfer to D.C. Memorial Hospital when they became concerned that the pregnancy was more advanced than presumed. Although Walter Barlow Wagner was too premature to survive for more than a few minutes, the teen parents opted to give their baby a proper burial.

The congressman, apparently unaware of these events, did not attend. Mark Wagner, who is the father of three daughters, has a long history of opposing women's rights. He is running for the U.S. Senate as a Republican. He's supported an Anti-Choice platform since his earliest days in Congress, and in his most recent campaign commercials in his home state, he's promised to bring to Washington 'respect for life from the moment of conception.'

Neither Congressman Wagner nor his wife was available to comment about their daughter's decision to exercise her right to choose.

The story went on with a list of women's rights initiatives Mark Wagner had not supported, and legislative attempts to restrict access to abortion that he had voted for. Rita also informed her readers that the largest population having late stage abortions is currently not teenagers, but poor women who already have more children then they can provide for, the same population that suffers from lack of access to reliable contraception.

~ Fourteen ~

Karida Robbins was mortified to see a picture of herself behind the baby's casket on the front page of the *Washington Chronicle*. She hid behind an umbrella when she walked from her apartment to her car. Her husband Peter didn't think it was anything to worry about. She was unidentified in the story and no one in Washington knew her except for this patient and some hospital staff. He reasoned that Karida would not be the focus of anyone's outrage; she was just a dedicated nurse trying to support a bereaved patient. Her association with the family of a congressman could turn out to be helpful.

Work allowed her to escape from her feelings of paranoia. After finishing up with a radical mastectomy, she grabbed a nutrition bar from a vending machine and tried to return a call to Pamela, but there was no connection. Then she got assigned to scrub in on an emergency gun shot case. Though a surgery team of six worked on the gang violence victim for five hours, there was little hope that the young man would survive.

She'd be so glad when this O.R. drama was over. At least working in Doctor Fox's office would enable her to interact with patients, instead of spending hours smacking scalpels into the hands of barking surgeons. More and more, hospital nursing seemed to be about vital signs, charting, bedpans, charting, regulations, charting, and more charting, no matter what department she floated through. After this grueling eleven-hour day, she took her letter of resignation to her supervisor.

"I'm so disappointed, Nurse Robbins. We've had great feedback about you from every unit you've worked in. Patients keep asking for you. I know for a fact that the surgical service wants to steal you away, and they only take the best. Let me find out if I can make you a better offer. Please, just give me until Monday and if I can't provide you with a big bonus, I'll accept your resignation."

Although she still had some anxiety about working for Doctor Fox, Karida was absolutely certain that she didn't want to be a full-time surgical scrub nurse. She said she'd wait, but if she did resign in spite of the bonus, it would have to be effective in two weeks.

She learned from Roland Fox's office that Pamela Wagner had not been scheduled for a follow-up exam as instructed. She tried to call Pamela again, unsuccessfully, and headed for home. "They're isolating that poor kid. Her phone's been disconnected and they're not even providing appropriate medical care," she complained to Peter.

"I don't really like you getting so involved with what's not your business," he replied. "I know you're just looking out for this girl, but don't you think you might be overstepping some bounds? I wouldn't assume that you know what's best for these people in their situation. They're certainly not idiots."

Peter was probably right, but she couldn't stop fretting about Pamela until the evening news gave her another problem to dwell on. Phil Dreyer was introduced as chief aide to Congressman Mark Wagner in a videotaped press conference. "Representative Wagner, his wife and children are dealing with a devastating family crisis. At this time, I can only say that he'll release a statement to the press after addressing family priorities."

Phil repeated the same words to every reporter's question half a dozen times until the waving microphones started to disappear. The clip got shown on multiple networks for the entire weekend, and every time the story was aired, a picture of Karida's face flashed across the screen. The *Washington Chronicle* had released a few more photos and a video clip of the burial to the major networks. By Sunday, her face would be recognizable to anyone in the nation who owned a TV. Peter also became concerned and Karida was scared to leave their apartment. Although she wore a hat and sunglasses, even in her car, she felt like people were looking at her. Walking through the hospital corridors, a bald man stepped right in front of her and glowered at her, making her flashback to the day of her abortion. Then she thought about the day after, when she was having horrible cramps and her mother told her to "just buck up, go to school and act normal. You'll get over the baby and the boyfriend." She was so sad her heart hurt. Then she got sick and was exhausted for months. If only she had had some support. The memory turned her thoughts back to Pamela. If she could just get through to the Wagners, maybe she could help Pamela avoid that.

When she got to the float desk, Karida was greeted by a hospital administrator and offered two thousand dollars to sign on to the surgical department or stay on as a float. She had to give it some thought, at least hash it out with Peter.

"Today, you're assigned to neonatal intensive care," the supervisor said.

"I do love variety, but please, not NICU. I never spent much time there and I'm not really current. I'll take any surgical case instead."

"Sorry, Karida. You have two more weeks of float responsibilities and today the NICU is desperately understaffed. Some nurses are out sick and there were two sets of premature twins born yesterday. That's where you're needed."

~ ~ ~

"Are you the float? Thank heavens. Follow me." The supervisor had Karida scrubbed up and into a gown, hat, mask, shoe covers, and gloves at lightening speed. You're going to be in Nursery C. No action in there today we hope. Bad times in Nursery A and B."

People in yellow surgical garb padded about everywhere, even visitors. Only the tiny little stethoscopes hanging over shoulders distinguished who was staff. Anyone who got caught coughing or sniffling behind their surgical masks got escorted to the nearest exit. The whole place vibrated with activity and drama. Karida was introduced to an older nurse in a small room with four incubators. "This is Adrienne. She's the mother of neonatal nursing around here, so you're in very experienced hands." The supervisor disappeared.

"Ever work NICU before? You look like a preemie yourself. Welcome to suction city. These little buggers are all weaning off ventilator support, but they still have tubes in their airways that get clogged up with mucous. Your job is to watch their monitors and if the oxygen level starts to go down, you need to pass this itty-bitty catheter down the itty-bitty breathing tube and suction out the mucous. Around here we call ourselves 'snot-busters.' Except normally, we each have two babies to care for and we're so short staffed today that right now I'm trying to snot-bust four of them. And Kelsey here is being a very bad girl and turning blue, even after I suction her. So am I ever glad they found you."

Karida figured she looked like a deer in the headlights after this introduction. She tried to overcome her dread of looking at each individual baby. To her great relief, none of them was as tiny as Pamela's.

"Let me introduce you to these kiddos," Adrienne went on. "These are all graduates of Nurseries A and B where the sicker babies are. These guys all have a very good chance of survival since they've beat their initial odds.

"This here's Harley, born at twenty-seven weeks when Mom bounced him out while riding on the back of a motorcycle. He survived a minor brain bleed and is now thirty-two weeks, due to be born in two months. He may come off his ventilator in about ten days if he has no further setbacks.

"This is baby girl Smith. We call her Smittens. She was supposedly twenty-eight weeks at birth but very small for her age. She's just about off of the vent at thirty-three weeks, but not gaining weight too well. The mother is a nineteen-year-old crack-head and hasn't named the kid or visited her even once. Like most crack babies, she's irritable and doesn't sleep well. It takes cocaine-exposed infants much longer than adults to clear the drug from their bodies, and it can take a good eight to ten weeks before they start acting normal."

"Doesn't cocaine cause birth defects?" Karida asked.

"Not typically. If the mother was using regularly, there's a high incidence of prematurity and low birth weight. The babies have small heads and a high incidence of learning disabilities. They also have a higher incidence of death in early infancy, probably because withdrawal is so hard on them that they can't deal with other stuff. The really sad thing is that when they do get sent home with their crackhead mothers, and the mom can't deal with the crying, she'll quiet the baby by giving it some coke. Then these poor things wind up back in the hospital, going through withdrawal all over again. Whether she goes home with Mom or straight to foster care, poor Smittens doesn't have a bright future."

Adrienne moved right along. "Over here's Kevin. He's Twin A of Kevin and Kelsey, born at thirty-one weeks and now thirty-three weeks old. He outweighed his sister by three hundred grams. The thief stole the lion's share of the placental blood supply. They were both doing well for the past few days, until today, when Kelsy turned blue twice. The nerve of some preemies after all we do for them! We've called for a chest x-ray to make sure she doesn't have pneumonia. Here's how you suction one of these critters. They can fight a little. Sometimes you have to manhandle them a bit, but don't worry. They won't break. You take Kevin and Smittens. They're the most stable babes, and I'll deal with Harley and crumping Kelsey. Cover up your gonads. Here comes the roving x-ray machine."

Karida saw Kelsey turn dusky blue just after her chest x-ray. Since the film didn't show pneumonia, a resident physician with an entourage of medical students crowded into the room, performed a spinal tap on the infant, and took blood and urine samples to check for hidden infection. After Kelsey turned blue again, she got moved back into

Nursery B and in her place arrived baby boy Tuttle, born three days ago at thirty-four weeks and rapidly weaning off of his ventilator. Mother was reported to be a single woman with no support system. She had to return home immediately to care for two other small children, and hadn't yet been back to give this boy a name.

The rest of Karida's day was what Adrienne called routine. She suctioned breathing tubes, administered medicines and nutrient solutions, and changed diapers. She watched Kevin's mother cry as she held his tiny hand. Premature twins on ventilators with one at risk of dying, was not what this young mother had dreamed of. Instead of the joy of taking two healthy babies home, her family's life would be all about a prolonged hospital stay, then: endless doctor appointments, huge medical bills, and years of anxiety.

Karida also watched people buzz in and out of the nurseries where babies were more critical. She watched a family process the news that their son had died. She bestowed blessings on Adrienne for dealing with this every day, and hoped that the NICU wouldn't need her again. It was just too heart wrenching.

After a second day in the NICU, Karida was relieved when the float desk sent her to the adult ICU. After a stressful day there, she took the opportunity to walk around the block and breathe some fresh air before heading to the parking garage. Just as she neared the entrance, she became aware of a brown car driving slowly in the street beside her. It also turned into the garage. She got a sudden panicky feeling that the vehicle had been following her. She walked back out of the garage and into the hospital without looking back. She waited for another person to leave the elevator at her parking level. She didn't see the brown car when she got there.

~ Fifteen ~

Greg Thatcher still couldn't concentrate on his schoolwork. When he wasn't pining for Colleen, he was consumed by Vivian's pregnancy. Fearing academic failure and feeling overwhelmed in general, he sought out a counselor in the campus clinic. After a short wait, he found himself explaining his situation to a grandfatherly man named Malcolm.

"So if she didn't come with a political father who's a Pro-Lifer, do you think your girlfriend would be amenable to abortion?" Malcolm asked.

"I wish I knew that, but I don't. The timing here is just so bad because her father's in a really tight senate race. If she did want to go against her family, there couldn't be a worse time to do it."

"If she's only a month pregnant, timing could be on your side. The election will be over in a few weeks and then she might be less bound by her father's politics, and there would still be time for her to consider terminating the pregnancy. If her father loses his seat, that could make it easier for her. Then maybe things will seem less colored by politics."

"I really hope that's what happens, and from all indicators, there's a chance her father will lose, and maybe they can return to life out of the public eye. The problem for me though, is that even if her father's stuff wasn't in play here, I think she's personally against abortion. What are a man's rights when a woman doesn't want to terminate a pregnancy?"

"I'm not a lawyer, Greg, but I'm familiar with that all-too-common problem. There's been more than a few lawsuits by potential fathers regarding their rights, and in every case they've lost. The courts consider an embryo to be a part of a woman's body, and therefore the decision of what is done to her body belongs to her. At the same time, if the woman decides to bear the child, the welfare of the child supersedes any rights the father might have, and therefore he will be held responsible for support. That's how the system works.

"Your best tactic is to try to convince your girlfriend that it's not in your mutual best interests to go forward with the pregnancy, and if she's dead set against abortion, try to persuade her to put the baby up for adoption."

"She's mentioned adoption, but I have this feeling that she won't go that route for two reasons. In the first place, I think she'd have a hard time giving the baby away, and secondly, I think she might see keeping the baby as a way to preserve our relationship. She's a really good person, but I don't feel the same way towards her as I once did, and I can't imagine having a good marriage if I feel trapped. I even wonder if maybe she deliberately got pregnant because she sensed that I wanted to break up."

"I can sympathize with you, Greg, but the world at large won't. It wasn't so long ago that if a guy got a girl pregnant, there was no alternative but to marry her. Some women do get pregnant to entrap a man, but if the man wasn't taking his own precautions, then he's jumped into the trap.

"The pill is very convenient for couples who are truly committed to one another, and mutually prepared for the 'what-if' the pill fails, but the pill takes away the man's responsibility and shifts it all to the woman. Think about it, Greg! For a few seconds of pleasure, and just a few hours of female fertility in a month's time, women are using expensive medicine every day that's associated with serious side effects and risks. From what you've told me, your girlfriend went on the pill with good faith that it would prevent pregnancy and enhance intimacy. It's a very sad statistic, but more than fifty per cent of women seeking abortions claim to have been using contraceptive measures when their pregnancy occurred. Even if half of them weren't complying one hundred per cent, the fact remains that there's no foolproof way to avoid unwanted pregnancy except to avoid intercourse; and if a man really wants to make sure pregnancy doesn't happen, or spare his partner the risks and costs of birth control pills, then he'll inconvenience himself and use a condom. Used properly, they're ninety-eight percent effective, better than the pill, *and* they prevent venereal disease.

"It's unfortunate in situations like yours that you and your girlfriend didn't talk or agree about your beliefs about this before you became intimate. I don't want to judge you, but I will tell you that now that you're in this pickle, you need to take responsibility for the outcome. I doubt that's of much help to you, Greg, but that's all I can offer."

~ ~ ~

Greg hoped the appointment with the birth control doctor would present another opportunity to convince Vivian that she shouldn't have the baby. But after picking her up at her house and hearing that she still hadn't had a period, they rode to the appointment in silence. As they entered the office, Vivian told Greg she was using the alias Sandra Johnson.

"Sandra, it's still kind of early to confirm your pregnancy with ultrasound, but I can tell you from your exam, symptoms, and tests, there's little doubt that you're pregnant," Doctor Myra Rourke told them. "From the looks on your faces, I take it that's not welcome news.

"I'm really sorry, Sandra. I know you had only just begun using the pills, but as I explained when we made that decision, no method of birth control comes with a hundred per cent guarantee. Even in the cases of men and women who have had their tubes tied, fertility can be the most powerful of forces.

"By the way, did you receive any free samples of your birth control pills? One of our patients told us that as a new user, they were sent a few months free supply, the source of which we're not sure of."

"No. I purchased them at a pharmacy."

"Have you had any vomiting or diarrhea? Occasionally we'll see pregnancy in a woman who took her pills, but then got stomach flu. The pills probably run through the digestive tract without getting absorbed."

"No, though I've been sick to my stomach since I'm pregnant."

"Were you put on antibiotics or other medicines by a doctor or dentist? Some drugs can interfere with the effects of birth control pills."

"Not at all. I haven't taken any other medicines, not even vitamins."

"I am sorry, Sandra, that apparently you are that rare woman for whom the pills failed. Have you two discussed what you plan to do?"

Their expressions said 'no' and Doctor Rourke sensed there was conflict.

"Let's talk about your options. I'd like to start by telling you about my own unplanned pregnancy. I was a little younger than you when I got pregnant by a summer boyfriend, whose family was gone before I even knew I was pregnant."

She showed them a picture of her twins. "My parents were very supportive and helped me to arrange an open adoption. We found a wonderful couple whose infertility had even sent them to Asia to adopt a baby. Then that baby died in spite of the heroics they went through to save her.

"The adoptive parents are very gracious people, and have allowed me to stay in touch with my children. When I was still in school, I only saw the twins on special occasions. My mother felt I shouldn't be too present in those early years so that the twins wouldn't have any confusion about who they belonged to. When they were twelve, they learned that I wasn't really Aunt Myra, but their biologic mother. They've accepted our arrangement, believing they are especially loved and wanted. They're adults now and I'm so proud of their successes. I could never have given them the opportunities that their adoptive parents did, and I couldn't have finished my education had I tried to raise them myself."

"That's interesting," Greg remarked. "I've never heard of anything like that. I always thought adopted kids were prohibited from knowing their birth parents."

"That certainly was true in the past but is less so nowadays. The idea that birth records should be kept confidential and forever sealed started in the early 1900s, and by the 1950s, just about every state had enacted laws to protect the anonymity of birth parents. Later on, it became apparent that secrecy was often the cause of distress in both the birth parents, and adopted children and in the 1970s, the trend to open adoption took off. Presently, we see three kinds of arrangements. The least open is when the birth parents are provided with a profile of the adoptive family and the adoptive family is provided with information about the child's heritage and family medical history. There's no contact between them thereafter. Then there's the mediated format, where the biologic and adoptive families communicate through a third party, and then there's open adoption, like the one I did for my twins.

"I can't tell you that they all work out so well. Even in open adoption, biologic parents can still have regrets; but emerging research suggests that the majority of people who exercise such options are satisfied, and have less stress than when they spend their lives wondering what's become of their children, or in the case of the children, who their biologic parents are.

"I also want to tell you that the media paints a rather undeserved picture of adoption. News stories about adopted kids committing crimes aren't uncommon, but you won't see stories about *biologic* kids committing crimes, nor will you read stories about adopted kids who achieve greatness. Did you know that Sara McLaughlin, Jack Nicholson, Faith Hill, and Willie Nelson are all adopted kids, just to name a few? In the U.S. there are about twenty-five thousand adoptions a year and possibly one and a half million abortions a year. One has to wonder how many potential great people are never born, and how many great people who suffer from infertility never get to have a family."

"What if we decided against continuing the pregnancy?" Greg had to ask for fear that Vivian wouldn't, and it seemed that Doctor Rourke had little intention of talking about options other than adoption.

"I need to tell you up front that I don't perform abortions except for medical indications, but if that's your choice, I'll refer you to someone who does. Sandra's pregnancy is still early enough that she could undergo medical abortion. That option remains on the table until about seven weeks. It involves taking some drugs that have proven to be very safe and effective."

Doctor Rourke handed them the cards of the local Planned Parenthood Clinic and Doctor Roland Fox. "Going to a doctor's office is more private but more costly. Even the abortion pills cost in the six-hundred dollar-range, and surgical abortion gets more expensive the more advanced the pregnancy is. Planned Parenthood reduces their fees for girls and women in need. I should mention that a normal delivery in a hospital can cost eight to ten thousand dollars. I know you're paying cash here, Sandra, but if you're considering having this baby, you might want to learn about any health insurance benefits your family might have for maternity. Can I answer any other questions?"

"What does it cost for me to come to you to monitor my pregnancy?" Vivian asked, as Greg took a giant gulp.

"Why don't you check on your family's health insurance benefits, Sandra? If there are none, I'll work with you, but you can anticipate spending a couple of thousand dollars if everything goes well. That would include office visits, ultrasounds, some lab tests and prenatal vitamins. If a problem should develop, costs could be much higher. Some things just aren't predicable."

"Like what?" Vivian asked.

"Unfortunately, the list of things that can go wrong in a pregnancy is quite long. Common problems are bleeding, elevated blood sugar and or blood pressure that can require medication. Also common are: coincidental illness or injury, needing a C-section, and worst-case scenario, the discovery of a birth defect. Then things can get expensive. Prematurity is another major risk. The cost of caring for a premature infant can range in the hundreds of thousands of dollars. That's why I'm encouraging you to look into your health insurance coverage as you consider your options."

~ ~ ~

"So what are you thinking, Vivian?" Greg asked as he started driving.

"I'm thinking this is a horrible mess. Without knowing whether you'll support my decision, I don't know what to think."

"Well I'll certainly support your decision if you decide to terminate. Even if I have to lose this whole semester of school, I'll take you to the appointments and pay for whatever it costs. Vivian, even if we decided to get married tomorrow, I'm not in favor of having this baby. It's my earnest belief that we are both supposed to do other things with our lives than become teenage parents."

"And if I do decide to have the baby, then what?"

"I don't know, Vivian. Since Sunday I've tried to consider every possibility, but the only option I'm comfortable with is terminating the pregnancy. I'm truly sorry if that's not what you're thinking, but that's how I feel about it and I can only ask you to please consider my feelings along with your own."

Observing tears streaking her cheeks, he tried to take hold of her hand, but she turned her face and pulled away.

"Hey, want to go get something to eat somewhere and talk about this?"

"I want to go home, Greg. Please just take me home."

~ Sixteen ~

Mark Wagner's congressional offices were barnstormed on the Friday that the Rodriguez story appeared in the *Chronicle*. Reporters from every media outlet in the country inundated his staff with phone calls. His home state office had to close to keep reporters from haranguing his local aides.

A police detail was assigned to keep the paparazzi and Pro-Life demonstrators from invading the Wagner home. Even with police protection, someone with a slingshot and rocks managed to break a window by sneaking past the gate of the house behind the Wagner's. They were able to get a glazier to fix the broken glass, but wound up having all the windows boarded over, both to protect themselves, and so that Pamela wouldn't be able to see the fracas going on around them. Poor Claire was accosted when she tried to leave to get some groceries, so a policewoman offered to take the shopping list and get the family some essentials.

By Saturday afternoon, reporters had figured out the Barlow connection and John and Wendy also had to call the police when a tabloid reporter tried to sneak in their back door. After that, Phil arranged for them to have a police escort to the airport, but because airport security procedures prohibited their using camouflage identity, it was only a matter of hours before leaks about their destination forced them to change their plans. Instead of staying with relatives they took refuge in an obscure motel.

All of the Wagner's kids were also targeted. Red paint had been splattered on Melissa and Cliff's house in Falls Church, Virginia.

Jackson and Alicia needed police escorts to leave their apartment, and demonstrators showed up at the townhouse where Roberta and Edward lived in Texas.

It wasn't until the following Wednesday that the swarm of reporters started to dissipate. Phil Dreyer's press releases had persuaded the majority that the Wagners were in mourning, and that the Congressman would give a statement the following Monday. It helped a great deal that there were a few other election scandals for the reporters to feast on while the Wagner story stalled, but Anti-Choice radicals still clogged the street of the Wagners' neighborhood, and a security team had to guard the house twenty-four/seven. Even Mark was surprised at the persistence of the demonstrators who had made his private business their chief occupation.

The talking heads weren't backing off either. If any of Mark's staffers tuned into any of the talk show radio hosts, it seemed that the Wagner story was the only issue in the world. The liberals were lambasting Mark for his hypocrisy, and the conservatives were screaming "baby killers".

"This is what happens when you have unrestricted access to abortion, for *children* no less," yammered a pundit. "This kid was so immature that she didn't even know when she got pregnant. Yet some mercenary baby killer legally murdered her innocent child. Pamela Wagner should be sterilized and the physician who murdered that child should go to the electric chair."

As he listened, Aaron McGraf wondered why the hate-mongers weren't also calling for the sterilization of the man who impregnated Pamela. She didn't get pregnant all by herself. Men were not being held accountable for being the cause of pregnancy; yet, it was men who wanted to deny women the right to choose.

Inside the Wagner home, Pamela was forbidden to watch television, listen to the radio or go on the Internet, while Mark and Lorraine immersed themselves in news. When Pamela wasn't lying on the floor with her ear on the vent, she played solitaire and cried in her bedroom. She was allowed to speak to Jeremy once a day from Lorraine's cell phone, but having her parents stand over her made those conversations brief and awkward. The Monday after the Rodriguez story exploded, a Pro-Life crowd had showed up at her school and harassed teachers and students on their way into the building. The principal sought legal counsel about expelling Pamela, because her attendance threated the safety of the other pupils. There was still a security team, at the school's main entrance a week later; even though multiple persons informed the demonstrators that Pamela was not in attendance. One of Mark's lesser-known aides picked up her school assignments.

Mark had intended to campaign back in his home state the week that their confinement began. Now he was torn between escaping from his imprisonment and staying put to escape the national rage. He and Phil had consulted numerous experts, but none of them had come up with a better plan than what Nora Sutton had proposed on the night after the burial. Most had counseled him to move away from the extreme stance he had come to be associated with, and adopt a more moderate position. Even if he held onto the more radical ideology that he believed his constituency favored, it was assumed that those supporters would desert him because of Pamela's choice. Jackson kept insisting that he was in a lose-lose situation if he continued to align himself with the position that even his own daughter had rejected. "You're going to lose the support of your base anyway, Dad, so you might as well try to gain the support of some of the Pro-Choice folks, as well as those who believe that there has to be a middle ground."

Nora Sutton was consulted again. After listening to people from both camps, Mark concluded that the irritating attorney best understood the issues.

"You will not succeed if you keep clinging to that sound-bite that life begins at conception," she insisted. "The very reason our whole society is divided into warring factions on this subject is that there is no way to resolve the differing opinions about what is 'life,' or when it 'begins'. Neither science nor religion has been able to develop universally acceptable definitions.

"Millions of devout Christians reference the biblical passage in Genesis 2:7, that states that 'God made Adam from dust, but only when God breathed into *it* the breath of life did 'man become a living person.' It's this very passage that enables so many people of faith to believe that the unborn are not persons until they're able to breathe for themselves."

"So what's the scientific definition of life?" Mark asked.

"Also ambiguous. Scientists can't agree on a definition either. Are living cells in a petri dish a life? If we aren't sure what life is, how would we recognize extraterrestrial life upon exploration of another planet? Doctors can't even agree on whether or not viruses are living things. A widely used scientific definition is that life is a self-sustaining chemical system with the capacity to reproduce and evolve, but prematurely born humans cannot sustain themselves.

"Prior to the days of microscopes, humans had little understanding of fetal development, and a young fetus couldn't be distinguished from other uterine discharge. And, before the relatively recent rise of neonatal medicine, which enables little beings with underdeveloped lungs to survive by being mechanically ventilated, there was nothing murderous about premature infants dying. It's only recently that fetuses who can't breathe on their own have come to be considered citizens whose rights need protection, and that's only occurred in medically advanced countries. In less developed regions of the world, newborns who are too immature to breathe independently follow nature's course, and nobody gets blamed for what biology intended."

Mark interrupted. "So you're saying that ignorance makes it okay to let premature infants die?"

"Not at all," Nora countered. "I'm saying that we do not have a universal way of determining when a 'life' is a life. Life, as it might be defined in a high tech neonatal intensive care unit, does not equal life in the back reaches of the world where humans can't access the miracles of modern medicine. The contention that a few cells multiplying after the meeting of sperm and egg cells is a 'life,' isn't any more valid than the biblical concept that 'life' begins when there is breath. If there were one universal definition of what is *'a life,'* there wouldn't be this fractious controversy about it. From all of the years I've studied this; I've come to believe that there may never be a universally acceptable definition, only the conflicting beliefs of opposing groups, which is why we must seek a middle ground. Neither side is right, neither side is wrong. There is no absolute truth here, only divergent opinions. This controversy will continue to rage, so the only question that maybe can be answered, is whether one side can can impose their beliefs on the other."

~ ~ ~

It was the Sunday before the Monday that Phil Dreyer had promised that Representative Wagner would issue a press release, and even after all the expert counsel he had availed himself of, Mark was still in a quandary. The extreme Anti-Abortion views promoted by the VP candidate had brought the issue into full focus, and whatever approach Mark considered, it seemed there'd be a firestorm.

Watching his father deteriorating under the pressure, Jackson got an idea. "Maybe we can stall and deflect by concocting another personal crisis to buy voter sympathy."

Mark put down his glass of bourbon and seemed pensive for a few minutes. Then he turned to his wife of thirty-three years and said, "Rainy, we need to publicize your alcohol problem as the cause of Pamela's problems and have you go to rehab."

~ Seventeen ~

For an instant, Eliza didn't recognize Karida when she reappeared on her ward. Her long, straight, jet-black hair was blond, short and spiked. She was wearing big eyeglasses and a lot of blush and lipstick. The new look only detracted from her natural beauty, but Karida said it had stopped the stares of strangers who recognized her from the news. She was hoping her new look would also squelch her fear that someone was stalking her. She thought she had seen the brown car three times, and it had caused her to change her driving routes and start coming to the hospital earlier and leaving later.

"Why do you think it's stalking you?" Eliza asked.

"Initially it was just a feeling I had. I first saw it on the Friday the newspaper article came out. It was going slowly when I walked on the street by the garage, just to get some fresh air after a long shift. Then I thought I saw it again Monday morning when I turned onto the street of the garage entrance. Then I'm sure I saw it again when I left the hospital on Monday. It drove right behind me when I pulled out of the garage, so I drove over to Burger Barn and got into the drive-up line rather than going home. It didn't follow."

Eliza looked concerned.

"When I first told my husband about it, Peter said I was just being paranoid. A day later he said he'd noticed that brown is kind of an unpopular car color nowadays, and it could be significant that I saw a brown car three different times. So I went straight to the salon to change my appearance and now I'm driving Peter's car and he mine.

Every time I've looked in the mirror, I've scared myself to death, but at least I'm not getting stared at so much."

"I think you look great," Eliza lied. "Did you notify hospital security?"

"I guess I should. Even if it isn't some Anti-Choice nut that's associating me with the Wagner case, it could just be a pervert. Someone in the surgery department told me a nurse was attacked in the parking garage here a few years ago. At least there seems to be good security in the garage. I'm starting to wonder who protects people who work in Doctor Fox's office."

"Are you reconsidering whether you should take the job?" Eliza worried that maybe Karida wouldn't become their ally.

"I've been thinking about it a lot and I really don't know what to do. Now Peter has to go do some depositions in Ireland, so he'll be gone most of the week, and that gives me way too much time to think. Boy, do I wish I hadn't gotten involved with Pamela Wagner, but now that I have, I still want to try to help that kid. I could really use some advice, Eliza."

Feeling a sense of guilt for having put Karida in the crosshairs, Eliza took comfort in the fact that she had done her earnest best to warn Karida that working for the abortion doctor could be dangerous, but Karida decided to go there. Eliza felt that somehow it was destined that this young nurse would become part of NEB.

"Being home alone does give you a lot of time to think, but just wrestling with your thoughts all by yourself could become a vicious cycle. It might be better if you had someone else's input. Remember my telling you that I have some friends that share our commitment to reproductive rights? It just so happens that a few of us are getting together tonight. Perhaps if you came along, it would help you to decide. We can walk over there this evening; it's real close to the hospital. Maybe we can even get out of here when the shift ends. I'll grab some take-out and we'll head over to my friend Lydia's."

~ ~ ~

When they arrived, Karida found herself in an upstairs apartment with two other women, a teenaged girl, and a dreadfully deformed child whose age and even gender were hard to discern. It was difficult not to stare. Karida was introduced to Roxanne Abraham, a private investigator, Tracy, her look-alike daughter, and Lydia Beery, who lived there.

After introductions, Lydia said "let me tell you about Willie. I know it's uncomfortable for people to just wonder. Please don't be embarrassed if you feel compelled to stare. It's a very natural reaction."

Karida had seen a few birth defects during her nursing career, but she'd never seen the likes of Willie. His head was misshapen and his ears were just fleshy little nubs. His eyes were wide apart and barely slits. There were surgical scars on his nose and upper lip. His arms were thin and it looked like his hands came out of his elbows. Brown goo in a bag suspended over his recliner trickled down a tube that stuck out of his belly. Medicine bottles and a pile of diapers sat on a nearby dresser. Willie drooled and rolled his head back and forth repetitively. He wasn't much bigger than a four-year-old.

"Willie's birth defects are due to the acne drug isotretoin, trade name Accutane," Lydia began. "As you can see, his head, face, and limbs are very deformed and so was his heart, although that got surgically fixed at seven months after he survived, against all odds. They fixed the cleft of his face too. Believe it or not, he's twenty-three years old.

"I was in my senior year of college and about to get married when I was offered a prescription for Accutane to clear up bad cystic acne. I spent my teens trying to hide my pizza-face with pancake make-up, until I met my husband, who was also a pizza-face. Who else could bear to look beyond my complexion? The hope of not being the pimpliest bride and groom on Earth seemed like a miracle to both of us.

"We were warned that the drug had a significant risk of causing birth defects. We were both raised Catholic, so it was a monstrous decision for us to use birth control. Still, I longed to not have people gawk at my face and I was assured that the drug would cure my hideous acne, so I took it and my birth control pills, faithfully."

Lydia put one hand on her abdomen and the other over her heart. "In spite of being extremely careful, I got pregnant. We agonized about having a child with birth defects, but we left our fate in God's hands and Willie was the result." She gazed at Willie for a minute and then turned back to Karida.

"My husband couldn't deal with having a profoundly impaired, monstrous looking child. He left after Willie survived heart surgery. Statistics show that fathers often flee when they're saddled with an imperfect child, while mothers bear the burden alone. Later on, when I got involved in a class action lawsuit against the drug manufacturer, my ex wanted to come back and reunite our family. Yeah right! When he found out it could take a decade to get a settlement, he took off again and married someone else. The new wife used to send Willie birthday cards, but that stopped when the court started to garnish my ex's wages for child support.

"Willie was born in 1985 and after years of litigation, I finally got some compensation in 1996. Some of it went to dermabrasion to get rid of the scars on my face, but most of it goes to paying off medical bills for Willie. He winds up in the hospital for something every couple of months. He gets an infection or has intractable seizures. Amongst his many medical problems, he can't swallow, so he aspirates saliva and gets pneumonia. They said he would die in infancy, but I guess God decided that my life purpose was to take care of him.

"Before Accutane caused birth defects like Willie's in the 1980s, thousands of children were born in the 1960s with terribly deformed limbs because their mothers were prescribed thalidomide. That drug was marketed as a mild sleeping pill, safe in pregnancy. Abortion wasn't legal in many countries in the 1960's, so affected women were forced to either bear deformed children or risk going for a back alley abortion.

"I have to wonder, what will be the next drug, or virus, or environmental toxin that will force another generation of women to bear defective children, if the right to choose is eradicated? Even Willie would want to know that that's not going to happen to other children."

"So let's see the surveillance set up," Roxanne said when Lydia finished her story. "I still can't believe we found this apartment."

Karida was surprised to see Eliza appear flustered. "Um...hold on a minute. Karida doesn't know about NEB yet, so we need to explain things first."

"I'm sorry, Eliza," Roxanne said. When you told me she was in our camp and going to work for Roland Fox, I just assumed she knew. Pardon my big mouth, Karida. Eliza, now that I've spilled the beans, you need to tell her."

"Remember when I told you, Karida, that working for Doctor Fox might put you in a position where you could reveal that an Anti-Choice politician's family member was having an abortion?" Eliza began. "Well, my friends and I like to see those secrets get exposed."

Karida glared at Eliza. "Did you call the reporter about Pamela Wagner?"

Eliza side-stepped her question. "We have a really hard time with the fact that some of these Anti-Choice politicians are denying other women the rights that their own families take advantage of. Each of us has had experiences that motivate us to want to see the right to choose preserved. Through our coincidental exposure to a certain person, we've come together to do that.

"If this is something you think is so unethical that you don't want to get involved, we'd respect that. It is unethical. Even if you said you'd be willing to take part, we'd have no problem if you changed your mind, should the issue actually arise because of your position with Doctor Fox. It would be your personal decision if you saw a case that fits our goals, but wanted to honor your professional duty to keep it confidential. After all, the bottom line is that an individual's reproductive issues are nobody else's business. NEB. That's what we call ourselves: Nobody Else's Business. Yet Anti-Choice advocates believe that other people's reproductive issues are their business."

Eliza paused to assess how Karida was processing this divulgence, just as a buzzer interrupted them. Tracy, the teenager, went to get the door, and Karida noticed the others looking a little anxious. "It's Nora," Tracy called out, and the others immediately relaxed. Once more, introductions were made, and Nora, who apparently already knew that Karida was the nurse that was going to work for Doctor Fox, was advised that she was first being told about NEB.

Karida looked at each person intently and frowned. "In my wildest dreams, I could never imagine myself getting involved with something that's illegal or unethical, but I kind of get what you're trying to do. The vice presidential candidate scares me. I read that when she was governor, rape victims in that state were forced to pay for their own medical evaluations. If you're poor and uninsured, that's like being told we don't care if you were raped. I think if I'm going to work for Doctor Fox, I should hear more about NEB."

"I'm glad you're here, Nora," Eliza said. "I think before Karida hears more, she needs to know the legal side. I don't want her to even consider getting into this without understanding her risks. She already knows that Anti-Choice radicals can be dangerous. We're even worried that someone might be stalking her because of the pictures from the Wagner burial."

Eliza turned back to Karida. "Nora Sutton's a child welfare advocate and an attorney who straddles the great divide between Pro-Life and Pro-Choice factions, but she's actually on the side of children. She's handled some cases for parents suing physicians and clinics for providing their kids with contraception or abortions, including some cases that came up for Doctor Fox. She's even been consulted by Pamela Wagner's father about his situation."

Karida's eyes widened. "Do you know how Pamela's doing? I feel so badly for her and I haven't been able to reach her. I'm really worried about her."

"I didn't actually meet Pamela, but I share your concerns. Hopefully she's with some relatives, because her family's way too preoccupied with their political stuff to deal with her issues," Nora answered. "Her father's a real piece of work. He's only interested in his career, not his daughter's welfare. I think he would have already made Pamela a scapegoat, except that he has a son, a law student, who seems protective of his kid sister.

"When I met with Mark Wagner, his son Jack was trying to persuade him to moderate his Pro-Life stance. If that should happen, then NEB has already scored a victory. Hard as we try, we rarely get an opportunity to influence a Pro-Life politician to publicly change his mind, although I think we've changed some minds privately. But let's talk about your legal risks here, Karida, because they are enormous. As a nurse, I'm sure you know about HIPAA."

"The Health Information Privacy Protection Act of 2003. I learned about it in nursing school."

"HIPAA actually stands for the Health Insurance Portability and Accountability Act, but it is about protecting privacy," Nora explained. "Do you know what the penalties are for violating it?"

"Well I know it's considered a crime, but I don't know the specifics of messing up. Up until now, I would never have even thought about violating a patient's privacy, so I guess I didn't pay attention to the penalties."

"It's a serious crime, Karida. If a health professional revealed something private about a patient just by being careless, she could be fined $50,000, spend a year in jail, or both; but if a privacy violation occurred for personal gain, commercial interest, or malicious harm, penalties could be up to $250,000, ten years in jail, or both. Even rapists are rarely treated that harshly."

Karida's hands clenched almost to the point of white knuckles and Eliza was worried she would back out. "Obviously, Karida, we wouldn't want that to happen to you, for our sake as well as yours. If the situation ever arose, we would have a way to protect you."

"But how? And wouldn't Doctor Fox be in danger too?"

"Yes, you both would, but we're pretty sure that we could make it seem that the leak came from somewhere else, and not from any of the staff in his office. We've been in this situation before and worked it out successfully. There was a case that we got to the media by a NEB member posing as another patient who identified the Senator's girlfriend in the waiting room. No one blamed Dr. Fox or his staff. That Senator lost his seat; so there's one less staunch Pro-Lifer in Congress, and his successor is a little more moderate. However, Doctor Fox changed his waiting room arrangements to better protect patient privacy after that, so our challenges grow."

The doorbell buzzed again and this time Karida was introduced to another woman named Maria, who was also anxious to see the surveillance set-up.

"So what is this surveillance you're talking about?" Karida asked.

Eliza explained that Doctors O'Ryan and Rourke across the street were the gynecologists who helped young girls with contraception. Tracy added that at her school, it was common knowledge that Doctors "O and R" are where you go if you want to go on the pill behind your parents' backs.

"But is that legal for those doctors to prescribe the pill to kids?"

Nora answered that in Washington D.C., and twenty-some other states, a minor of any age can independently consent to contraceptive prescriptions. Some states have no laws on this issue, and about twenty-five states require parental consent. "What's bad about these laws," Nora continued, "is that when states require girls to have parental consent to obtain contraceptives, half of them simply forgo pregnancy protection. Money is another hurdle for this age group. Girls of means can find a way to access the pill, but most girls can't."

Sensing that Karida was still in tune with their goals, Eliza decided to reveal more. "Here's the worst thing we do. One of our NEB people, whose high school sweetheart was killed by a back alley abortionist six months before the passage of *Roe v. Wade*, used to work for the FDA. He was able to obtain some cases of counterfeit Jaz and Jazmin, which are the birth control pills that most of the O and R patients are prescribed. Nationwide, these particular oral contraceptives outsell most all others combined."

"Jaz can even clear up acne," Lydia added.

"I take Jaz myself," Karida commented. "I think it really helps my premenstrual symptoms, kind of a mood smoother."

Roxanne, the detective, took over the conversation. "It's always the most popular drugs that the counterfeiters profit on, like Viagra. These drugs have markets all over the world and China doesn't intervene in the manufacture of counterfeit drugs. The operation that produces the bogus Jaz is so expert that even the FDA people couldn't distinguish between the real and the fake pills without chemical analysis, which showed that the fakes contained little of the active ingredients. Our FDA liaison, an analytic chemist, investigated the pills when they appeared in an Eastern Europe market, and found that they were basically sugar pills with a tiny bit of estrogen and no toxins. So far, their distribution in American markets has not been reported, but our FDA man was able to obtain a trunkful of them when he was stationed in Europe. The hard part has been getting the counterfeits to our political targets.

"We think we've succeeded in getting the pills to a handful of Pro-Life political wives by a NEB member that works as a pharmacist, but if those women wound up with unwanted pregnancies, we don't know. They probably travel to terminate, rather than risk exposure in D.C. or their home states. We're pretty sure none of them gave birth. These are resourceful women, so this was a waste of our limited supply of fake pills. That's why we decided to target the kids of the Anti-Choice politicians, because the kids are more likely to seek help locally, rather than involve their parents."

"This was an agonizing decision for us," Eliza interjected. "We don't really want to hurt young girls, but the young girls we're targeting have parents who want to take away the right to choose. We're not going after the girls who aren't engaging in premarital sex behind their parent's backs. And, if we were to see an Anti-Choice kid exiting O'Ryan's office *with* a parent, we wouldn't target them. Those parents are helping their kids to avoid pregnancy.

"The girls we're targeting have options that poor girls don't. If they choose to have their babies, their families have the means to support the girl and her child, or arrange a private adoption. Meanwhile, the poor girls don't have those options. They can't get the high priced contraceptives, and if they wind up pregnant and happen to live in one of the more restrictive states, they may not have access to abortion. They may not even know about families wanting to adopt. Some of them have never even seen the want ads in a newspaper. So while we're not comfortable with this decision to go after kids, we believe that making things difficult for a handful of privileged girls, who are already risking pregnancies, justifies our goal of protecting the right to choose for all."

"But how do you get the fake pills to them?" Karida asked.

Lydia took over the conversation. "It's pretty devious, Karida. One of our associates has a professional cleaning service. About a year ago, she was able to get a contract to clean the doctors' office across the street. Once there, she found that they aren't yet computerized. They keep patient sign-in sheets in a folder, and in violation of HIPAA, they leave keys to the medical records file in an unlocked drawer. She also found a loose-leaf with weekly lists of the prescriptions that get phoned to pharmacies. Our cleaning lady can sneak a peak at the charts of everyone who gets Jaz called in, but we never saw the name of a political kid on those lists because apparently, these girls use aliases when seeking contraceptives.

"Then this apartment became available. For me, it's the best thing that could have happened; first of all because I can get Willie to the hospital faster by foot than trying to drive in this crazy city, and secondly because we now have a way to identify people who go in and out of the O and R office."

Lydia took the group into the front bedroom where the surveillance camera was set up. It was too dark to see the office across the street, but the tapes she played demonstrated how well they could see the faces of women as they exited the front door.

"But how do you know who they are?" Karida asked.

"That's the biggest part of this operation. It's come together largely because Willie has imprisoned me for twenty-three years. Of course I can take him wherever I want to go; pushing him in his wheelchair isn't physically difficult. It's the horror of his appearance that keeps us at home. It's not much fun to see children go screaming to their parents that 'there's a monster in this store.' I have an aide who comes three times a week so I can get out and tend to errands. Beyond that, I'm a pretty much a shut-in.

"The Internet has saved me from going mad and I've become a whiz at it. For years, I've been compiling a database with pictures of every political wife and kid I can find. There's almost always a hometown newspaper picture of political wives. It's also very convenient that some put family pictures on the Internet. Also, my nephew works for a yearbook publishing company. He can get us student pictures from schools all over the place. We also obtained some face-matching software, so now I download the surveillance tapes to see if any of the faces that come out of that office belong to the people from Anti-Choice political families in my data base. The very first day we ran the program we got a match. That night, our cleaning lady found a name on the patient sign-in sheet that correlated to the time of entry and exit on the videotape. Then she checked the girl's chart. Sure enough, she was there for contraceptives. It's amazing how much privacy cell phones and Email can give these kids, and girls who have access to cash can keep their contraception issues very secret from their parents. Roxanne's daughter, Tracy, hears conversations about it in school all the time."

Karida frowned. "This is unbelievable. I just don't know that I want to have any part of this." She looked at Tracy. "Who are these kids in your school?"

"It's a very expensive private school and I wouldn't even be going there if NEB web wasn't paying my tuition. I'll bet I'm the only kid there whose parents aren't politically important or just filthy rich," Tracy said. "Probably more than half of the girls in my school talk about being sexually active, and I'd guess there are others who do it but don't blab about it. I can talk that lingo too.

"Growing up the daughter of two private investigators has rubbed off on me, and I really believe in NEB. When I was in public school in eighth grade, one of the kids in my class told another girl that she got pregnant by her stepfather. She died trying to self-abort with a knitting needle in the girl's bathroom. She punctured her uterus and bled to death before the ambulance could get there. I was the one who found her on the floor in a pool of blood, and I will never, never get that picture out my head."

"Oh my God, Tracy. No wonder you're in to this." Karida turned back to the others. "So how do you actually get the phony pills into these girls' hands?"

"That's the trickiest part," Lydia responded. "Typically I send them a text message that advises them that as a new user of the product, they are entitled to three-month's worth of the pills for free. It appears that while these girls will use a phony name and address, they use their real cell phone numbers. We then give them a website they can go to. Since the cost of the pills is about $60 a month, and these girls are paying cash to keep their secret, they usually go for the free pills and give their real address. We mail them the counterfeit pills tucked into a innocent looking sample box of tampons.

"We're risking mail fraud here, along with other crimes, but it's the best scheme we've been able to come up with. It could take months before anyone winds up pregnant, if any do, and even then, their families might whisk them off to who-knows-where, and we'd never know if they had an abortion. We're always brainstorming for a better way. Meanwhile, if we could just impact one or two more prominent politicians or judges, we'd probably shut down the whole operation, because of the risks. The craziest thing is that the Wagner case came up without any effort on our part, and it's the best case we've ever had."

"This is just too much," Karida grumbled. "What a lot of risk and effort for maybe no results. All of you must have had some wicked experiences to go to these extremes."

"My mother was killed by a Pro-Life radical when I was fourteen," Roxanne volunteered. "It was 1979 and abortion was perfectly legal when a maniac bombed the clinic where she was a receptionist. She had burns over most of her body and she died in sheer agony."

Karida shook her head. "I'm so sorry, Roxanne, but I'm starting to understand why NEB is what it is. She turned to Nora. "Now I'm wondering what radicalized you?"

"I lost my sister Barbara to an illegal abortion in 1967," Nora said. "She had two young children and was pregnant with her third when her husband was drafted. He was in Viet Nam for about three weeks when he was killed. Barbara couldn't see any way she could care for another child. She could barely function with the two she had. Neither her in-laws nor my parents were in a position to be of much help. We were blue-collar families, just barely scraping by. Barbara wound up in the hands of an illegal abortionist who caused her to suffer an infection that killed her, and my parents wound up raising her kids, without enough money to eat and keep the house warm. That's how it was in the days before *Roe v. Wade*. I was able to climb out of the cycle of poverty because I was just lucky enough to have a good brain. I won a scholarship that enabled me to pursue a college education."

The group looked to Maria to tell her story.

"Two experiences brought me to NEB. The first was that my high school friend Cathy bled to death when she naively thought she could do her own abortion, just like the girl in Tracy's class. Cathy was the daughter of Doctor O'Ryan, whose office we're spying on. Dr. O'Ryan became a big advocate of contraception for teenagers after Cathy's death.

"The other thing that brought me here, brought all of us together in fact, is my association with a young woman named Lorena Green. For comic relief we call her 'Lee Green, the Baby Machine,' but it's no joke. I've been a social worker with the D.C. Department of Juvenile Protective Services for eighteen years and Lorena has been one of my most challenging cases. She was one of five children born to a her-oin-addicted prostitute. At least there were five that we knew about and of those, two are in jail and two are dead, due to drug overdoses. Lorena's mother is dead now too. Lorena was thirteen years old when her mother's pimp taught her to turn tricks, and fourteen when she first gave birth. The baby died of dehydration when it was six weeks old and that's when this dynasty came to the attention of Protective Services.

"Lorena is cognitively impaired, but she's pretty and very sweet. She can converse a little, but her ability to reason is severely limited. We estimate her to have the intellect of a six-year-old. After her mother died, we got her into a group home. When she had another baby, we worked very hard to help her learn how to care for it, but there was just so little she grasped. After weeks of coaching I asked her what should she do if the baby has a fever, and she said, 'call a baby sitter.' In spite of all the teaching and supervision, we had to take the second child away when it wasn't gaining weight.

"After that, we tricked her into Norplant. Karida might be too young to remember Norplant, but that was a birth control pellet that got sewn under the skin of the arm and worked pretty well for about five years. It came onto the US market in 1990 and got pulled off the market in '99 because of lawsuits over side effects. I think there were something like fifty thousand lawsuits.

"Lorena was fifteen when we got the Norplant in her and it apparently stopped working after four years. She gave birth to another baby at age twenty and after a few months, we again had to rescue the infant for neglect. The following year she gave birth to a very premature baby that probably cost the taxpayers half a million before it died. After that she had two more, including another sick preemie. Once, I asked her why she kept having babies when she knew she couldn't take care of them. She answered that she was going to keep having babies until we let her keep one.

"After another birth, we went to a judge to see if we could get a court order for involuntary sterilization, but the judge denied our petition because Lorena said she really wanted a baby. We tried to appeal, but out of nowhere, a Pro-Life attorney came to her defense and the judge ruled in her favor. Lorena is now thirty-three-years-old and she's had twelve pregnancies resulting in the birth of thirteen children. Three died in infancy and two have found permanent homes. The rest are in the foster care system. Most of them are cognitively impaired and one of her sons has already been in trouble with the law. I suspect the majority of them will be dependent on social services for life. The good news is that Lorena may now be infertile due to pelvic inflammatory disease. No births for the last three years."

"So how did this Lorena bring you all together?" Karida asked.

Eliza spoke first. "I've been in attendance for some of her deliveries and I met María when she was trying to persuade Lorena to give one of her babies up for adoption."

"I'm the attorney who Protective Services hired to petition the court. I still can't believe I lost that case," Nora lamented.

"I met Lorena when Willie was in the hospital one time, and she was there for one of her deliveries," Lydia explained. "She saw me pushing Willie in his wheelchair in the hallway and got so scared, she went running down the hall and tripped and fell. I went to help her get up and she seemed like such a lost soul, that I escorted her from the pediatric ward back to labor and delivery. I met Eliza there who told me Lorena would frequently go to the pediatric ward to see if any of her babies were there."

Only Roxanne's connection was still missing from the story. "I'm the private investigator that Nora hired to find out how the Pro-Life attorney came to Lorena's defense. My husband Daniel and I both used to be detectives on the police force, but after twelve years of that, we started our own business. What I found out in Lorena's case, was that her boyfriend of that season, a nice nineteen-year-old kid who was also cognitively impaired, came from an influential Anti-Choice family, and his parents hired the attorney, who would have defended a mass murderer if it paid well. This lawyer could have cared less about Lorena or the offspring she was producing. We did get Lorena to put that baby up for adoption when it was four months old, because she had a new boyfriend then. The family whose son impregnated her and hired the lawyer to fight her sterilization, wasn't willing to adopt her baby when she lost interest in it."

Maria spoke again. "The saddest and scariest part of all of this is that there are about two dozen Lorenas in our system, and finding homes for the children they can't care for is an enormous burden to society. Many of these unwanted children wind up in our corrections system as well as in the social services system. It's heartbreaking to work with people who have been unwanted their entire lives."

~ Eighteen ~

"There's no way I can go to rehab now," Lorraine protested. "If nothing else, I need to be here for Pamela. Create some other crisis, Mark, if that's what you have to do to take the heat off yourself. Let your mother be sick. Wouldn't that arouse more voter sympathy then your wife being an alcoholic? Why not go to rehab yourself? You're a worse alcoholic than I am anyway."

"That's brilliant, Lorraine! That will really save my career. I'm sure my constituents will be happy to elect a Senator who's in rehab. And my mother's healthy as a horse. What am I supposed to do to validate that she's sick? Break her leg? Our daughter is not my mother's problem, Lorraine. I'm sure if my mother had been raising Pamela, we wouldn't have a fourteen-year-old sneaking around having sex and abortions. If you had done your job as a mother, we wouldn't be in this sinkhole."

"What about your role as a father? What have you done lately to be a parent? It's always about your career, Mark, not your family. Our needs are pretty low on your priority list. You think I like having to make appearances at political functions ten times a month and entertaining the ambassador from Timbuktu? I'd be much happier being a stay-at-home Mom or selling real estate. I'm not the one who chose to go to Washington, Mark."

"I don't see other congressional wives being neglectful parents, Lorraine. I'm not hearing about their kids having sex and abortions, maybe because they're not drinking martinis all afternoon. This isn't about being in Washington, Lorraine. This is about being a sober mother."

"Ha! That's a laugh! You're not hearing about other congressional kids because you're too busy solving the world's problems. Believe me, there are plenty of congressional families with kid problems. Talk to any Washington mother and you'll hear about them. You wouldn't know, because family issues aren't important to you. Other than making appearances and furthering your career, you have zero interest in family, maybe less than zero. We're just adornments to you, Mark, and I'm altogether sick of it. That's what's driven me to drink, Mark, your selfish ambition and indifference to me and the kids."

From the floor vent in Roberta's bedroom, Pamela cried while she listened to her parents argue. She so desperately wanted her mother to be better. Her mother used to be fun. She missed the mom who was always doing stuff with her girls. Just two years ago, when the plans for Roberta's wedding were getting under way, her mother wanted to know her daughters' thoughts about everything: the guest list, the invitation, the cake, the flowers. They had such a good time when they went shopping for dresses.

Even last year, when Melissa and Cliff were getting ready for their baby, her mother wanted Pamela along to help her pick out things for the nursery. She and her mother went on shopping excursions and went horseback riding together. Now her mother just spent her afternoons drinking, and they hardly ever went anywhere together anymore.

Pamela had also noticed that her mother was taking some pills fairly regularly. Lorraine had said it was to help the hot flashes, and Pamela got a lesson about menopause. Now she wondered if that was really what the pills were for. Lately, her mother's mood and alertness seemed unpredictable. Sometimes Lorraine appeared energetic and happy, but then she'd get lethargic and crabby, even if she hadn't started drinking her martinis.

While her folks continued to shout at each other, she became more curious about the pills. She went to her parents' bedroom and started going through her mom's dresser. Finding nothing interesting there, she explored the cabinet over the sink in her mother's bathroom and found a vial of pills she suspected was for sleep, because it said to use at bedtime.

Then she started looking in the pocketbooks that hung from pegs in Lorraine's closet. In a gray leather purse that she'd seen her mother using when they first went to see Doctor Fox, was an almost empty vial with her sister Roberta's name and 'dextroamphetamine' on the label. It was dated from a few weeks ago, which didn't make sense. Roberta hadn't lived at home for more than a year. Pamela didn't know what dextroamphetamine was, but she knew that amphetamines were uppers and that people used them to lose weight. Her mother was obsessed with her weight. She so wished she could go to the Internet and find out more, but she was still being restricted.

Curiosity got the better of her. She next went rummaging through both of her parents' nightstands and the cabinet in her father's bathroom, where she found a vial of Viagra and a bottle of bourbon under his sink. Absorbed in her mission, she hadn't noticed that the shouting downstairs had ceased, and she was caught totally off guard when her father suddenly appeared behind her.

"What the hell are you doing in here, you little sneak?"

For a minute she was speechless. Her father's tone and expression said she had better come up with a very good answer, but the only one she could think of was the truth.

"I heard you tell Mommy that she needed to go to rehab and I think you're right, Daddy. She's not only drinking too much, but she's taking some kind of pills, and I came in here to see if I could find the pills to show you."

It was Mark's turn to be speechless. If Pamela was right, Lorraine was more messed up than he had even ventured to guess. He softened his tone considerably. "Did you find any pills?"

"I don't know, Daddy, but let me show you what I did find." She went back to her mother's closet and pulled the vial from the gray purse. "I just don't get it that Mommy would have Roberta's pills. I'm sorry I'm in here looking through your stuff, but I'm scared that Mommy has a drug problem. She's just not like she used to be."

Mark sat down on the corner of his bed and rolled the pill bottle in his hand. "What's different about Mommy, Pamela?"

Pamela explained the mood changes and nervousness she'd been noticing. "Also, she's never hungry anymore. We used to have supper together most evenings that she's home, but now I wind up eating by myself most of the time. Claire says the two of us don't eat enough to feed a bird and she doesn't know why she even bothers to cook. I'm sorry I'm in your room snooping, Daddy, but I'm totally worried about Mommy."

After a few moments of contemplation, Mark asked Pamela if she'd help him confront Lorraine. "I haven't been the best father, Pamela, but, now you've helped me to see that I haven't been paying enough attention to either you or Mommy. I'm sorry I've been so angry with you. Come! Let's go see if your mother can tell us what's going on with her. You've done right by telling me."

Pamela bit her lip. "Now Mommy is going to be furious with me. It was a sneaky thing for me to go through her purses."

"Yes, but you did it out of love and concern, Pammy. I'll tell her I found this. Okay? If you don't want to help me get to the bottom of this, I'll do it without you, but the things you just told me mean more coming from you. I'm afraid I've been wearing blinders, and maybe you're the only one around here who's had their eyes open. I'm sorry I haven't given you more credit, Pamela. If you're right about Mommy, this might save her life."

"I'll go with you, Daddy. Are you going to tell her now?"

"There's no time like the present. She drank herself unconscious a few days ago. I don't think we can take the chance that she could take an overdose of alcohol and pills with all the stress she's under. And this is not your fault, Pamela, it's mine. I'm sorry I haven't been a better father, Sweetheart."

Pamela chewed her lower lip. Mark put his arms out for a hug and she rushed to him and soaked up the affection. As he embraced her, Mark found himself feeling grateful that her sleuthing would give him the ammunition he needed to force Lorraine to go to rehab. When she broke away, they descended the stairs together and found Lorraine in her office. She had her martini glass next to her mouse as she surfed the Internet. Mark looked over her shoulder to see that she was looking at home state news. He picked up the martini glass and put his other hand on her shoulder. "We need to talk, Rainy."

"You mean there's some insult you haven't yet hurled at me today?" she said without looking up.

"Pamela's here too," he responded.

Lorraine whirled around in her chair, surprised by the presence of her daughter. Other than the once a day supervised phone call Pamela was allowed to make to Jeremy, Lorraine had barely seen her.

"Did you eat, Sweetie? Claire made a wonderful soup."

Pamela shook her head no and chewed on her lower lip.

"What?" She looked at Mark. "What's up? You both look like the cat that swallowed the canary."

"Pamela told me she's worried about you taking pills is what's up. Is she right to worry?"

Lorraine looked back and forth at her husband and her daughter. She addressed Mark. "As I told Pamela, I've been taking an herbal formula for hot flashes. I'm also on an estrogen patch. Menopause hasn't been much fun."

"Well, when she told me, Rainy, I went looking around upstairs and I found this." He handed her the pill vial. "Can you please explain why a prescription for Roberta was in our bedroom?"

Lorraine had thought she had been exceptionally careful to conceal her pills. "Where'd this come from? It must be really old."

"The date on the label says it was dispensed last month."

Lorraine looked at the small print. "That's ridiculous! The pharmacist must have put the wrong date on it." She grabbed the martini Mark had put down when he took the pill vial from his pocket, and cradled the glass in her hands. "Where'd you find that, anyway? Roberta stopped taking that two years ago."

"What was Roberta taking amphetamines for?"

"Well if you ever paid attention, Mark, you'd remember she was diagnosed with attention deficit when she got to junior high. First they put her on Ritalin, but she complained it gave her a stomachache so they switched her to this. She took it only on school days right up until she went to business school. Then she went off of it, but she went back on it when she started studying for final exams. After that, she went on and off it, depending on her school demands."

"So how come Doctor Orton isn't the prescriber on the label?"

Lorraine looked at the vial again. "I don't know. Maybe he was on vacation and this Doctor Thomas called it in to the druggist."

"You know, Rainy, I don't think doctors can prescribe a controlled substance like this over the phone. I think pharmacists have to have a written prescription to dispense amphetamines, barbiturates and narcotics."

Lorraine drained her martini glass. "Well, I don't know. Maybe they fax the prescriptions in these days."

"So if I call the pharmacist and ask him when's the last time he filled this prescription, do you think he'll verify for me that he put the wrong date on it?"

It was Lorraine's turn to look like she swallowed the canary. "Do we have to discuss this in front of Pamela?"

"I'm the one that's worried about you, Mommy. You're not the mommy I used to know. Lately, I've seen you get real nervous for no good reason. If you have a drug problem, Mommy, it could kill you. I don't want to lose you too."

Once more, Lorraine and Mark watched their daughter burst into tears. "I'm sorry, Mommy. I just don't want anything else bad to happen."

Lorraine chewed her lower lip. She put down her glass and extended her arms to Pamela, but her daughter didn't come to her and she dropped them. She looked back at Mark. "Don't you think she's had enough trauma for one week?"

Mark grabbed the pill vial off the desk. "I think it's high time we all started to confront the problems around here, Rainy. Don't you? Or are you okay with me checking this out with the pharmacy?"

Lorraine's face flushed. "Okay! All right! Yes, I've been taking the pills once in a while, but just when I'm exhausted and I have to be awake and alert for some event I have to attend. Menopause has shattered my ability to sleep and some days, I'm so tired I can't think straight."

"So why are you getting pills in Roberta's name?"

"Because she was on them already for a legitimate diagnosis and I didn't want to sully your precious reputation. I told Doctor Orton that Roberta was doing some more coursework and hadn't yet found a doctor in Texas, and I was sending them to her."

"So who's this Doctor Thomas on the label here?"

"Just what I said; he was covering for Doctor Orton last month."

"Please, just tell me, Lorraine, that if I go looking into it, that I'm not going to find that multiple pharmacies are filling prescriptions from multiple doctors for this and other pills. Please tell me that in addition to the booze and the amphetamines and the sleeping pills, that I'm not going to find out you're also taking narcotics. Can you tell me that, Rainy? Please, please tell me that."

A long silence and tears welling up in his wife's eyes gave him his answer.

"It's okay, Rainy. It's okay. We'll get help. If you don't want to do it for yourself or for me, do it for Pamela. Please, Rainy! Go for help! It's one thing for your daughter to come home and find you unconscious, quite another if she comes home to find you dead."

~ Nineteen ~

Greg drove back to campus from the Dr. Rourke appointment, stewing all the way. He scrambled to get notes from the Thursday classes he missed. After a few hours of procrastinating, he made the phone call he had promised to make earlier, but dreaded. "How are you doing, Vivian?"

"How do you think I'm doing, Greg? Not only do I feel physically and emotionally lousy, but I feel very alone with the hardest decision of my life."

"Have you talked to you mother about it?"

"You've got to be kidding me. My parents are running themselves ragged trying to get my father re-elected and it's looking worse and worse for him through no fault of his own. I really don't need to throw a bomb at them right now, especially since I haven't gotten any closer to making the decision about what I'm going to do. If I were to tell my parents, I can guarantee you that the option of abortion is off the table."

Greg felt a glimmer of hope that maybe she was considering it. "Are you thinking that would be the best thing to do?"

"All I can think about, Greg, night and day, is what I should do, and I still don't know. It would be a hell of a lot easier for me to make a decision if I knew your intentions if I don't opt for abortion. Maybe it's easy for you to sit on the fence, but it's sheer agony for me to not know if I still have a partner in this decision, or in life, for that matter."

Silence on the other end of the phone made Vivian's heart sink. "Greg? Are you there?"

"Sorry, Vivian. It's not my intention to make this harder on you than it already is. But, it's just that I don't know what to do either. All I can tell you at this point is that I'm just not ready to be a parent. If you opt for abortion or adoption I can support that, but if you plan to keep the baby, I can't say that I can be supportive of that. I mean I'd help financially, but I haven't yet come to grips with being a father or a husband."

"So you're saying we're through. That's it. I'm pregnant and you want to move on."

Greg could hear anguish in her voice. "Vivian, I'm not abandoning you. As I told you when we left Doctor Rourke's office, I'll leave school and cover all the expenses to help you get rid of this problem. Money is not an issue. If you absolutely insist on having this baby, I'll do what I should to support you both. I don't know, Vivian. Maybe when I've had time to really process this, I'll feel differently about getting married, but right now that's not a comfortable decision for me. I'm so sorry, but I have to be honest about this. I'm just not ready to get married and have a family."

The silence on the other end of the phone could not have been louder.

"Viv? I know this is terrible for you and I'm so sorry. Why don't we both sleep on it and I'll call you tomorrow after school."

Greg couldn't wait until his Friday economics class. He had decided that whatever Vivian planned to do, he had to preserve this weekend after last weekend had turned out so badly. He needed the time to study, but he also hoped to be able to get a date with Colleen. Every time he saw her in class or in a hallway, his desire grew more fervent.

He took the seat in which she sometimes sat next to him. She arrived in the room ahead of most and smiled at him, but she took a seat in the front of the room. When the class ended, she was out the door before he even had his laptop unplugged and he hustled to catch up with her. Then his pace was interrupted when another classroom of weekend-stoked freshmen emptied into the hallway in front of him. When he got past the throng and exited the building, he caught sight of Colleen as she greeted another one of those thick-necked football types who appeared to have been waiting for her. His heart sank as he observed them walk away with the big guy's arm around her.

As he sulked back to his dorm, he chastised himself for being more upset about having missed his chance with Colleen, than having emotionally abandoned his high school sweetheart. Still he couldn't even think about Vivian. His brain was obsessed with Colleen. He tried to hit the books, but his concentration was nil. He told himself he'd be able to think more clearly if he followed up on his promise to call Vivian. Maybe she'd decided to go along with abortion. He tried to call her twice but she didn't answer and he was puzzled. Then he left his dorm for the library with the hopes that the environment there would be more conducive to studying. It wasn't, and he opted to assuage his ego by hitting on a girl who he had noticed eyeing him. She was cute and flirtatious and she seemed like just the distraction he needed from his problems. She introduced herself as Donna from Kentucky.

~ ~ ~

With her parents campaigning in their home state over the weekend, Vivian was alone. After school on Friday, she was dreading returning to an empty house and wallowing in her dilemma, so she was relieved when her friend Glenna invited her over to get the notes she had missed from Thursday's classes. She was even more grateful for the opportunity to talk to someone, and Glenna was someone she trusted.

"I can't believe the pill failed you. That's horrible. I'm on the same pill and Mike and I never talked about what we'd do if I got pregnant. I'm really angry but not surprised that Greg Thatcher could be so irresponsible and inconsiderate. Geez, you guys have been together forever. I've only been going with Mike for six months. I'm really sorry, Vivian. You don't deserve this."

They were interrupted by Vivian's cell phone. "That's Greg now."

Glenna clasped her hand over Vivian's. "Don't answer it, Viv. Let him sweat a little. Push him off of his fence. If you let him talk you into abortion, you won't have made the decision that's best for you, and he won't have to really consider the consequences of the pregnancy. He's a coward and you need to be the strong one. Let him wonder for a while."

"So you think I should go through with the pregnancy?"

"Actually, I think you'd be crazy if you did, Vivian. Even if Greg wakes up tomorrow and says, 'Let's get married,' I don't see a happily-ever-after for the two of you. Just the way he's treated you since you told him, says he's not mature enough. To be perfectly honest, Viv, I always thought you were too good for Greg. A lot of guys at our school are as good-looking, smart and rich as Greg, but he's always seemed too full of himself for my taste."

"Are you Pro-Abortion Glenna?"

"I know your father is a big Pro-Life guy, Vivian, but being Pro-Choice is not the same thing as being Pro-Abortion. I do consider myself Pro-Choice, only because sometimes abortion is a better option than having an unwanted child. I very strongly believe that children should be wanted. I don't think I ever told you this, Viv, but my half-sister on my father's side, Shelly, had an unintended pregnancy her junior year of college. She's sixteen years older than me so we didn't grow up together. Anyway, she and her boyfriend opted to get married and have the kid. Five-year-old me was the flower-girl at her wedding, and seven months later she delivered a healthy baby boy, Skyler. Then they wound up getting divorced when Sky was five, and he became one of those footballs that went back and forth between Mom and Dad every other weekend. I know Shelly loves him, but I also know that from early on, she resented him. Whenever it was her weekend to have him, she would get all down and ornery. After she moved out of our house and was trying to date, she would drop him off for the weekend, and you could just tell the little guy was insecure and confused.

Even though my parents did all kinds of wonderful things with him, I'm sure he felt unwanted by his parents. Then when he was nine, his father remarried and moved to Miami. Sky doesn't get along with the stepmother or her kids, and he became enraged that his father was taking care of other children instead of him. Then he became very rebellious. He's twelve now and he's turned out to be a real problem, and my sister resents him more than ever. He hangs out with rotten kids and he won't even come here anymore, which is fine with my parents, because he was stealing stuff. My folks have been paying for Sky and Shelly to get counseling, but so far it doesn't seem to have made a difference. I don't know what his future will be, but if he's any example of what happens to unwanted kids, I'd say abortion is the lesser of two evils."

Vivian's phone rang again. She took Glenna's advice and decided to let Greg just wonder. His voice mail message said he thought maybe she'd gone out to dinner with her parents and he hoped she was feeling okay. He'd call again later. He didn't. When he did call on Saturday she also didn't answer. She spent Saturday alone at the shopping mall, looking at maternity clothes.

Glenna's sister's story was weighing heavily on her. She also wanted desperately to not disappoint her parents. Regardless of whether or not her father was re-elected, having an unmarried, pregnant teenage daughter would be a huge black eye for him, and hurting her parents would be the worst thing she could do. She had almost come to the conclusion that she'd go for an abortion, but she wasn't sure enough in her own mind to tell Greg yet. When he called Sunday, she told him she was still considering her options. The conversation was brief and there was no "I love you" at the end.

When her parents got back to Washington Sunday afternoon, her mother ordered take out from one of Vivian's favorite restaurants. Their dinner together was full of talk of how badly Roger's campaign was going. The missteps of the current administration were killing the whole party, the opposition was gaining traction everywhere, and the

VP candidate was turning more people off every day with inept television interviews and mean spirited rallies where no effort was made to dissuade followers from calling for the death of the opponent. Roger Evans's competitor was a Congressman with only two years of experience on the national stage, yet he seemed to be riding the wave of enthusiasm for change, a wave that Roger felt was going to drown him.

Roger normally didn't take phone calls during meals but the one that came through on this occasion got his attention. When he returned to the dinner table, he announced that he had just been contacted by Congressman Mark Wagner's office to consult on a statement they were preparing for a press conference on Monday and they were very solicitous of his opinions.

"I think I'll go help the poor guy out. His chances are starting to look as poor as mine, and he thinks what he says at this press conference tomorrow is his only hope. I can't imagine being in his shoes. His little girl sure screwed things up for him. I just can't believe kids are having sex so young, and then making these monstrous decisions; though I heard that Lorraine Wagner actually signed consent for their daughter's abortion. I guess you never really know what you'd do as a parent in their situation. If Rita Rodriguez hadn't caught them, no one would ever have known. I have to say, you make me proud, Vivian. I know you'd never do something like that."

~ Twenty ~

I t took Phil Dreyer a few hours to get back to Mark with recommendations for a rehab facility. There were numerous options, but most weren't dedicated to serving important people. Phil's contacts recommended some programs frequented by celebrities. Mark called two local clinics and both recommended immediate admission. "Bring your loved one here now if they've admitted they need help. If you wait until tomorrow, there's an overwhelming chance that the addiction will overpower the motivation to recover."

When Mark called the Betty Ford Center in California and another high end program in Utah, counselors there said the same thing. "People suffering from addiction rarely admit they need help until they're confronted by a crisis. As soon as the crisis passes, they retreat from facing their problems." While Mark made anonymous inquiries, Lorraine packed a suitcase. As soon as Mark told her he wanted her to enter a local program immediately, and then transfer to a more appropriate one, Lorraine changed her mind about going. Mark was about to explode when Pamela intervened.

"Please, Mommy, please," she begged. "I'll be fine here with Claire. When Daddy goes back to campaign, I'll stay with Jack and Ally, or Melissa and Cliff. All of us just want you to get better. Please, Mommy. You need to get better."

Lorraine wavered. She hated having a drug problem and a problem it was. Initially, she took the dexies just when she was exhausted, or before attending an event where food was plentiful. The pills killed her appetite really well. She used to be able to control her weight with vigorous exercise and moderation in eating. She prided herself for maintaining a size six, while her parents and sisters had become obese; but it was a constant struggle. Then menopause came on, and so did the pounds. She had a closet full of fabulous clothes that no longer fit. She increased her exercise and hired a personal trainer, but her midsection kept expanding and even her newest clothes were too tight.

It was during the stress of planning for the wedding that she started to use the pills. Roberta had promised Edward she'd stop taking them, and she proudly announced to her mother that she was done with them, as she tossed a vial into the trash in their exercise room. That evening, Lorraine couldn't close the zipper on a recently purchased skirt, which prompted her to rescue the pills to see if she could just shed a few pounds to fit into her gown for Roberta's wedding. She planned to use the pills just for a week or so. When she easily shed five pounds and felt more alert and energetic than she could remember, she started taking them more often.

She learned about Doctor Thomas from another congressional wife. "All you have to do is tell him that you have attention deficit disorder, go through his tests, and he'll write whatever prescription you want. He's good for pain pills too. You don't even have to give your real name if you pay cash. To check for attention deficit, he'll have you draw a line through a maze, and if your line squiggles when he makes a noise, he'll document that you tested positive for attention deficit. He knows we're all on the pills for weight control, but he plays the game. Just make sure your line in the maze squiggles."

At first Lorraine just took one of the pills in the morning. It helped offset the hangover from the sleeping pills, and made the tasks of the day seem less daunting. It definitely suppressed her appetite and even at catered events, she could resist the fabulous hors d'oeuvres. When the effects of the medicine started to wear off sooner and sooner, she found herself feeling tired and anxious. It didn't take long for her to start to need a second pill in the afternoon. Then she realized that if she took a dexie later in the day, she'd be unable to sleep at night, even with the sleeping pills that Doctor Orton was prescribing. That's when she came to rely on having more martinis. They took the anxiety away and helped her sleep. Most recently, she found herself taking higher doses of the pills in the morning and more martinis in the afternoon and evening. Also recently, she had asked Doctor Thomas for something for headaches, and he prescribed an opioid pain reliever that she found herself using more frequently, whether she had a headache or not. It just kind of mellowed her out. Intellectually she knew she was caught in a vicious cycle that would only get worse. Emotionally, she couldn't imagine going off the pills and regaining the weight.

She chastised herself for her vanity, for being a lousy parent, and for being an addict. It was time to stop. Still, the thought of checking herself into rehab was just too humiliating, and having to go public with her problem to salvage Mark's career, infuriated her. Ultimately, it was the depth of despair in Pamela's pleas for her to get help, and maternal instinct, that made her acquiesce. Besides, the consequences of not going could be worse.

Her ride to the rehab facility was in a police car. Even late Sunday afternoon, a few Anti-Choice protesters straggled outside the Wagner home. Lorraine ducked down as a heavily bearded man tried to take her picture. The last thing she saw before she ducked was an enormously obese, unkempt woman waving a crude sign that said "Baby Killers."

~ Twenty-One ~

P hil, Aaron and Jack got police escorts to the Wagner's house. They rejected meeting elsewhere to keep the protestors from descending on others. Pamela got sent upstairs. She hung a jingly bracelet on the doorknob so she'd be warned to get her ear off of the floor vent if someone came looking for her. The sound conduit kept her from going insane in her isolation.

"Do you really think this is going to work?" Mark asked his cohorts.

"It's your best chance, Sir," Aaron replied. "It's astounding how forgiving the public is when a renowned figure admits they've got a drug problem and goes for help. Even the Florida congressman who was sexually exploiting interns, got kid glove treatment from the media after checking himself into drug rehab. Then there's Rush Limbaugh who spent hours lambasting others with drug problems, until he got busted for illegally obtaining narcotic painkillers for himself. His followers still love him. The list of recovered addicts is full of actors, musicians, and comedians, but also remarkable for the number of politicians who are still respected, from Ted Kennedy's alcoholism to Governor Arnold's passion for pot. Don't forget President George W. Bush is a recovered alcoholic, and the wife of our presidential candidate is recovered from narcotics addiction.

"The public even immortalizes those who kill themselves with their addictions: Elvis Presley, Marilyn Monroe, Jimmy Hendrix, John Belushi, Jim Morrison, Chris Farley, River Phoenix, Heath Ledger, to name a few. The list is very long. I think there's a good chance that when we announce Lorraine's hospitalization, the abortion issue will fade into the background. If we can get just the right statement out, you might receive an outpouring of sympathy that will carry you to the Senate."

For the first time since learning of Pamela's abortion, Mark felt hopeful. "Have you drafted a press release yet, Aaron?" His suspicion that McGraf was gay no longer bothered him. What mattered now was that this young aide was a gifted political thinker and great wordsmith.

"I haven't, Sir, not in print anyway. Every time I start to write it in my head, I stumble on how to address the issue of your daughter."

As Mark seemed to ponder this, Phil offered an opinion. "If our goal is to take the focus off of Pamela and put it on Lorraine, why mention her at all? Aren't we trying to distract?"

"True," Aaron said, "but if we leave her out completely, the media may keep speculating about her, and that can keep the dead baby image in the public eye. What I'm thinking we have to do is change her image from villain to victim, paint her as a child adrift without a functional mother. But that puts the onus on you too, Congressman, so we have to be cautious."

Jack sensed Aaron was correct, but he resented how low Pamela's issues seemed to be on his father's priority list. "Dad, how do you plan to protect Pamela? Whether we do or don't mention her in this press release, it's likely that the media or the Pro-Life radicals are going to keep coming after her. Her security has to be paramount in whatever we come up with."

"Good thought, Son," Mark responded, somewhat guiltily.

Aaron asked: "Are you planning to give a news conference or just issue a statement to the press, or to a particular reporter?"

Again Mark looked unsettled. "What does the spin doctor advise?"

"A distressed appearance could be helpful if you give a news conference," Aaron said, "but then you'll have to take questions. The press isn't going to stop hounding you if you just make a statement and turn your back, like Phil did on Friday. Let's craft a written statement first, to nail what we want to say, and then we can figure out whether or not to do it in front of cameras. Like a classroom exercise; let's each write up what we think should be said and then we can select the best phrasing."

Three of the men started tapping on their laptops. Mark, who had never learned to type, penned his draft in a small notebook. After merging and editing their versions, Mark was still unsatisfied.

"Phil, go see if you can get another consult with that annoying Nora Sutton. We need someone more objective to judge how our statement comes across to people on both sides." Although public speaking was the reason Mark was so successful in life, something about Nora Sutton made him feel like an elementary school kid in front of a demanding teacher. He was craving a shot of bourbon, but too embarrassed to pour himself one, having just shipped his wife off to rehab. Once Nora was updated, he read his version.

> *It is with great dismay that I stand before you today to announce that my Senate bid has been unexpectedly interrupted by personal crises. As you already know, my fourteen-year-old daughter suffered a horrific outcome due to termination of an unplanned pregnancy last week. Today, my wife of thirty-three years, entered a rehabilitation program to fight her addiction to alcohol and prescription medicine.*

> *I am terribly guilty of having been oblivious to these developments in my own home, and blame myself for the grief and suffering that has befallen the people I love. In my exuberance for serving this great nation, I neglected my duties as a spouse and a parent.*

> *It is my sincerest hope that because of these failures, I will become a better man, and that those who elect me to represent their interests in government, will forgive me for these failures*

and allow me the privilege of continuing to serve. I believe the
humbling lessons that my wife's and daughter's issues have
· *taught me, will ultimately make me a better representative of*
all the people.

"That's it?" Nora remarked as Mark looked up from his notebook. She shook her head in disbelief. "If you shed a few tears on camera with those words, you'll arouse sympathy, but the press will still be clamoring for where you stand on abortion, and there'll still be plenty of time for you to be decimated by people on both sides of the debate. I'm sincerely sorry that you now have to deal with your wife's addiction, but I still want to know why you think you should deny other women, the right to choose as exercised by your daughter."

She was just so irritating, Mark thought, but he needed an honest critic and she sure fulfilled that function. He turned to his son. "Why don't you read your last version, Jack?"

"Okay, here goes:

My fellow Americans, I stand in shame before you. While
preoccupied with the critical issues our country faces, I was
blind to critical issues my own family was facing. I have only
just come to understand how oblivious I was to the struggles
of my youngest child, as well as those that were consuming my
partner in life. Yesterday, my wife Lorraine, mother to our four
children and a tireless advocate for education, was hospitalized
for dependency on addictive medicine.

Lorraine and I have long strived to protect the rights of the
unborn. In this crusade, we didn't always consider the plight
of women with unintended pregnancies. Because of the
tragedies that our own family is now suffering, we hope to be
able to work on a new front to reduce the practice of abortion.

Our children are constantly bombarded by media messages

about sexuality, but we've done an awful job of educating them as to how to deal with their sexuality. We've presumed that teaching them to just say 'no' somehow protects them from the dire consequences of not saying no. We've failed to assist them in resisting cultural and peer pressure to engage in premarital sex. They are woefully under-educated about contraception and the poor prognosis of teen pregnancy, and pregnant teens are often ignorant about adoption.

If my constituents see fit, I promise to work to change the climate that leads children like my daughter to terminate their pregnancies. I will seek legislation to expand health coverage for women and children and bolster childcare, and to make adoption a more available option. We must do everything possible to discourage premarital sex, but we must also do what's possible, to encourage women to bring their pregnancies to term.

Nora clapped her hands. "So when are you running for office, Jack? I'd not only vote for a legislator who made those commitments, I'd go out and campaign for you." She turned back to Mark. "That is the speech you should deliver. What's preventing you from adopting your son's position?"

Mark sighed with frustration. "I just don't think it will appeal to the people in my state who want to overturn *Roe v. Wade.*"

It was Nora's turn to sigh. "Ah yes! The zealots who are joining the anti-abortion armies. How do we placate them?"

"What do you mean by armies?" Jackson asked.

"Surely, as Pro-Life advocates, you've heard about these ultra-violent groups. They have the potential to derail the whole Right-To-Life agenda. These radicals not only seek to reverse *Roe v. Wade*, but to take over the world. They are militant and fascist. In the US, they attract the heavy metal, Goth element of the teen and young adult population, who they transplant from moderate Evangelical churches to their more radical fold. The people they are most successful at recruiting are already angry and disenfranchised from mainstream society. These groups also run so-called Christian summer camps where they train very young children how to use weaponry, so that they'll be ready to kill those who stand in the way of their goals. Children younger than six have been brainwashed to be warriors."

"Well that's certainly not the voting block I'm trying to appeal to," Mark retorted.

"Really? Do you know that our party's VP candidate has belonged to congregations that are suspected of being aligned with this movement?"

Mark shook his head. "I find that very hard to believe."

"So do I," Nora retorted. "Yet every time this candidate makes reference to going into politics to answer God's call, I have to wonder. Such very extreme Anti-Choice views can only hurt the party and the Pro-Life cause. We have to be on guard against our ideals being commandeered by radicals who would actually maim and kill people to advance a Pro-Life agenda. These people are anything *but* pro life."

"What specifically about Jack's speech seems incompatible with the views of the voters you want to appeal to?"

"Teaching kids about contraception. I mean personally, I wish my daughter was much better informed on the subject, but I think that's viewed very unfavorably by my constituents."

"Why do you think so? If one looks at church positions on contraception, there are almost no bans, and the bible also says nothing specific about contraception, although the story of Onan spilling seed has been interpreted that way. Even in denominations that eagerly promote large families, such as Mormonism and Catholicism, some forms of contraception are acceptable. Only in fundamentalist Judaism and Islam is contraception prohibited. Let me clarify that. Only one of nine subgroups of Muslims actively oppose contraception, and the writings of Mohammed suggest that he favored it. Even amongst very Orthodox Jews, abortion is mandatory if the mother's life is in danger."

"So how did contraception come to be so taboo?" Jack asked.

"Great question, if you don't mind a little history lesson." Mark, Aaron and Phil signaled they wanted to hear more.

"Artifacts from many cultures show that humans have long been invested in trying to prevent unwanted births. Anthropologists have found foreign bodies in the uteruses of mummified Egyptian girls. Ancient writings indicate that women used crocodile and elephant dung as spermicides, and the alkalinity of these substances was probably fairly effective. Cervical barriers made from silk fibers and spider webs have been found in exploration of ancient Rome and Asia. Men were developing condoms as early as the 1500s, and fashioning them out of sheep intestines by the 1700s. Diaphragms and cervical caps made from a variety of materials were widely used in Europe in the 1800s, at least by the upper classes. Am I boring you with my lecturing?"

They all seemed engrossed, so Mark said, "please go on."

"Well, we presume that people were highly motivated to not produce children when food was scarce. But then, as agricultural productivity and industrial manufacturing evolved, children became valuable as laborers. At least children of the lower class were coveted for the labor force. Consequently, by the 1800s, leaders started restricting contraception, especially for the lower classes, which provoked a backlash.

"For example, in the 1830s, an English immigrant who called herself Madame Restell, opened a clinic in New York for the sole purpose of providing medicinal and surgical birth control. In the 1840s she expanded her operation to Boston and Philadelphia. By the 1870's she was so successful, she was spending more than $60,000 a year just to advertise her services. Ads from a Syracuse, New York clinic from the 1870s, indicate it was providing abortion services by injecting water into the uterus, claiming that even a servant girl could afford the ten-dollar charge. In response, a man named Anthony Comstock, started a personal crusade to shut these clinics down. Madame Restell was brought to trial and committed suicide. Thereafter, an anti-contraceptive movement took full root in the United States with passage of the Comstock Act of 1873, which outlawed mailing of contraceptive devices, medicines, and even information about birth control. Politicians were worried that if poor people didn't produce children, there wouldn't be enough laborers.

"Fast forward a generation, and a nurse named Margaret Sanger challenged the illegality of contraception. She'd seen too many women who already had too many children, die during childbirth. She became a community organizer and enlisted the help of ministers and rabbis to advance her cause. In 1916, she opened a birth control clinic and on the very first day, one hundred and forty women came seeking her services. When the police came on day nine, she corralled her supporters to petition the government to at least allow physicians to prescribe contraceptives to cure or prevent disease. Today, Margaret Sanger is viewed as the founder of Planned Parenthood.

"With that history in mind, the more recent role of religion is better appreciated. It was 1934 when the Episcopal Church decreed that birth control was acceptable for married couples. Other denominations also started to liberalize their policies and even the Catholic Church gave it's blessing to the rhythm method, but barred Catholics from using 'unnatural' birth control. Meanwhile, the birth rate amongst Catholics is no longer higher than other populations, so there may not be many adhering to the church's teachings. It should also be noted that the abortion rate amongst Catholics is slightly higher than among non-Catholics. Perhaps the church is currently spending so much compensating the victims of pedophile priests, they don't have enough resources to provide better teaching to the faithful. None of this speaks well to their goal of reducing abortion, especially promotion of the unreliable rhythm method.

"But back to the timeline. Although society and churches were finally acknowledging that intimacy between married persons served purposes other than procreation, poor people were still unable to access reliable contraception. Up until 1958, New York hospitals would not provide contraceptives to the poor until a protest by *clergymen* fostered a policy change. Legal access to contraceptives for all women finally came about with a Supreme Court decision in 1965, in the case of *Griswold v. Connecticut*, whereby the court determined that the right to privacy exceeded government restrictions on contraception. The next breakthrough also came in 1965 when once more, *clergymen* supported the distribution of contraceptives to the poor in Baltimore. Then in 1967, fifteen hundred clergymen came together to help one hundred thousand poor women find access to safe abortion. That was six years before *Roe v. Wade*.

"The point is, Congressman Wagner, modern religious leaders have been fighting to allow their flocks to control the size of their families. On a more global scale, contraception is directly related to the standard of living. When people can limit the size of their families, they can prosper. In disadvantaged cultures where women keep birthing, we find the highest levels of poverty and human suffering. Before China's birth control policy was forced on its population, the country was burgeoning to the point of starvation; but that's another whole dissertation. The bottom line, Congressman Wagner, is that we'll never reduce abortion if we don't promote contraception."

Mark looked at the floor more than he looked at Nora as he said "You've made your point exceedingly well, and while I appreciate the wealth of knowledge that you're sharing with us, I still think that promoting contraception for teenagers is what could cost me the election. I just don't believe that works for the social conservatives I represent."

"Then maybe we should talk about the adverse outcomes of teen pregnancy, because as a group, the kids from such pregnancies do poorly. They have more school dysfunction, mental illness, substance abuse and criminal behavior, and even if they don't have those problems, they tend to have lower levels of education, lower employment rates, and increased risks of becoming teenage parents themselves. That's what the voters need to understand, and that's what we ought to be teaching our children before they become sexually active. We can't hold onto the delusion that Victorian morals are compatible with our highly sexualized culture. Our children need a much more relevant education; but you're the politician here. If your constituents want to substitute creationism for science, and continue to promote abstinence-only education, then I suppose you have to kowtow to their prurient interests. On the other hand, if your goal is to reduce the killing of unborn babies, then you'll have to modify your approach."

Mark had no arguments to contradict the knowledge and verbal prowess of Nora Sutton, and decided he'd leave it at that. As he eyed the door, he said, "I truly appreciate your input. Are there any other cautions to heed?"

Nora sensed she'd made some progress with him, though he needed a lot more education. It was probably enough for one encounter though. Instead of answering him, she said, "Well, actually, I'd like to know how your daughter is doing. In fact, I'd like to meet the young lady. Is she here?"

Jackson didn't wait for a gesture of approval from his father. It was bothering him that Pamela was so isolated. "She's upstairs. If she's awake, I'll have her come down so you can see what a fine young woman she is."

~ Twenty-Two ~

When Jack didn't find Pamela in her room, he looked in Roberta's room, thinking she was probably listening through the floor vent. Her absence in all of the bedrooms led him to the bathroom.

"It's Jack, Pamela. Are you in there? There's a very interesting lady downstairs who'd like to meet you."

"I'll be right out."

Jack became concerned. "Pammy, are you okay?"

"Just a minute. Jack? Can you get me a pair of jeans from my closet?"

Jack handed the jeans in. "Is everything okay, Pammy?"

"I'll be right out."

After another minute he asked again if something was wrong. Finally she emerged and answered, "I don't know. Doctor Fox said I probably wouldn't have a real period for another month or two, but I've got one now. Do you think I should be worried?"

"Melissa would be a better resource on that. Did you try to call her?"

"Daddy took my phone away, and I'm not allowed to talk to anyone."

"Hmmm! Let me try to call her right now. No answer at home. She's not answering her cell either. She's probably bathing the baby or something."

"Maybe Alicia knows," Pam suggested.

"I don't think so, Pammy. Your situation isn't in her realm of experience. We do happen to have a very smart lady downstairs though.

Maybe she can help. Do you feel okay enough to come down and meet her?"

Like everyone else, Nora Sutton was appalled at Pamela Wagner's appearance. She was way too thin and maybe too pale. She smiled when introduced, but red-rimmed eyes and her general demeanor screamed 'depression'. How could she not be? On top of her father's and her own predicaments, she'd just lost her mother to rehab, and what distress preceded that, Nora could only wonder.

Jack whispered about Pamela's problem to Mark and then turned to Nora. "I hate to bother you with something beyond the political issues here, Ms. Sutton, but right now, my sister could really use some womanly advice, if you wouldn't mind."

While her father and colleagues continued to banter, Pamela and Nora retreated to Lorraine's office. Pamela explained her problem. Nora didn't know how concerning the bleeding was, and she placed a call to Doctor Fox.

"Doctor Fox is presiding at an emergency in the hospital", his answering service said. "Until he's available, he asks that any patient with an emergency go to the E.R. at D.C. Memorial."

"My father will have a cow if I attract attention in an E.R. right now. He's got enough to deal with already because of me, and now things are even worse because of my mother. I can't just go to the hospital."

Pretty altruistic Nora thought. "I wouldn't want to see you in the E.R. either. Perhaps we have another option. I have a friend who's an obstetric nurse. If I can just reach her, she'll know what to do." She scrolled to Eliza's number.

"It's Nora. Really glad I caught you. Look, I'm doing a legal consult right now and there's a young woman here who had a premature delivery about a week ago, and now she's having some bleeding. Should we be concerned?"

"You're kidding. You're at the Wagner's right now?"

"Yes, as a matter of fact. I'm consulting here, and by coincidence, I happen to be with the young woman right now. There's a lot going on for her family and her mother isn't available. We tried to call the obstetrician who delivered her, but he's taking care of an emergency. Due to circumstances, it would be quite awkward to have her sit in an E.R. Do you think this can wait?"

Eliza had Nora check Pamela's pulse, which wasn't too rapid. She instructed Nora how to examine her belly, which didn't seem tender. From Pamela's description, they decided the bleeding wasn't too serious. Eliza recommended a follow-up exam with the doctor at earliest convenience, unless more symptoms arose before then. Pain, fever or heavier bleeding could constitute an emergency.

"This is a very interesting development," Eliza said. I know you can't really talk, but how do you think she's doing? "Say 'yes' for well, 'okay' for okay, 'no' for not so good and 'no, no' for we need to be concerned."

"No, no. I'm even wondering if you could check her out."

"Would that be safe? The news said there are still demonstrators at the Wagner's house. I don't need them stalking me."

"What if we could somehow sneak her to see you in the hospital?"

"How would you do that? Even if you could sneak her there, she'd recognize me. It's too risky. How do you keep the crazies from targeting you?"

"I come and go by cab in wigs. The last time I left, I had the cabbie drop me off at the police station to shake someone tailing me. Then I took another cab home."

Eliza fretted. "Pamela was supposed to be rechecked by Doctor Fox this past week. I bet that didn't happen. Now that I think about it, getting her to Doctor Fox might be too risky for him. Then the crazies would be demonstrating outside his office. We've got a problem here. By the by, what are they planning to do to protect Pamela anyway?"

"That's a great question. Let me go talk to the family some more and get back to you. Keep your phone free."

Pamela told Nora that she was unaware of any plans or even discussion about when she could go back to school. She knew her father had to make a statement to the press and that was supposed to get the demonstrators off their backs, but now that her mother was hospitalized, she had no idea what the plans were. Together, Nora and Pamela interrupted Mark and his colleagues.

"We tried calling her doctor but he's dealing with an emergency now, so I spoke with an obstetric nurse I know who helped us assess things. We're confident that it's not an emergency now, but she needs medical follow-up for these symptoms. How can we arrange that?"

Mark looked embarrassed. Here he was, blabbering about how he was going to make his family his top priority and he hadn't given Pamela's situation any consideration beyond confining her.

"We're making plans with a relative," he lied, "and while I'm giving the press conference tomorrow afternoon, we'll sneak Pamela off to her destination. My wife's problem only came to light earlier today and I have to call her mother and sisters before this gets broadcast tomorrow." He turned to Jack.

"Why don't we take a break and order in some food? Jack, I'd be really grateful if you'd call your grandparents and Aunts Nancy and Teresa. If Teresa's okay with it, that might be the safest place for Pamela until this blows over."

Jack looked flustered. "You know, Dad, except for pecks on the cheek at weddings, I don't think I've had any contact with Aunt Teresa in my conscious life. I wonder if they've even heard of this fiasco up in Canada. I'll be glad to call Grandmas Wagner and Ellis but I'd really prefer it if you'd speak to Aunt Teresa. She's pretty much a stranger to me."

"To me too," Pamela echoed. "Can't I stay with Melissa or Jack, or go to Texas and stay with Roberta?"

"It's not safe to stay with close family, Sweetheart. These people who think you've done a terrible thing could make it dangerous for your brother and sisters. It's only for a short time. We have to do what's safest."

Pamela's tears started to trickle. "But what about school, Daddy? I have to go to school, don't I?"

"We'll get you a tutor. I'm sorry, Pamela. I wish it didn't have to be this way, but I have to get back to the campaign and you can't stay here alone."

"But I won't be alone. Claire can stay here with me. Please, Daddy, I don't want to go to Canada. Mommy always says Aunt Teresa married a jerk and has made a sorry life for herself."

"Well, maybe we can make some other arrangements. The important thing is that we need to make sure that you're out of harm's way."

"We also need to get her proper medical attention," Nora interjected. "I was advised that if the bleeding got worse or she becomes feverish or has any pain, then it *would* be a medical emergency. Excuse me for a moment, but I want to call my nurse friend back and ask her something else."

Nora retreated to Lorraine's study and called Eliza again. "They're going to ship this poor kid off to whatever relative will take her. She's a really sweet kid, Eliza. I wish I could help her somehow."

"I've been racking my brain about this, Nora, and I'm thinking that no one from NEB should get involved. If the congressman realized there was a connection between you and the rest of us, your cover could be blown as well as NEB's. The family's going to have to find her the support she needs, and I'm just grateful you're there now to endorse that. They should get her out of D.C. and get her to a gynecologist and counselor who won't be sitting ducks for the demonstrators."

~ Twenty-Three ~

Since he had no real inclination to read a textbook, Greg Thatcher left the library with Donna from Kentucky. Together they went to the campus snack bar and shared a pizza. She was a freshman too, majoring in business administration. She was a lively conversationalist and Greg enjoyed her company. She wasn't nearly as pretty as Colleen or Vivian but she was cute in a sexy sort of way. They walked around a bit after their meal and as it got dark, they proceeded to Greg's car with the intention of going to a movie in town. She was the ideal diversion from his turmoil.

Greg didn't even have the key in the ignition when Donna unzipped his fly. When he was maximally excited she started to take off her clothes, and within seconds he was following her over the seat into the back of the car.

"I don't have any condoms with me," he confessed.

"No worries, Big Boy. I'm on the pill."

Those four words had a chilling effect on Greg. Having a pregnant girlfriend on the pill made him balk.

Picking up on his reluctance, Donna asked "Ever gone in the back door?"

He wouldn't admit he hadn't, but saw it as a convenient opportunity for new experience. After that, she wouldn't let him rest. They never left the parking lot until she had coaxed more performance out of him than he knew he was capable of. When he was totally spent, she gave him her phone number, and he dropped her off at her dorm before returning to his own, totally exhausted. After reading one paragraph in his economics textbook, he fell fast asleep.

Saturday he did as much as studying as he could. He tried to call Vivian, but she didn't answer, and he felt relieved. He didn't know what to say to her anymore. He was also looking forward to another hot night with Donna. He called to see what time he should pick her up, but the number she gave him was disconnected. He returned to the dorm he had dropped her off at, but no one there seemed to have any idea who he was talking about when he described her to other residents. He then went looking for her in the library and the snack bar, to no avail. He even tried finding her in some of the other girls' dorms, but no one he asked knew a Donna that fit her description.

He meandered over to the stadium and bought a ticket, but football didn't interest him. He walked around looking for Donna and surprisingly ran into Colleen. She looked more stunning than ever but was only briefly friendly. "Doing anything after the game?" he ventured.

"You're so sweet to ask, Greg, but actually, I've got a date with one of the guys on the team. Maybe some other time."

Defeated, he again tried to call Vivian, but she still wasn't answering. Maybe she had gone back home with her folks for her dad's campaign. It momentarily occurred to him that maybe she didn't want to talk to him, but he discarded that thought quickly. What he really suspected was that she was simply waiting for him to tell her they would get married and live happily ever after, and that was the last thing on his mind. He retraced his steps looking for Donna, but never found her. He spent the night alone, trying to study.

~ ~ ~

By Monday, Greg started to suspect that something was wrong. It hurt a lot to pee. He figured it was just a result of the sexual workout that Donna had given him, followed by his self-stimulation as he fantasized about Colleen when Vivian hadn't taken his calls.

By Tuesday he knew something was really wrong. He felt feverish and achy and he noticed some pus in his underwear. He made a beeline for the infirmary, but was embarrassed to find the doctor on duty was a woman. He'd never seen a woman doctor. He decided to come back when there was a male physician on the schedule the following day.

By the time he got in to Doctor Paul Freitag on Wednesday, not only was he feeling sick, but he'd also noticed blisters on his genitals.

"Did this girl bite at you at all?" Doctor Freitag asked as he swabbed Greg's urethra with a few different Q-tips.

After the intense pain subsided, Greg admitted that she did seem to use her teeth quite a bit and maybe she kind of nipped at him. He wasn't sure if she broke the skin. When it was all over he was pretty raw and irritated.

"Was she kind of petite and did her name start with D?" the physician asked as he drew several vials of blood.

Greg was dumbfounded. "Yes. Why do you ask that?"

As Greg rolled down his shirtsleeve, Dr. Freitag motioned him into a chair in an inner office.

"I'm worried that you may have hooked up with a very vicious person, Greg. Here at the infirmary, one of the other doctors and I have each seen a case of a student with a story like yours, and neither of us thought much of it until yesterday morning, when we coincidentally got into a conversation about it. The stories seemed way too similar, so we contacted the Public Health Department and spoke to an investigator there, who was aware of some other cases that fit this perpetrator's pattern, so now the police are also investigating."

"What are you saying?" Greg asked, not wanting to even think of the possibilities.

"In each of these cases, all of which have presented with acute symptoms of sexually transmitted infections, the patients have now been called back and asked for details. This morning the investigator told us that this perpetrator seems to hang around college campuses and entice men with witty conversation and seductive behavior. She uses different names. I wrote them down."

He grappled with a huge pile of papers on his desk and found a scribbled list. "Here it is. So far, she's called herself Darcy, Debra, Denise, and Diedra. It seems she's going through the the alphabet and we can only wonder how many men she's infected using names starting with A, B and C. She's also told each victim she's from a different state. She told you Kentucky. I think the investigator said Georgia, Arkansas, and other southern states. Now they're looking into possible cases in other colleges, because of a suspected case in Virginia, so a federal investigator has also been called in."

"Infected with what?"

Doctor Freitag grimaced. "Well, Greg, I'm sorry to tell you that so far victims have had positive cultures for chlamydia and gonorrhea. Three of the victims presented with herpes blisters, one with genital warts and one of the victims has tested positive for the AIDS virus. Now that person wasn't here on campus, but showed up at the Public Health Department more than a week ago, so I don't know all the facts in his case. It's possible he had AIDS from some other source, so that isn't necessarily a risk for you. We just don't know yet.

"Your sores appear to be herpes, and the painful urination and pus suggest gonorrhea. Of course we'll know more when the cultures come back. The AIDS tests may not be reliable for another week, and even then, we can't be sure if the initial test is negative. Sometimes it takes a few months before we can identify an AIDS infection with any certainty. Gonorrhea we can cure, and we can get rid of genital warts if you develop them. Sorry to tell you there's still no cure for herpes or AIDS, though this prescription will help reduce the severity of the herpes outbreak. The antibiotic shot we'll give you here, along with oral antibiotics should clear up gonorrhea and chlamydia and cover for syphilis. We'll also need to check for hepatitis, but we can't cure that either."

Greg felt like he had a million questions at the same time that he felt like his mind had gone completely blank.

Doctor Freitag continued in his matter-of-fact way. "You also need to know that with herpes, you're now contagious on an ongoing basis, and you can infect others you engage in sex with. This pamphlet has information about precautions you should take. Ethical herpes sufferers generally restrict their unprotected sexual activity only to others who are already infected. We estimate as many as one in five people in your age group has the virus, although many don't know they have it unless they've had painful eruptions. The incidence could actually be closer to one in four persons. There are some medications that can reduce the frequency and severity of outbreaks, but, unfortunately, this is a chronic disease. The moral of the story is: you need to always use condoms unless your partner accepts the risk of being infected.

"I'm also sorry to tell you, Greg that you'll need to come back to be interviewed by investigators when we get that set up. A police illustrator will be working with our victims on a sketch, so we can get warnings out in our dorms and fraternity houses. This dangerous person must be stopped.

"Here's some prescriptions and please make a follow-up appointment to come back in about a week for the AIDS test. We'll contact you when we have the meeting set up with the investigators, probably tomorrow or Friday."

Greg finally found his voice. "What will happen to this girl if she's found?"

"I'm not sure. Some states put people like this in jail, but not a lot of states have laws to protect victims unless they were *forced* to have sex by the infected person. Of course the first problem is finding her. Apparently she's very crafty and she could already be in another state."

"What would possess someone to do something like this?"

"It's hard to say, Greg. I've researched that a little since we became aware of our cases and it seems most of the people who have been caught doing this sort of thing are sociopaths; that is, they harbor deep rage. They don't see others as people, only as targets and opportunities. They lack the capacity to feel love, shame, guilt, or remorse. Instead of friends, they have victims and accomplices who usually end up as victims. They can be very cunning and our jails are full of sociopaths. It's not very curable.

"In the case of your attacker, it appears she knows what she's doing. My guess is that when she learned she'd been infected, she adopted a fatalistic attitude that if she's going down, she's going to take as many men with her as she can. Infecting others satisfies some need for revenge or power.

"You do know, I hope, that nowadays most people with AIDS live a long time if they take their medicine; but then again, we don't know if she even has AIDS. We may never know what motivated this person, and all I can really say is that I'm sorry you fell victim."

"Not as sorry as I am." The physical pain now seemed less significant than the lifetime of humiliation he was anticipating. He couldn't think of anything else to ask and found himself holding back tears. As he turned to go, Doctor Freitag added that he could come back tomorrow and speak to a counselor.

"Sometimes it's helpful to have someone to talk to when you've received bad news like this. It's not something most people like to discuss with friends. There's also a support group on campus for herpes sufferers. It's all there in the papers I gave you. Please call if you have any problems with the antibiotics. And don't forget the AIDS test. I'm so sorry, Greg."

~ Twenty-Four ~

Mark Wagner's press conference was scheduled for two o'clock on Monday afternoon. He and his aides worked for hours Sunday trying to prepare, but by Monday morning they still needed to sharpen their position on several issues.

Phil Dreyer had scouted out the schedules of some of their allies on The Hill. "I've arranged for Roger Evans to join us. His voting record is similar to yours, though his seat is in jeopardy. There's a very strong challenger coming after him. He should be here shortly."

Aaron McGraf had prepared a list of questions the reporters might hurl at Mark. He read them as soon as they got down to business.

"Do you believe that women should have unrestricted access to the emergency contraceptive, PLAN B? What about teenage girls?"

"Do you believe that parents should be notified if a minor seeks contraceptives?

"Should a man be able to stop a woman from having an abortion if he agrees to take full responsibility for raising the child?

"Should gays and lesbians be allowed to adopt? I'm sure you're aware that there are several state referendums this election to prohibit such adoptions.

"What's your position on the proposed regulation to allow health care professionals who disagree with *Roe v. Wade,* to refuse to provide contraception and abortion services?

"Where do you stand on stem cell research?"

"And here are some questions that a Rita Rodriguez type might ask:

"How do you plan to help your daughter recover from her tragedy?

"Did Mrs. Wagner support your daughter's decision to have an abortion?

"Would you have helped your daughter obtain contraceptives if you knew about her relationship with her boyfriend?

"Should schools be providing better education regarding contraception?

"What kind of sex education was your daughter's school providing?

"Why didn't you attend the burial service for your grandson?"

Aaron looked up from his laptop. "I'm very concerned that even with the speech we concocted yesterday, these reporters are going to grill you until you sizzle. They've had the better part of a week to look at your record. I've prepared some statements to try to answer some of these questions, but I don't have answers on the more personal ones."

Mark looked perturbed. "Can't I just back away from questions that are too personal?"

"I don't think so, Sir. You're using your personal problems to garner sympathy. You need to have some statement other than it's 'none of your business.' Here are some potential responses."

"I take full responsibility for the problems that have befallen my wife and daughter. Parents need to talk to with one another and their children about these critical issues. I learned the hard way and hope that by publically airing my mistakes, I can help others to avoid them."

"Good Aaron. I like that. Let's work on some of these other questions."

"May I ask, Sir, where Pamela's going to be staying? She seemed so fragile yesterday that I felt like offering her refuge myself. Well not myself actually, but my sister's a nurse and a stay-at-home mom. She lives in Baltimore, and, if it's of any help to you, and we could somehow sneak Pamela there, it could maybe give her a safe haven as well as some nursing assistance. My sister has a good heart and I know she would want to help. Also, when she was still actively nursing, she worked with patients with anorexia."

The word anorexia stunned Mark. Pamela couldn't have anorexia he told himself. It was just the stress of the pregnancy that caused her to lose weight. Wasn't anorexia a potentially fatal disease? Maybe if she did have it, he'd glean even more sympathy.

"That's a very generous offer, Aaron. Jack has been working on arrangements to get her to his wife's grandparents, but I actually like your offer better. I have to see what Jack's come up with."

A secretary voiced in, "Senator Roger Evans is here."

"Thanks for taking time out of your campaign, Roger. I really appreciate your coming by. How's the family?"

"Glad if I can help you, Mark. We're fine. Amelia keeps promising she'll give up private practice, but she still spends too much time as a consultant for severely disturbed patients. Maybe if I lose the election, she and I can actually get to spend some time together. Then there's my son Chris, a junior at Princeton. He seems to be majoring in girls and minoring in political science, but he's basically a good kid. My pride and joy is my daughter Vivian. She's a high school senior and plans to be a doctor, but she could have a future as a concert pianist, if her boyfriend didn't take up so much of her time. She's so talented that her teachers keep saying they have nothing more to offer and we should find a more advanced teacher. All's well considering I'm in the political fight of my life. I'm spending as much time thinking about my next career as I am trying to salvage my campaign, but I still have a small lead. I'm really sorry to see your campaign in such a tailspin."

"I had a good lead before Rita Rodriguez stuck her cameras into my personal life. Now my lead has dwindled considerably. On top of my youngest daughter's missteps, yesterday, I had to admit Lorraine to the hospital for detox; diet pills and martinis. She totally lost control. Now she's on her way to a rehab facility in Utah. I promised a press conference today to address the abortion issue, but now I'm also going to publicly admit to Lorraine's addiction. Either the voters will take pity on me or they'll dance on my political grave. We've been brainstorming for the last few days, trying to figure out what to say, and I'd be truly grateful if you'd critique the statements we've come up with."

While Roger looked at the drafts, Phil firmed plans to transfer Lorraine to the Best Hope House in Utah, a favorite rehab facility for celebrities. Mark called Jack about the newest option for where to hide Pamela. Baltimore would be convenient. They could go back to the first plan if Aaron's sister didn't work out.

"I'd go with this one here." Roger selected Jack's version of the speech.

"How do you think the Pro-Life voters are going to react to the idea that teenagers need education about contraception?"

"I struggle with that myself, Mark. My state requires parental consent for young girls to get contraceptives and we have a terrible teen pregnancy rate. We don't allow unmarried couples to adopt, while there are thousands of unwanted children in the foster care system. Many of these kids have been abandoned, neglected or abused by their heterosexual parents, while our voters refuse to allow homosexual couples to open their homes to a child in need. Look at Nebraska where dozens of parents just rushed to dump unwanted children on hospital doorsteps before the state legislature outlaws this behavior.

"Did you know that in the 2000 census, barely half of children in this country were living with a married mother and father? New data shows that births to teens under age seventeen costs society about eight billion a year. That figure reflects the lower taxes teen families pay, as well as the extra social services they often require. Without public assistance, children of teen families might be vulnerable to malnutrition and preventable crippling diseases like polio."

"At least my state isn't that restrictive about adoption," Mark said, "but we've got a hell of a lot of kids in the foster care system anyway."

Roger shook his head. "Just this August, Amelia was consulted on a case in which a ten-year-old boy had become mute. He was sexually molested by his grandpa in his own home and sent to foster care, where another child molested him. Amelia wound up in a conference with the boy's court-appointed guardian who ranted that licensure should be required for becoming a parent. The guardian gave Amelia a whole written dissertation on how people who perform far less meaningful jobs have to prove their competence. An unlicensed plumber can't touch your pipes and beauticians can't even trim your nails without demonstrating that they have the proper training and skills. Why do we allow people with no training, no skills, and insufficient resources, to take on the hardest job in the world, child rearing? People should at least be given a parenting course as part of their basic education, have to intern in a daycare setting, and have to pass a parenting knowledge test before they start producing kids. This frustrated guardian was trying to get Amelia to push me to legislate for parenting licensure. Imagine that!

"I actually agree with Jack. There's something inherently wrong with voters who want to end the right to safe abortion, but oppose educating teens about reproduction. It's even more illogical that these are the same voters who don't want to expand adoption options for unwanted children. I detest having to appeal to voters who are anti-sex education and anti-child welfare, but my biggest donors are extreme conservatives and I have to champion the goals of my supporters or lose my seat. That's politics."

"So why do you think I should chance giving this speech Jack wrote."

"I think Jack's speech could work, but I have another idea for you. Why not use Lorraine's hospitalization as an escape from the bite of the rabid press, and have Jack deliver the speech as a proxy while you escort her to rehab. That way, you really do look like a devoted family man, and the press won't hold you up as a dartboard. Maybe tip off Rodriguez to photograph you at the airport to capitalize on the scandal of it. I doubt the reporters will give Jack a hard time if he's stepping in at the last minute, especially if their phones are showing a picture of embarrassed you and Lorraine on the way to the hospital."

"Hmmm. I like that idea. Thanks, Roger. I should be with Lorraine anyway, and that could give Jack a jump-start on his political career. I really appreciate your help.

"You know, my daughter Melissa's father-in-law is a manager with the symphony, and he's helped some young musicians to get orchestral auditions. Let me know if your daughter would like to audition some time and I'll arrange it. I hope you can keep your seat, Roger, and please give our regards to Amelia. Thanks again."

~ Twenty-Five ~

At first, Jack balked about being proxy for his father. He had already taken the day off in order to take Pamela to his wife's grandparents, so it wasn't a question of availability. He just felt wholly unprepared to stand before a host of reporters who seemed to want to draw blood.

"They won't do to you what they'd do to me, Jack. When they see your fresh young face and learn about your mother's troubles, they'll be much more compassionate. Aaron took the speech you wrote and reworked it so that it comes from you instead of me. We've even expanded a little on your ideas. By the way, Senator Evans came to help us out with this earlier this morning, and after reading all of the drafts; he thought yours was the best. Jack, this is an opportunity for you to make a name for yourself on the national political stage."

"What about Mom and Pamela?"

"Phil's arranged for Mom and I to fly to Utah where there's a very good rehab program. He's also tipped off someone from the *Washington Chronicle* so we get photographed on our way. We have to be at the airport about an hour before the press conference has been scheduled. That's maybe just enough time for a reporter's pictures to get out on the Internet."

"And Mom knows about this?"

"I talked with the physician at the hospital. He said her physical withdrawal will not be too difficult. She might only need a few days of detoxification followed by a few weeks of counseling. She's on some medication now to allay the physical symptoms. He also said that the program in Utah should be just right for her because she won't be in group therapy sessions with street addicts. She'll be working with people from her own social class who know what it's like to suffer public humiliation. I spoke with Mom briefly and she's willing to go along with this. She said she's actually relieved that it's all come out, and that she's afraid of how much worse things might have become."

"So how do I get Pamela to Alicia's grandparents in New Jersey if I'm doing a press conference?"

"We have a new option for Pamela. While you're speaking and the press is trying to catch Mom and me on the way to Utah, McGraf is going to come to the house in a rug cleaner's van and carry Pamela out of the house wrapped in a rug. He'll get her to his sister's house in Baltimore. She's a nurse, and since no one knows her connection to us, Pamela should be safe and well cared for there. Her name is Gail Furness. Aaron says she wants to help."

"And what does Pamela think about this arrangement?"

"She's okay with it. She was actually afraid of involving your in-laws; that a reporter could figure out the connection."

"Me too, Dad. Okay. I'll do it, but I need to be comfortable with the speech. Are you in your office now? Where's the press room?"

"I am, and the reporters will be in the conference room across the hall from my office; about a dozen of them. How long until you can get here?"

"If traffic isn't too bad, I can probably get into a suit and be there in an hour. But have Aaron E-mail me the speech before I get on the road, so I can give it some thought."

~ ~ ~

With multiple microphones in his face and bright lights flashing, Jackson Wagner stood before an audience of journalists for the first time in his life. He was both surprised and delighted at how at ease he felt.

Good afternoon, Ladies and Gentlemen of the Press. For those of you who do not know who I am, please allow me to introduce myself. I am Jackson Wagner, the son of Congressman Mark Wagner. I stand here before you in my father's place, because another family crisis prohibits my father from being here at this appointed time. At this very moment, my father, Congressman Mark Wagner, is admitting his wife Lorraine, my mother, to an addiction treatment facility.

It took a few minutes for the buzz in the room to subside before Jack could continue.

Since I no longer live at home, issues concerning my parents and baby sister came to light for me, as they did for the press and the public, in just the past few days. Apparently, while my father was preoccupied with the multiple, enormous and difficult challenges that our country is presently facing, he failed to notice some serious problems that were developing at home.

As my father labored night and day to attend to matters on the House floor, my mother, a tireless advocate for literacy and education, developed a dependency on addictive medicine. Then, while coping with the events surrounding missteps taken by my baby sister, my mother revealed her own problems to us just yesterday. She was hospitalized last evening and is now on her way to a specialized facility to start the difficult journey to recovery, with my father at her side.

As you already know, my parents have long strived to protect the rights of the unborn. In this noble crusade, they now recognize that they didn't always give fair consideration to the plight of girls and women who are the victims of unintended pregnancy. Because of the tragedies that our family is now suffering, my father intends to commit himself to developing a new frontier to reduce the practice of abortion.

Children, such as my fourteen-year-old sister, are continuously bombarded by media messages about sexuality. What they are not provided with is essential information as to how to behave in a highly sexualized culture where intimacy is not only the basis of relationships, but also the basis of entertainment. We've failed to develop effective education to assist youth in resisting cultural and peer pressure to engage in premarital sex. They are sorely undereducated on the subjects of contraception and the unfortunate outcomes associated with teen pregnancy. Those that do get caught up in the tragedy of unplanned pregnancies do not know enough about adoption.

If the voters see fit to re-elect my father, he promises to work to change the climate that leads girls like my sister to terminate their pregnancies. He promises to seek legislation to expand health coverage for women and children, to bolster childcare for single mothers, and to make adoption more accessible for those families who have the love in their hearts, but lack the financial resources to provide for a needy child.

Because human sexuality is a fact of life, families, schools, churches, and government must come together to help guide youth to develop responsible sexual behavior. They must also join forces to help people prevent unplanned pregnancies, so that abortion becomes unnecessary, and so that every fetus becomes a wanted child.

My father is deeply embarrassed by our family's tragedies, and sincerely regrets that he is not standing here in person to present these issues and his intentions. But he believes that the politician, who takes full responsibility for the welfare of his loved ones, is best able to serve all of the people of this great nation.

Thank you.

With almost every journalist in the room shouting questions, Jackson responded that his father would be available to answer their questions as soon as the situation allowed. He thanked them for their understanding and turned away as cameras flashed and reporters yammered on their cell phones. Just as he exited, he heard a reporter shout that he had a picture of the Wagners at the airport. "They're admitting her to the Best Hope House in Utah."

From a microphone left in the conference room, Jack and Phil heard more murmurings about the Best Hope House. Maybe Lorraine's addiction had supplanted the fixation on Pamela's abortion. They could only hope.

~ Twenty-Six ~

It was Karida Robbins's last week at D.C. Memorial, and she had already seen enough trauma to make office practice seem all the more inviting. At the same time, she was having second thoughts about working with NEB. As much as she shared the goals of these women, she wasn't sure she wanted to be a part of their devious schemes. Peter thought she should take the position with Doctor Fox anyway. She was under no obligation to violate anyone's privacy and if it turned out to be terrible, she could go elsewhere. The demand for nurses was up, and even the D.C. Memorial administrator has said she'd be welcomed back if she changed her mind.

On the Monday of her last week, she spent another heart-wrenching day in the NICU. There was another baby in the unit who had been abandoned by its drug-addicted mother. "These women's only concern is getting back on the street to get a fix," her mentor Adrienne explained. "Sometimes they'll come back to see if the baby is doing well, because someone's tipped them off that healthy white babies command a pretty penny on the black market. Then they'll act like they're going to be good moms, promise to get off the heroin or whatever, and reform themselves; when all they really want to do is take the baby out of here and sell it to the highest bidder so they can buy more drugs."

"Can't the hospital deny them access to the babies?" Karida asked.

"Not if the mother makes a good show of reforming herself. Besides, who wants to adopt an addict's baby anyway? Any girl who has anything on the ball knows there are infertile couples out there who will pay for their obstetric care and maybe even their college education, and provide good homes for their babies. They survey the ads, pick out a nice couple, and do a private adoption.

"The babies who get left in big city hospital nurseries like ours, for social services to find homes for, are the offspring of girls who have nothing going for them. They're either drug addicts or mentally ill or impaired, and their kids are at risk. Whenever I hear of a couple looking to adopt, I encourage them to adopt an older child. Everyone wants newborns, but with newborns, you don't know what you're getting. If you adopt a three-year-old, you have a reasonable chance of knowing whether or not you can deal with that child's health issues, disposition and developmental potential. Of course older children also come with more emotional baggage. It's still a gamble."

"So what will happen to a baby like Smittens?" Karida asked.

"Her mother's still a no-show. She'll be big enough to discharge in another few weeks, probably to foster care. If she's not the delightful child some foster family chooses to adopt, she may never have a family to call her own. It wouldn't surprise me if fifteen years from now, she'll deliver another unwanted baby that you and I will be snot-busting. Even if Smittens finds a good foster family, once she turns eighteen, funding for those families ends. Most foster kids get turned out with nothing more than a pack of a few personal belongings on their backs, and more than half of them wind up homeless. It's no wonder they turn to prostitution and dealing drugs. Smitten's future is so bleak, it makes you want to cry."

"Part of me wants to take this poor little thing home myself. Have you ever felt like adopting any of these babies, Adrienne?"

"Oh, sure! Just about every other month there's one here that I get attached to, but I long ago figured out that I could help a lot more of these kiddos by being their nurse. When I first came to the NICU, one of the nurses fell in love with an unwanted girl, and left nursing to parent her. She knew the baby had all kinds of problems, but she had this strong rescue compulsion and she took her on. Last I heard, she wound up divorced because her husband couldn't deal with having a child that needed constant medical attention and had little potential for becoming a self-sufficient adult. Although I very much admire the loving people that foster and adopt special needs children, I'm just not that much of a sacrificial lamb myself."

After another day in the NICU, Karida was happy to be reassigned to labor and delivery. She and Eliza managed to grab a few minutes to talk. "Did you happen to catch the speech Mark Wagner's son gave Monday?" Eliza asked.

"I saw excerpts on the news after my shift. He's quite the dish, Jackson Wagner. Maybe the speech was will help get the media off of the Wagners' case, but I still worry about Pamela."

"Nora says she thinks she's with relatives. She had a lot of praise for Jack Wagner. She thinks if Mark Wagner does turn around, it's because of Jack.

"Did you see the Rodriquez story about political celebrity drug addiction yesterday? No wonder Pamela Wagner got into trouble. I guess her mother was pretty impaired, but now at least she's getting help. Maybe the exposure of Pamela's secret even saved Lorraine Wagner's life."

"I hadn't thought of it that way." Karida said. "Even when I saw Mrs. Wagner at the burial, I sensed she was troubled in some way beyond her reaction to Pamela's situation. Still, I wish this hadn't happened to Pamela."

"It sounds like you have mixed feelings about NEB, Karida. Please believe me when I tell you that we would never want you to do anything that your conscience says you shouldn't. Perhaps you should take advantage of someone else's perspective. There's going to be a lecture about Anti-Abortion propositions on state ballots tomorrow evening at the Sewall-Belmont House. Both Colorado and South Dakota have scary propositions on their ballots."

"What's the Sewall-Belmont House?"

"Sewall-Belmont is a museum and research center dedicated to the cause of equal rights for women. It displays mementos of those who led the fight, people like Susan B. Anthony, and Alice Paul, who wrote the Equal Rights Amendment. It's also a very historic building. The British burned it during the war of 1812, just before they set fire to the White House.

"If Peter's free, maybe he could attend too, so he'll know more about the issues you'll be dealing with working for Doctor Fox. Do you know what's going on in these states where they're trying to restrict abortion?"

"Not really. If I'm going to work for Doctor Fox, I guess I should learn."

"Nora and Maria will be there too, and maybe Roxanne and her daughter Tracy, but we'll sit apart to keep our association private. I'll Email you the details. I've heard this speaker before and she packs a punch."

~ ~ ~

Karida and Peter were surprised at how many people were streaming into a small lecture hall on a chilly Wednesday evening. The seating couldn't accommodate them all, and even some very well-dressed people sat on the floor in front of the lectern. The speaker introduced herself as an attorney for the National Women's Party and dove right into her topic.

"Proposition Eleven in South Dakota is an attempt by the state legislature to make abortion inaccessible except in cases of rape, incest and life threatening maternal illness. Two years ago, the legislators there tried to pass an even stricter version of this bill, but the voters defeated it. Now the legislators believe that if they make these exceptions, they can get the bill passed and create a challenge to *Roe v. Wade*.

"Proposition Forty-Eight in Colorado seeks to extend the state constitution's definition of a 'person' to include a fertilized egg, and thus provide the egg with inalienable rights, equality of justice, and due process of the law. Proponents of this bill claim it's intended to protect women as well as unborn babies. Let me illustrate for you how 'baby protection laws' can be used to violate women's rights.

"In 1996, a Florida woman named Laura Pemberton sought to have a vaginal delivery, though she had previously given birth by C-Section. She researched her options and chose to deliver her baby at home. Her physician decided that she didn't have that right because of the risk of complications. When Laura went into labor, a sheriff barged into her home, handcuffed her, tied her legs together, and took her to the hospital. A judge assigned a lawyer to represent the fetus, but Laura wasn't provided with legal counsel and she was forced to have her abdomen and uterus cut open to surgically deliver her baby.

"In 1998, a twenty-seven-year-old pregnant Maryland woman named Angela Carter, was dying of cancer. Pro-Life physicians decided it was their duty to save her fetus and obtained a court order to force her to have a C-section. The procedure killed Angela and the baby.

"In 2004, a physician providing care for Amber Marlowe, a Pennsylvania mother of six, decided that her baby was too large for natural delivery and when she refused to consent to surgery, the court awarded the hospital custody of her baby before, during and even *after* delivery. Amber was also forced to have a C-section against her will.

"Also in 2004, a Utah woman named Melissa Rowland refused to consent to surgical delivery of twins. When one of the twins was still-born, she was arrested and charged with murder.

"If Colorado should pass Proposition Forty-Eight, there would be numerous ways for the state to criminalize the behavior of pregnant women. Taking medicine or having a glass of wine could be construed as reckless endangerment; even if the woman doesn't yet know she's pregnant. Missing a doctor's appointment could be considered neglect. A pregnant woman with cancer who chooses chemotherapy could be accused of feticide.

"For decades, Pro-Life zealots have been pushing for incarceration of pregnant women who abuse drugs. Proponents argue that if such a woman is in jail, she won't be smoking dope. Opponents say that testing pregnant women for illicit drug use would prevent many women from seeking prenatal care or delivering their babies in hospitals, greatly reducing the chances that they or their babies would receive medical assistance if needed. Arresting, convicting and incarcerating pregnant women would not provide justice for the unborn.

"For the thirty-five years since the US Supreme Court determined that women have the right to choose, people who disagree with that decision have succeeded in restricting women's access to safe abortion. Perhaps the state of Oklahoma is the most restrictive. With their policies and proposed laws as of 2008, no public facilities or employees may assist women with unwanted pregnancies. Private providers may refuse to help such women and if they choose to help, they must meet demands not imposed on other health professionals. Insurers and public assistance programs are prohibited from paying for abortion services, unless a woman is a rape victim or has life threatening illness. Women under eighteen may not obtain abortions without parental consent. There's mandatory delay as to when the procedure can be performed, and it's required that the woman who chooses abortion be given *biased* counseling, while it's simultaneously *against the law* to provide her with supportive counseling. However, the most imposing Oklahoma regulation requires a woman seeking abortion to first undergo an ultrasound examination during which the technician must describe in extensive detail, what fetal body parts are in what stage of development, even though these body parts are typically too tiny to be seen without a microscope.

"Now, in states where fetal ultrasound pictures are mandated, clinics report that women do not change their minds based on fetal ultrasound pictures. So why has this expensive, time-consuming and ineffective practice, which can only humiliate the ultrasonographer as well as the woman, become a weapon in the Pro-Lifers' arsenal? It's just a waste of precious resources."

The speaker paused and took a sip of water.

"History shows us that women the world over, always have and always will, seek to terminate pregnancies when they don't believe they can provide for a child. When safe abortion is unavailable, women die in enormous numbers resorting to unsafe methods, and, abandoned and dead babies turn up in garbage cans. Where's the concern for dead women and dead babies by those who claim to be Pro-Life? And why is the life of a fetus more important then the life of a mother, or her already born children who need her?

"When Pro-Choice advocates argue that we need to provide unwed single mothers with assistance so they see a way to provide for a child, Pro-Lifers vote against the health and welfare of children. They are only concerned with the life of fetuses, not the children they become. Do they really want to reduce abortion by helping women and children, or do they just want to punish women, which ultimately punishes children?

"It is my hope that those of you who can, will reach out to voters in South Dakota and Colorado to enlist their help in getting these propositions defeated. Thank you and let's take questions."

"Do you think it was okay that Congressman Wagner's daughter had a late stage abortion"? A man in the back of the audience asked.

"My knowledge of that case is limited to what I've seen in the media and apparently, this young woman misunderstood the course of her pregnancy. The only comment I can make is that when investigative reporter Rodriguez surveyed the teachings of some of the local private schools, including the school where this young woman was a student, she found that there was no teaching about contraception or pregnancy.

"It would be a wonderful thing if kids this age weren't sexually active, but they are. In recent surveys, more than sixty per cent of high school seniors have admitted to having had sexual relationships. It's the norm. More than three million teenagers are diagnosed with sexually transmitted diseases every year, and that's just the cases we know about. If we're ever going to reduce abortion, we need to educate young people as to why they shouldn't rush into sexual relationships, as well as teach them how to prevent pregnancy. Obviously that's not happening in enough family settings. What I'd like to know is why is it that the very same people who want to outlaw abortion, don't want young adults to have a greater understanding of reproductive risks and outcomes?"

"Don't you think Pamela Wagner is going to suffer psychological damage from killing her baby?" an older woman asked.

"There's almost no evidence to support the supposition that abortion causes inordinate distress in women if they're not taunted by others. This poor young woman has people all over the world pointing fingers at her, which is far more likely to cause her distress than having chosen not to become a parent at age fourteen. Might she have regrets? Of course! Everyone's done things they regret, from lying to parents to marrying the wrong person. We're all human. We all make mistakes. If we're not beaten down, we get past these trials and we make better decisions later on because of our experience. If others who sit in judgment of us scorn us, then we're more likely to suffer."

"How could a physician, in good conscience, perform an abortion on such a young child?" asked a pregnant woman.

"Washington D.C. does not have an age restriction on abortion. Unlike in some states, here, if you're old enough to be pregnant, you have the right to choose. As far as the physician's conscience goes, terminating an unintended pregnancy can be much less devastating than trying to take care of unwanted children who are starved, beaten, burned and raped, if not murdered by parents who should never have had them. If you'd like to get in touch with your own conscience on this matter, I urge you to visit the neurological trauma unit of the Crippled Children's Hospital where there are always multiple comatose children on respirators because frustrated parents bashed their brains in."

"If you're a moral person, why wouldn't you want to protect the most vulnerable of human beings?" a young man asked.

"I don't believe fetuses *are* the most vulnerable. In times of famine, such as the one in Europe in the mid 1800s due to a potato blight, starving women continued to birth. The fetus can actually steal its mother's reserves when there isn't enough nutrition for two. Fetuses have guaranteed life support systems. They are not the most vulnerable. The most vulnerable human beings are the newborns that get tossed in garbage cans and the children who nobody loves. Unwanted children are far more vulnerable than fetuses."

"How can you not respect the life of the unborn?" an older woman asked.

"You know, there's an old saying: you're loved when you're born and you're loved when you die, but in between, you just have to manage. It's a challenge to love the living and show compassion for people burdened by unwanted pregnancy."

Fewer hands waved, and people started to leave. Those that shared the viewpoints of the speaker had few questions, and those that came to challenge her, perceived that they had met their match. Karida and Peter stayed to hear her effectively respond to a few more questions before they exited.

"I'm starting to feel better about this cause you've stumbled into, Karida," Peter was saying when Eliza approached them in the parking lot.

"You must be Peter," she said, extending her unscarred hand. "I'm Eliza. Karida never told me she's married to a Brother. Welcome to our nation's capitol, where we blacks outnumber the whites by a nice fat majority. Would the two of you like to join Nora and me for some decaf over at Lydia's?"

Peter nodded yes.

"I'm delighted to finally meet you, Peter, and I'd really like to know what you think of your wife's new career option. See you at Lydia's."

~ Twenty-Seven ~

Karida and Peter left their car in the hospital garage and walked the block to Lydia's. On the way, Karida reminded Peter about how shocking it was going to be to see her son Willie.

Eliza, Nora, Roxanne and Tracy were already there, and Peter and Karida were introduced to two other women who Karida hadn't previously met. Harriet seemed to be the oldest. She was introduced as a librarian. Sherry's age was hard to assess. She was elegantly coifed and dressed. When Lydia explained that she was the cleaning lady who spied on the medical records of patients who turned up in the office of Doctors O'Ryan and Rourke, Karida and Peter were struck by the incongruity of her moneyed appearance with her profession.

"I've heard all about you, Karida," Sherry said. "We still can't quite believe we're going to have a link to Doctor Fox's office. This is an extraordinary break for NEB. What did you think of the lecture tonight?"

"It was a real eye-opener for me. I knew some states made it pretty difficult for teenaged girls to get abortions, but I didn't know how hard some make it for all women. It does seem that those kinds of regulations will just drive desperate woman to resort to unsafe abortions."

Trying to figure out how this elegant woman could be a cleaning lady, Karida said, "I have to ask you, Sherry, how you came to be involved with NEB. I've been telling Peter about the remarkable experiences the others have shared, and I'm wondering about your story." She turned to Harriet. "And yours too?"

"Well, like the rest of our group, I have a very personal reason for wanting to protect the right to choose," Sherry replied. "I was eight years old and I had a five-year-old brother when my mother was diagnosed with multiple sclerosis. Her disease advanced very quickly and my father said they were warned to avoid another pregnancy because sometimes, the disease progresses rapidly after a pregnancy. Of course this was back in the days before birth control pills, legal abortion, and immune therapy to prevent worsening MS. As my father told the story, they were victims of a broken condom, and my poor mother wound up pregnant. Her doctor petitioned the state to permit her to have an abortion, but whoever reviewed her case didn't think her condition warranted an abortion because multiple sclerosis isn't always fatal. They weren't impressed with the fact that my mother's case was so severe. My parents were law-abiding citizens and wouldn't consider an illegal abortion, so she carried the pregnancy to term. Unfortunately, her disease got so bad about six weeks after delivery, that her breathing became impaired, and she died in her sleep. You never really recover from losing your mother, especially when you know her life could have and should have been saved.

"My father didn't handle her death very well. My grandmothers helped out initially and then my father hired a nanny. A few years later his dry cleaning business started to go under as permanent press clothes were becoming popular, and he could no longer afford the nanny. By the time I started junior high; I wound up being mother to my brother and my baby sister. I guess I was always a bit of a 'neatnik', and my father was kind of a slob, so if there was anything I knew how to do really well, it was clean house.

"One day, when I was sixteen, my father and I took my little sister to a nearby dentist for a toothache, and I was freaked out by how dirty his office was. I told the dentist that I was an excellent cleaning girl and I think he knew my family needed the money, so he said if I did a better job than the service he already had, he'd hire me. His office was in walking distance of our house, so it turned out to be a very convenient job for me, but also an opportunity. It only took me about an hour and a half to walk over there after dinner and get his office absolutely sparkling. He was very pleased, and before I finished high school, I was cleaning three other offices in his little professional building and I hired a classmate to work for me. Today, I have one hundred and fifteen employees, and contracts to clean about four hundred and thirty professional offices in the District. Doctors O'Ryan's and Rourke's office is the only one I clean myself these days, and that's only on special occasions when NEB needs me to look something up."

"That is so remarkable." Karida shook her head in awe and Peter was nodding with admiration.

"As long as we're telling our stories, you really need to hear why Harriet became a part of NEB," Sherry said. "It's the most personal story of them all."

Harriet moved her chair a little closer to Karida and adjusted her hearing aides. "You see, Karida, my father was a radio salesman before he joined the army in 1944. He was one of the first to land at Normandy on D-Day, and he never made it out of the water, leaving my mother alone with three children. I was ten, the youngest. We moved into a boarding house on the south side of Chicago, and my mother went to work in a meat processing plant. She worked twelve hours a day and my brother quit school to take care of my sister and me. He was fourteen at the time, and my sister was twelve. When my brother turned fifteen, he also went to work at the meat processing plant, while my sister and I attended school and did what we could to prepare meals for my mother and brother. We lived in a single room and shared a small kitchen and bathroom with two other families, who had rooms on the same floor. One of those families had two boys. Albert was a year older than me, and when I was sixteen and absolutely ignorant about sex, Albert gave me an education.

"It was Albert's mother who noticed my ballooning belly. I had no idea what was going on. She explained pregnancy to me and said she was going to get me to a doctor to fix it. She gave me one hundred dollars, which was more money than I'd ever seen, and told me to wait on a street corner in our neighborhood on a Saturday morning, and that someone in a turquoise Chevy was going to come by and pick me up and take me to a doctor.

"When I got into the car, a man took the money and then he blindfolded me. He said it was important that I didn't know where the doctor was because he could get in trouble if anyone knew he was helping girls like me. He gave me a cup of something and told me to drink it. At first I thought it was beer, because Albert's father was always drinking beer, and I recognized the smell. Of course it was laced with something else, because I felt really dizzy after drinking it. It must have knocked me out because I don't remember much of anything after that, except waking up in that car and being in a lot of pain. I was told to get out of the car and as soon as I did, it sped away. I remember looking down and seeing myself covered in blood and blood trickling onto the ground. The next thing I remember was waking up in a hospital and being told that it was miraculous that I survived, but they had to take my uterus and I'd never be able to have children.

"When I was released from the hospital and managed to find my way back to the city, I learned the police had been looking for me. Albert's family had moved away in the middle of the night and nobody knew where they'd gone. That's what abortion was like for an ignorant kid like me in 1950.

"It took me eleven years after that to work my way through college. Whoever punctured my uterus also damaged my bladder and left me without control of my urine, so I never dated or married, but I did get a degree in library science, and I've been fortunate to have a career at the Library of Congress for the past four decades. That's where I met Nora. She was always coming in to research the voting records of legislators with regards to child welfare and we connected long ago. That's how I wound up in NEB."

"How did you get involved with NEB, Sherry? Karida asked.

"We can blame that on Nora as well. When she used to work at a big law firm, I got a contract to clean their office. I always checked out an office before sending my employees in, and the night I went to check out that one, I happened to notice some articles about abortion on a desk. I didn't get much done in the manner of assessing the cleaning needs that night, but I sure got interested in what one of those lawyers was up to, so I came back during the day and met Nora Sutton. We've been friends for decades. It's always been my belief that someone in government has absolutely no business telling a woman what she should or shouldn't be able to do with her own body, like they did to my poor mother when she was just trying to survive multiple sclerosis. It really is nobody else's business."

"Karida," Lydia said, "we have a new development that could involve you. Eliza thought both you and your husband should hear about it because it could be a very major case for NEB, but a very delicate situation for you. Have either of you ever heard of Senator Roger Evans?"

Neither Peter nor Karida knew of him, so Nora gave them an intro. "He's one of those politicians who professes that a one-millisecond-old fertilized egg has more rights than the woman in whose body it might grow. Roger Evans not only thinks that American women shouldn't have the right to choose, but he's trying to restrict reproductive rights globally by pulling US support for UNFPA, an international relief agency that tries to help poor mothers and children around the world, like starving refugees. We think that Senator Evans needs to have a much better understanding about the situation of a woman who is dealing with an unintended pregnancy, and we have reason to believe his own daughter might be in that situation. I'm going to let Tracy explain."

NEB's youngest member seemed eager to tell the story. "So, it's like this, Karida. Vivian Evans, the senator's daughter, and her boyfriend go to my school. Well the boyfriend, Gregory Thatcher, did go, but he graduated last June. Anyway, last week I went to the girls' room before class and all of the sudden, Vivian Evans came running in with her hand over her mouth. She barely made it to the sink before she started throwing up. I asked her if I could help her, maybe get the school nurse; but she said she already felt much better and didn't think it was anything except some bad milk she had in her cereal. She acted real nonchalant about it, and I thought that was kind of weird. She and her boyfriend are one of those infamous couples that everyone at school knows about and I wondered if she could be pregnant.

"So I told my mother about it and brought home a yearbook from last year that had a good picture of Vivian and Greg from his senior prom. Mom knew about her father's Pro-Life politics, so she brought the yearbook over here for Lydia to scan in the picture and see if the face-match software might show Vivian going to Doctors O'Ryan and Rourke."

Lydia was almost dancing. "I got a great match for the boyfriend Gregory Thatcher. They were there just last Thursday. Ain't technology amazing?" She brought up an image on her computer screen. The others gathered around.

"You can see here, Vivian had her head down when they came out of the office so you can barely see her face, but we can see Greg clear as day." She shuffled back and forth between the prom picture and the video image. "When I enlarge this photo from the surveillance tape and look closely, we can identify Vivian fairly well, even though the face match software didn't pick up on it. Tracey! Look again! Are you sure?"

Tracey bent over Lydia's shoulder. "Unless Greg is two-timing her with a double, that's Vivian Evans," Tracey confirmed.

"So, we put Sherry to work and of course she didn't find Vivian's name on the sign in-sheet, but she checked the charts of all of the women who were signed in during that time period, and we're confident that Vivian used the alias Sandra Johnson. Doctor Rourke's notes said Sandra was there with her boyfriend, that her birth control pills failed, and that the boyfriend, but not Sandra, was asking about abortion. They were counseled about adoption and given phone numbers for Planned Parenthood and Doctor Fox."

Karida shot an accusatory glance at Eliza and she picked up on it.

"Karida, you need to know that Vivian was not a victim of our counterfeit birth control pills. We're certain that she got pregnant without any intervention on our part, just one of the unfortunates for whom the real pills were a bust, or who, by accident or by intention, missed a pill."

Eliza kept watching Peter and Karida's faces and she thought Peter seemed to be nodding approval.

"A real budding private investigator my daughter," Roxanne said, putting her arm around Tracy. "We'd never have known about this case if not for her intuition." Tracey ducked out of Roxanne's embrace and looked humble.

"But of course," Roxanne cautioned, "there are several reasons as to why Vivian won't show up in Dr. Fox's office, the foremost being that her family is very Anti-Abortion. Also, these two young people have apparently been a couple for several years, so they might marry and have their baby. Another possibility is that Greg Thatcher's family is richer than a chocolate sundae, and they might arrange an abortion on their own terms. We've learned that Greg's father is a lobbyist for a drug company and a commodities trader, and he probably has all kinds of connections. Vivian could also show up in Doctor Fox's office using a different alias, or maybe she'll go to Planned Parenthood. So who knows if she will show in Doctor Fox's office, but if she does, Karida, we have a plan. If we know when she has an appointment, we could have Tracy show up coincidentally, and she could spill the beans and give Senator Roger Evans a whole new perspective regarding choice."

Karida felt really conflicted and she watched Peter to gauge his reaction. His expression was neutral, so she guessed he wasn't rejecting the idea, which made her feel like she should at least give the scheme some consideration. "So essentially, the only thing I'd be doing would be letting you know if and when this girl has an appointment."

"That's it. It would be up to us to arrange the rest. It's all a long shot. You're only going to be starting there on Monday and for all we know; Vivian could already have an appointment for Monday, or could show up there before you even get there. There's lots of possibilities," Roxanne conceded.

"Well I could go over there when he has office hours Saturday morning and look at the appointment schedule. I wanted to talk to the office staff some more anyway and I also wanted to find out if Pamela Wagner ever got her follow-up. When I went there last weekend to finalize things with Doctor Fox, there was no record of Pamela having an appointment. If this Vivian, or what's her other name, Sandra, is on the schedule and there's no room for Tracy to get an appointment, maybe she could just appear at that time on the pretense that she came in to make an appointment."

"You're a step ahead of me, Karida," Roxanne said. "I went to case out the office this morning. I was wondering how this doctor manages to keep things confidential and was expecting an off-the-main-road private building. But then, I thought about how we're spying on Doctors O'Ryan's and Rourke's private little office so easily from this apartment, and it dawned on me how much easier it would be for women to be less noticeable entering a big office building from a shopping mall parking lot. Unless someone is hanging out in the hallway, they're not going to notice which person heads for which door. So, we're thinking Tracy could be in the hallway on the pretense that she's looking for the dermatologist's office. There are other doctors in the building."

"Aren't you worried about Tracy though?" Karida asked. "Having a reputation in high school as a snitch might not be much fun."

Roxanne turned to her daughter. "Tracy, why don't you tell Karida what you told us?"

"Thanks for worrying about me, Karida. Mom and Dad and I have talked about this a lot, ever since Lydia got the match on Greg's picture. I have absolutely nothing against Vivian Evans. I'm a junior and she's a senior, so I don't know her really well, but from what I do know, she's a nice girl; much less snooty than some of the other kids who come from political families. If she and Greg were to decide to have their baby, I would only wish them the best; but knowing Greg Thatcher, I'd be very surprised if that's what they'll do.

"I should say I don't know Greg all that well either. He was two years ahead of me, but he has a reputation as a conceited rich kid who always gets his way. He wears the most expensive clothes and drives one of the most luxurious cars of anyone in our whole school, and it's a school full of rich kids. Rumor has it that he gets a thousand dollars a month allowance. I've also heard that even though he and Vivian are supposedly a tight couple, last year he was also dating another girl from another private school. I don't know if that's true, but I do know that some kids think Vivian could do a lot better than Greg Thatcher. One of my school friends who knows them both says he'll manipulate her to do whatever he wants."

"But where does that leave you, Tracy?" Karida asked.

"Well, I'm not the only one in school who thinks Vivian is pregnant. Someone else saw her vomiting in the girl's room and the rumors have been flying all week. It's a pretty small school and stuff like that gets around fast; and everyone knows you get the pill or PLAN B from Doctors O'Ryan and Rourke, and if you need an abortion, you go to Doctor Fox. Girls talk about this stuff like they're talking about where to buy a prom dress.

"Anyway, Karida, the whole reason I even agreed to go to this school, is because I want to contribute to the defense of the right to choose. I saw a classmate die from trying to not have to deliver her stepfather's baby. Why should Vivian be able to opt for a safe abortion when her father would like to make it so that other girls won't have that choice? There's hardly anyone in my school that I know of who supports the opinion of people like Senator Evans. So if I spilled the beans, maybe I'd be a rat, but my guess is that I'd more likely be a hero. I'm not looking to be a hero, but I'm willing to take the chance of being a rat if we get the opportunity to turn politicians like Vivian's father. It's just so wrong for people like him to be fighting to deny women, maybe even his own daughter that right; just like it was so wrong for my grandmother to have been burned alive because she worked where women had a choice."

"Wow! Tracey. You're inspiring me!" Karida appeared less unsettled.

"So, lawyer to lawyer Peter, what do you think of our scheme?" Nora asked. "Karida has been put in a difficult situation by stumbling into our little organization. It's our hope that by including you in the planning for this caper, that she won't have to wrestle with your dissent along with the wrestling we think she's already doing with her own conscience. We all struggle with the illegality and immorality of NEB's methods, but we agonize more over the fate of unwanted children."

Peter didn't hesitate. "I'm with you. Between hearing Karida talk about wanting to bring that little cocaine baby home from the NICU because no one would ever want it, and then hearing that speaker tonight, talking about children on life support because their parents beat them half to death, I think what NEB is doing is justified. When I was a law student, I learned about *Planned Parenthood v. Casey*, the 1992 Supreme Court decision that allowed states to put restrictions on abortion. It seems that most of the states that have taken advantage of that decision, have enacted regulations that discriminate against the young and the poor, the people who are least able to provide for children. I really fear what will happen if our next president appoints judges who will overturn *Roe v. Wade*. Desperate causes sometimes call for desperate measures. If Karida feels she can take this on, she'll have my support. I'm impressed that you thought to include me. You ladies are very brave. I especially applaud you, Tracy. At your age, I don't think I ever, even for a minute, considered working for a cause outside my own personal interests. You inspire me. But I'm also worried that what you do could be dangerous."

~ Twenty-Eight ~

Even though he started his antibiotics Wednesday night, Greg felt much too ill to attend classes on Thursday. He wanted to go back to the clinic and talk to the counselor, but he couldn't even drag himself out of bed. He felt feverish, achy and more depressed than he'd ever been in his life. He spent the morning surfing the Internet in attempt to learn more about the infections. It only made him more depressed.

His mother had always said to drink a lot of fluids if you have fever and he did his best to keep chugging down water and juice. The trouble with that was it made him have to pee a lot, which hurt like hell. Even more distressing, each time he went to the bathroom, he saw more of the herpes blisters, and seeing them seemed to make the pain even worse.

Just as he was starting to give some serious thought to suicide, his phone rang. It was the infirmary advising him that the investigators from the health and police departments wanted to interview him at four o'clock if he didn't have a class then. In an odd sort of way, it was something to live for. He considered that getting revenge on Donna, or whatever the hell her name was, was worth hanging on for, for at least another few hours. He could always go back to his suicide plans after the interview.

He swallowed another Tylenol and pondered what to wear to present himself to these authorities. He wanted to look more sophisticated than the typical college freshman. He settled on a charcoal gray Coppley suit with a crème colored cashmere turtleneck and a pair of dress shoes. His mother had laughed when he decided to bring that executive suit to college. "From what I know about campus life, you're never going to wear that thing," she said as she watched him pack up his Mercedes. "Save it for when you're really going to need it for job interviews." What did his mother know anyway? She certainly wasn't anticipating his being interviewed by the police or the state health department.

The suit didn't help him feel any better about himself as he sat in the waiting room of the infirmary. He was the only guy amongst several girls and his apparel made them eye him suspiciously. Just before he got called back, a guy emerged from the clinic wearing a ragged sweatshirt and tattered jeans. Greg wondered if he was another of Donna's victims. He'd been told that each of the patients would be interviewed individually to protect their privacy, but now it seemed, they'd see each other going to and from the interviews. Stupid, he thought. Maybe, we should all get together and start our own support group: 'Stupid Guys That Got Screwed by a Sexual Predator.' But, would it really help to know he wasn't the only stupid one? When he thought about the disheveled looking guy who'd just walked out, he concluded that if *that* dude was one of the victims, they'd have nothing in common except stupidity; so how could it possibly help to sit around and cry on each other's shoulders?

He was taken aback by how many people were in the room when he got to the interview. In addition to Doctor Freitag and a police detective, he was introduced to two other campus physicians, a physician and an epidemiologist from the state health department, and a police sketch artist. The crowd sitting around him, and the presence of tape recorders on the desk, made his spine tingle. The whole set-up felt more like an interrogation than an interview.

"How are you feeling today, Greg?" Doctor Freitag asked.

"Not very well, thank you. Some of the symptoms seem worse."

"I'm afraid it will take at least forty-eight hours of antibiotics to get some of the infection under control, and it looks like we only got those prescriptions to you yesterday. Have you started them yet?"

"I started them immediately," Greg reported.

The public health doctor said, "I know this is very difficult, Greg, but we would like to start things off by your telling us exactly what you told Doctor Freitag. Please try not to be embarrassed, and let us hear the details of your encounter; not just about the girl's sexual behavior, but how you met and what she talked about. Our purpose here is to find a dangerous criminal, and even some insignificant little detail could prove to be valuable in our attempts to track her down. Unfortunately, this morning we saw another suspicious case. After you met Kentucky Donna on Friday, Dorothy from Texas seduced another student here on Saturday. We just haven't gotten the warnings out fast enough."

After describing the whole experience as best he could, the police artist showed him a sketch. "That's her all right, except her hair was darker than that, kind of a dark brown. It did look like it was dyed, now that I think about it."

"She seems to change her hair as readily as her name," the detective said. "It was reported to be longer by the patients who showed up last week, so either she had hair extensions or she's cut it shorter since. One of our patients said she was blond with a pink streak, while another victim said the streak was blue. Do you think she could have been wearing a wig?"

"I doubt it. If she was, it was glued on pretty tightly relative to the acrobatics she was doing in my car. Does she always get victims in their cars?"

"Location seems to be whatever's convenient. Look carefully at the sketch, Greg, and tell us if there's anything else that looks different from the girl you saw. Take your time. We've had differing opinions about the shape of her chin. One victim thought it was rounder than this."

Greg studied the sketch more closely. "Actually, I think her eyebrows weren't quite that arched, but I'm not really sure. I guess she could change the shape of her eyebrows. The chin looks like I remember. I think it's a very good likeness of her except for the hair. I'd be able to recognize her from this picture."

"Describe her clothing as best as you can recall."

"Nothing very remarkable. A black sweater, a black leather jacket with fleece trim, and a short gray skirt."

"Did you notice any birthmarks, scars, tattoos, anything like that?"

Greg shook his head no.

"How about any distinctive piercings, jewelry, underwear, pocketbook, cell phone? Anything at all that caught your attention beyond her outer clothing."

Greg tried to re-envision her, but nothing stood out. He best remembered the low cut black sweater that showed cleavage, a black bra and black thong panties. "I think the bra was padded. That's all I remember."

"Did she have a purse or backpack?"

"As I recall, she had a small black pocketbook that she put a paperback book into when we left the library. The purse wasn't much bigger than the paperback and I don't think I saw the book title."

"What about her shoes?"

"That I remember. Hooker shoes. Pointy toes and skinny high heels, much higher than most girls wear around here, but then she was kind of short. I thought maybe she was just trying to look taller. In retrospect, I don't usually see girls on campus wearing shoes like that, not even the really short ones."

"Would you say her clothes and shoes were expensive? Your suit suggests you know a little about clothing quality."

Greg stroked the lapel of his jacket. "I can't say I paid much attention, but my impression is she wore cheap stuff. I do recognize better quality fabric and clothing cuts on people, and nothing she was wearing looked like anything of value. I don't remember seeing any labels."

"Tell us about her voice quality and speech pattern. Anything distinctive that you recall?"

"A slight southern drawl. Maybe she talked a little faster than most southerners. I can kind of hear her voice in my head and the only word I can think to describe it is ordinary."

"Thank you for your time and cooperation, Greg. You can go now. We may call you back though, and if you think of anything else, please call." The health department investigator and police detective each handed Greg a card.

"May I ask if you have any leads?"

"I can tell you this is not the first campus or state where she's victimized students," the investigator said. Several students showed up on a Maryland campus last month with infections attributed to Barbara, Beth, and Bonnie. The physicians there are looking for other cases, and we now have investigators checking out other campuses. The state lab is investigating whether the gonorrhea cases are all due to the same bacterial strain."

"Have any of the other victims tested positive for AIDS?"

"Only one so far. We're also worried about hepatitis. It's too soon for students here to be showing hepatitis, but two cases from the campus from last month are testing positive for hepatitis B and E. We can cure gonorrhea, chlamydia and syphilis, but not hepatitis and herpes. Herpes is a terrible nuisance and a risk to newborn babies, but people with herpes can live relatively normal lives. AIDS and hepatitis B are more devastating infections. For some sufferers, it means a lifetime of expensive medication, if not serious illness.

"Please understand, Greg, that not everyone who's exposed to HIV, the virus that causes AIDS, contracts an infection. We don't know why some people get overwhelming infection from a tiny needle stick, while someone else who was exposed to large amounts of the virus never shows it in their system. This is also true for hepatitis. That's why it's important that you be tested. What we do know is that those who have contracted AIDS who are treated quickly, have a much better chance of never developing clinical disease. You were exposed last Friday, so you should get tested next Monday. If the first test is negative you'll need retesting, but if it's positive, then treatment can be started right away and improve your chances."

"What will happen to this girl if you find her?"

The police detective took the question. "It kind of depends on what state she's caught in, as state laws vary. I can tell you she'll be much safer in jail than if she's caught by one of her victims. Be assured, you're not the only one who might be fantasizing about strangling her, or worse. What she's done is as heinous as any crime we see in my line of work, and we see some awful things."

"There is a sexual crimes victim support group on campus, Greg," the woman doctor said. "It's called SOS, Sexual Offence Support. Most of the attendees are women who have been raped, but I think male victims of this predator would also find attendance at SOS is a healthy way to deal with their justifiable rage and depression. It's certainly a better route than contemplating suicide, which is what many sexual offense victims do when they're first coping with having been assaulted. I'll find out if any of the other guys in your situation would be interested and let you know. We're also here to provide individual counseling. Please don't think you have to deal with this all by yourself."

"Thank you. Will you let me know if you find this girl?"

"Absolutely. We'll need her victims to identify her, press charges, and assist in prosecution. Thank you, Greg."

Doctor Freitag walked him to the door and patted him on the shoulder as he exited. Greg fought hard not to cry as he walked back past the waiting room, where he saw another miserable looking guy, anxiously waiting.

His thoughts turned back to suicide.

~ Twenty-Nine ~

Pamela Wagner took an instant liking to Aaron McGraf's sister Gail and her husband Brian Furness. Brian was a nursing supervisor on the night shift at a psychiatric hospital, so he was home during the day. He slept until mid afternoon, so everyone kept real quiet. Pamela learned that Gail had also been a nurse before she left her career to be a full-time mom. Their kids were adorable. Emily was in fourth grade, Douglas in second grade, and four-year-old Molly practiced singing every afternoon, so she could be on *American Idol*.

In Pamela's eyes they were a real family, unlike her own, where what was going on at home seemed wholly unimportant compared to what was going on in the world. There was no housekeeper. Gail cleaned, cooked, played with Molly, and helped Emmy and Doug with their homework. Each night one of the kids got to choose a mom-approved TV program, which they watched together as a family. At bedtime, Gail read them a chapter from a *Doctor Dolittle* book, and Pamela found herself looking forward to it as much as the kids did.

On the Tuesday after she arrived, Gail took her to a beauty parlor where her blond hair was cut short and colored dark brown. Then she saw Gail's gynecologist, who did an ultrasound to make sure there was no retained placenta as the cause of her bleeding. The doctor thought her bleeding was due to hormonal shifts provoked by stress and weight loss. She was very concerned about Pamela's weight. "Your hormones may not straighten out if you don't give your body better nutrition. Here's a diet plan I want you to take very seriously. We'll see you back in one week, and if you haven't gained a pound or more by then, we might even have to hospitalize you. I'd like to see you gain more weight by then, but I want you to eat healthy food, not junk food."

From the doctor's office, Gail took Pamela grocery shopping and helped her make selections for her diet plan. Once home, they made a big pasta chicken salad and a tuna salad with lots of mayonnaise. Her mother, who made sure everything Claire prepared was lean and low calorie, would have been horrified.

Wednesday night, Jack came by with textbooks and assignments that he had asked the school to have her teachers prepare on the premise that she'd have a prolonged absence. Jack also brought her a laptop and a cell phone. "Daddy doesn't know I'm giving you these so please, Pammy, do not talk to anyone except Jeremy, Roberta, Melissa and me. Please do not tell Jeremy where you are, other than at the home of a family friend. I think it would be a good idea if you didn't even talk to Meghan. There are still tabloid reporters out there looking for all of us, and we don't need them to hassle our friends. I know Jeremy and Meghan would never betray you, but a reporter like Rita Rodriguez could trick them, like when she cornered Jeremy.

"Your principal said you're going to need the Internet to do some of your homework and Brian Furness says he'll hook you up to his wireless connection, so I need to prepare you for what you're going to see if you search your own name. There's a lot of hate out there, Pammy, and some of it is really vicious. You are the subject of hundreds of newspaper articles and editorials. Just to get here, I drove like a paranoid person looking over my shoulder at every corner, because I was afraid someone might be following me."

"I'm so sorry, Jack. I've made such a mess of everything."

"It's not your fault, Pammy. I think it's Mommy and Daddy who made this mess, and what you did probably saved Mommy's life. And you know what, Pammy? What you did may prove to save thousands of women's lives if it helps to preserve a woman's right to safely terminate an unintended pregnancy. In spite of all those demonstrators and bloggers who think that your personal decision was wrong, the majority of people in this country support the choice you made. In addition to all of the nasty stuff you're going to see, you'll also find that many people think you're a hero.

"Let's get back to the issue of your communications though. You have to be extremely careful. If the wrong person got hands on Jeremy's computer or cell phone, anything written could be a matter of public record. Other than discussing schoolwork, you should say absolutely nothing about Daddy, the Furnesses, or the demonstrators. No texting either, under any circumstances. Phones get lost too easily. Absolutely no texting."

"Thanks, Jack. I promise I'll be very careful. Do you know how Mommy is?"

"You're such a good kid, Pammy, always worried about someone else. I talked to Daddy last night and he said the rehab center is a really special place in a spectacular mountain setting. Mom has a beautiful room, more like a fine hotel than a hospital. She can't have a cell phone there, but later in the week she'll have phone privileges. Don't be upset, though, if she doesn't call you. At this point, neither Mom nor Dad knows that I got you this phone, so that's our secret. I'm going to be the go-between you and Mommy and Daddy so they don't know I've restored your access to the outside world. Dad's really not ready to let you in on what's happening out there, so I'm crossing a line here; but from my point of view, you're going to have to deal with all of this stuff anyway. I know you're smart enough and mature enough to handle it. You just have to remember to not take any of it personally. It's not about you, Pammy. All those people who have a problem with what you did, don't know you or anything about you. What they're all upset about is just that your beliefs aren't the same as theirs. The other thing you should realize, Baby, is that some of these people, who think it's their business to judge you, are probably projecting onto you, some guilt they have about something they did in their own lives that they regret. Most healthy, sane people don't need to spend their precious time throwing rocks at someone whose beliefs differ from their own. These people who are pointing fingers at you are mostly lonely people who need some cause to fixate on, rather than deal with the messes in their own lives."

Pamela threw her arms around her brother. "You're the best, Jack. Thanks for always looking out for me. I could never get through this without you. Do you know how long I'm going to have to stay here?"

"Is everything okay here with the Furnesses? They seem really nice."

"Oh they are, Jack. They're great. They're like a model family and they're making me feel like I'm one of the family. Gail has already helped me a lot. She took me to her doctor and now I understand that I have to gain weight. She's going to help me learn to cook. Even the kids are cool. You should hear the little girl sing. If I had to stay here all year, I wouldn't mind. I just don't want to be a burden. And I so want to go ride Moon Flower. Jeremy's sister is going to ride her this weekend so she gets some exercise."

"I don't really know how long this is for, Pammy, but I'm sure you're not a burden. Daddy will take good care of the Furnesses in exchange for them helping us out. But if some reporter or crazy realizes you're here, we might have to make other arrangements. Phil is working on a back-up plan if that should happen. A lot depends on the election, so maybe, just a little longer until we know if we're going to be left alone. If Dad loses, we could all be leaving the Washington spotlight and getting back to a normal life.

"Hey! Did I tell you I like your hair this way? Even I had to look twice to recognize you, except your dimples and your skinny arms gave you away. If you put on a few pounds, Pammy, trade in your name for a new one, and we sent you to a new school, no one would ever know who you are."

"Could I be Dawn? I really like the name Dawn."

"Of course you could be Dawn, but hopefully none of that will be necessary. The news vultures will have lots else to focus on after the election and the crazies will eventually forget your story. You just have to hang in there a little longer."

As Jack pulled out of the Furness's driveway and drove down the block, he noticed a brown car behind him and got a feeling that it was following him. Not really knowing where he was going, he made some turns wherever a cross street presented, only to see the car make the same turns. He saw a school at the end of the street and pulled into its parking lot. The brown car drove on past him. He sat there for a while and then called the Furnesses to be sure all was okay.

"That was probably my neighbor down the block," Brian said. "One of his kids drives an old brown jalopy. I forget what make. Sometimes I see the kid at night when I'm leaving for work."

"He stayed pretty far behind me," Jack said, "so I couldn't tell, except I could see the distinctive color when the headlights of another car shone on it. He's gone now, but let's keep Pamela out of sight, just to be on the safe side."

~ Thirty ~

The fever and burning urination seemed considerably better by Friday, while the herpes lesions became more painful and numerous. Greg had three classes, but he didn't feel like going to any of them. He especially feared walking into his economics class and seeing Colleen. Even if she showed interest, there was no way he could pursue her now. Unless she was part of the Herpes Club, he'd just have to forget about her.

He decided not to go to class at all. Although no one on campus except the doctors in the infirmary knew anything about what he was dealing with, he felt like a marked man. The most stylish and expensive clothes in his closet didn't overcome his sense of shame. He spent some time reading about hepatitis on the Internet. There were multiple types and Hepatitis B seemed to be the worst. Even people in the Herpes Club wouldn't want Hep B.

He again started to think that life was not worth living and wondered who would miss him if he killed himself. His mother would be upset. She'd no longer have him to show off to her tennis friends. He was pretty good with a racket, though not as good as his mother or his sister. Although he was the good-looking one, his sister got the lion's share of the athlete genes. She was also a competitive figure skater, while he could barely balance on the ice. His sister definitely wouldn't miss him. She was four years older, selfish and self-centered, and she'd treated him like a pesky little brother their whole childhood. Although she was their father's favorite, she clearly resented Greg for being their mother's favorite. The last time they were both home on the same weekend, she barely talked to him.

His father would miss having someone to lecture to about how to invest money. To his father, he was primarily a pupil, and he couldn't remember there ever being much else to their relationship. If his father wasn't working he was golfing, and Greg wasn't good at that either. He concluded that his death wouldn't be that tragic for his family.

He thought about his friends from high school who all went to different colleges. His friend Ted still sent him funny Emails, and Randy texted him now and then, but it was just idle gossip about another kid from their high school. Since graduation, he'd hardly had contact with any of them. He certainly hadn't made friends on campus, but he blamed that on having had to run back and forth on the weekends to see Vivian. When he really thought about it, the only truly good friend he had in the world was Vivian. Good old pretty, smart, faithful Vivian, who he'd been ready to drop like a hot potato because a prettier girl smiled at him. Poor Vivian. She was struggling with the most monstrous decision of a lifetime all by herself, and he hadn't given her a smidgeon of emotional support. If anything, he'd made it worse for her. He was so like his father whose solution to every problem in life was "whatever it costs, I'll pay for it."

Vivian truly loved him and just a few days ago, she would have sacrificed her whole future to marry him and give him children; but would she still want him now? Why on earth would she want a guy with herpes, hepatitis and AIDS, all of which he contracted while cheating on her at the same time that she was struggling with an unintended pregnancy all by herself? He didn't deserve Vivian and she certainly didn't deserve to have a stupid prick like him for a partner. Ending his life seemed like the solution.

A gun would be easiest, but he didn't have a gun. Pills would be easy too, but not only didn't he have any pills, but he thought it was too wimpy. He could crash his car, but that was risky. He might wind up crippled instead of dead, and he couldn't handle being crippled any better than he could handle being a sexual leper. He thought about hanging himself, but there were no rafters in his room, he didn't have any rope and he didn't know how to make a noose anyway. He went looking through his roommate's stuff to see if he had any pills, but only found allergy pills. He'd just have to go out and buy a gun.

Then he started to think about a suicide note and he couldn't come up with anything meaningful. "I caught a sexually transmitted infection" didn't seem like a justifiable cause for killing oneself. "I'm a miserable son of a bitch and I couldn't live with myself anymore," sounded more truthful, but it didn't explain anything to anyone who might actually care. Suddenly, he got curious about what other people's suicide notes said, prompting another Internet search. He was astonished by what he found.

The words 'suicide note' brought up more than two million postings. Apparently, there were tons of people who wanted to tell the wide web world why they were so miserable that they had to entertain ending their lives. He found himself reading a collection of notes from a forensic psychologist. Many of these people seemed motivated to kill themselves to punish someone else. It certainly wasn't going to matter to Donna if he committed suicide, so who would he be punishing? Others were deathly ill with no hope. His illnesses, if he even had them, were not necessarily deadly, and a medical breakthrough could arise in the future. Some notes suggested the writers were just plain crazy, and he didn't think he had become insane because a more carefree sex life had been spoiled by a moment of indiscretion. He even found a website that would write a note for you. You just had to input the recipient(s) and your reason(s) for killing yourself. Options included: bankruptcy, broken heart, chronic pain, dementia, illness, immobility, loneliness, politics, religion, revenge, and self-hatred. He figured unintended pregnancy might make the list if abortion became illegal.

Researching suicide methods also proved interesting. He learned that slitting one's wrists was largely unsuccessful and often left survivors with paralyzed hands. Carbon monoxide poisoning hadn't occurred to him either, but the probability of being rescued and winding up as a vegetable instead of a corpse was discouraging. The best rate of success was definitely bullet to the brain. He wondered if he'd have the courage to pull the trigger.

Once he decided on method, he went back to thinking about writing a note. It occurred to him that the person he would most owe an explanation to was Vivian. Would he even want to tell her he didn't want to go on living because he had contracted venereal disease? What purpose would that serve? But it certainly wouldn't be fair to let her think that her pregnancy was the reason. What if that motivated her to commit suicide? What if she did have his child and had to tell that child that its father was such a coward that he killed himself rather than become a father? What a horrible legacy! No! If he was going to kill himself, it had to look like an accident. No note. No gun. No guilt on Vivian's or his child's shoulders. He'd just have to get more creative. He needed more time to think, but he also needed some sleep. Between being sick and hating himself for ruining his life, he had slept very little in the past few days.

He pulled the shades, turned off his computer and got back into bed, but sleep just wouldn't come. Maybe the infirmary would give him something to help him sleep, and something to help with the pain. The over-the-counter stuff he was taking wasn't doing much of anything. Maybe he should even go back and talk to the counselor at the infirmary. Then, his thoughts turned back to suicide.

~ Thirty-One ~

Mark Wagner found a quiet little motel a short drive from the Best Hope House. After initially ducking around in the shadows, he concluded that either no one there recognized him, or they didn't care. It was a great reprieve from his daily life in the Washington limelight, and he took the rest of the day to read about drug addiction and alcoholism while simultaneously sipping bourbon. In some part of his consciousness, he realized that he wasn't very far away from needing rehab himself, but for the most part he was in denial. Lorraine had a serious problem with alcohol and pills, but he could control his drinking so that it didn't interfere with the multiple roles in life that he was trying to fulfill.

The next morning he flew back to Washington to vote on emergency measures regarding the economic crisis. He needed his constituents to know that he was not neglecting his congressional duties, even as he was attending to family matters. Phil made sure that there were reporters present at the airports to photograph him coming and going, and even managed to squeeze in a photo-op of Mark laying a flower on the grave of Walter Barlow Wagner at the Potomac Gardens Cemetery. Only a few reporters were tipped off about that event and Rita Rodriguez wasn't one of them.

Whenever a reporter shouted, "Where's Pamela?" Mark responded that his daughter had a great deal of healing to do and that she needed to do it privately. "She's just a confused little girl right now. If you must attack someone, attack me. I take full responsibility for the crises that have befallen my family."

After he had given this response a few times, the reporters seemed to back off, at least with regards to Pamela. Instead they hollered questions about how Lorraine Wagner was doing in rehab and where was his surrogate, Jack?

"I'm the one who's running for office. My son is a full time student with a family of his own, and my wife is seriously ill and fighting to regain her health. Please respect their privacy and focus your questions on my congressional duties and me. America's problems are of far more concern to the public right now than are the private lives and tribulations of my wife and children."

That statement brought a chorus of shouted questions about his views on abortion relative to his daughter's decision; but Mark backed away from these inquiries with the announcement that he planned to give another press conference to answer those questions before Election Day. "I owe that to the voters of my home state and I will address those issues very directly at another time. Today I need to focus on the critical issues before Congress and those that are consuming my family."

When he returned to Utah at the end of the week, he met with Lorraine's counselor. Lorraine was past the physical part of her ordeal and tapering off the medicines she was taking to allay the symptoms of withdrawal. However, the counselor felt that she needed at least another few weeks to deal with the psychological issues that were underlying her drug dependency, as well as the cravings that could be very strong when she returned to her stressful environment. "She needs more time to be ready to face her world without chemical crutches," the counselor said. "The majority of people who suffer from alcoholism need some kind of support on a lifetime basis to overcome the very high risk of relapse. It's extremely difficult for a recovering alcoholic to resist the temptation to drink if they are continuously exposed to settings where alcohol is flowing freely. It's even more difficult for them if alcohol is flowing freely at home."

Mark felt like there was a noose around his neck. Rationally, he knew that Lorraine's situation was intricately tied to his own, but emotionally he wanted to punch the counselor for insinuating that he drank too much. He felt his face flush and wondered if he smelled of alcohol. He had a few drinks on the airplane.

It had been his idea to send Lorraine to rehab, not so much because he was concerned about her drinking, but because it was a politically convenient diversion from the other issues that threatened to unseat him. Now that she was here, he had to play along. "I'm truly happy for Lorraine's progress and want to do everything I can to facilitate her making a complete recovery, but is there any way we can interrupt her program for just these final days before the election? If she and I can get out on the campaign trail together and meet our obligations there, then she could return to the program afterwards, and work on the issues that will insure her complete recovery."

"That's totally up to Lorraine," the counselor said. "This is a voluntary program. No one's held here against his or her will. I would recommend against her being put in a stressful situation at this point, but it's her priorities and choices that matter, not mine."

Lorraine took a deep breath. "I've had a lot of time to think in the last few days, Mark. I'm not doing this just to please you. I'm doing this because I really need to do this for myself and Pamela. Have you spoken to her today?"

Mark felt the noose tighten a little. "Didn't have a chance this morning. I talked to Jack last night and he said that she's in a great family environment, possibly the best we could have arranged. The people she's with are giving her great support. The woman took her to a doctor who helped her to understand that she has to eat better and gain weight. Jack says she's doing well there."

"So when did you last speak to her, Mark?"

The noose tightened. Mark hadn't spoken to Pamela since the day he told her that one of his aides was going to wrap her up in a rug and smuggle her to the home of people neither she nor he knew. Since then, he had relied only on Jack's assessment. "Jackson went to see her there on Wednesday and he's very impressed with the stable environment the

Furness family is providing. No demonstrators or paparazzi either. It really is fortuitous that McGraf came up with this option."

"Mark, I haven't been able to make phone calls, but I find it entirely unacceptable that our fourteen-year-old daughter is hiding out in the home of complete strangers, emotionally and physically ailing, and in six days, her only available parent has been too busy to even call her. That in itself is reason for me to interrupt my program here and return to Washington. But to tell the truth, I don't want to do it unless you're also going to stop drinking. I can live without the pills, Mark. I've only had a pill problem for the past year or so, but alcohol has been a long time problem for me, as it has for you. If we're both going to go around smiling at voters, I need to do it in an atmosphere of sobriety. Otherwise, I'm going to stay right here and you can just go hit the campaign trail by yourself. I don't really care if we wind up back home or stay in Washington. To be perfectly honest, I'd be happier and healthier out of Washington. What I care most about at this point is becoming a sober parent who is available to support our daughter."

The noose was almost choking him now. He didn't know if he could stop drinking and still deal with the pressures of home, Congress and the campaign. He couldn't even remember the last time he'd gone through an entire day without a drink. He wondered if he did, if he'd go through physical withdrawal. He knew for sure he'd have to fight cravings. Sometimes he had to fight them through the morning just to get to his bourbon at lunch. The prospect of not drinking at all seemed overwhelming. Perhaps he should have Lorraine stay at the facility for another week while he'd taper down.

"Why don't we talk about this some more over dinner, Rainy? I haven't had lunch, and my stomach's complaining a bit. How's the food here anyway?"

"Very good actually. I'm surprised as to how many choices are on the menu for such a small dining room, and everything is fresh and well prepared. It makes me wonder who they pay better, the counselors or the chef? They do emphasize good nutrition as part of the program, but of course you're not going to be able to order a drink."

"Would you rather we go out to a restaurant? I had a pretty good meal at a local steak house after I first dropped you off."

"Actually, Mark, I'd rather eat here. It would be very difficult for me to sit in a restaurant and not order a martini. I'm actually glad you asked the question because it makes me realize I'm not ready. Even if I wanted to get out of here and go help Pamela and campaign with you, I don't think I could do it just yet, and not wind up undoing the hard work I've just done to get through withdrawal. My counselor is right. It's too soon."

Mark nodded. "It would be foolish for you to do it if you're just going to wind up back where you were a week ago. I'll go home tomorrow and I promise I'll go see Pamela, as long as I can avoid having a reporter follow me. At least the demonstrators have stopped hanging around the house, but there are still some that wait on the Capitol steps for me. A few were there yesterday."

"What are you going to say about abortion when the time comes, Mark?"

"When I've had to time to think, that's all I've thought about. I met with that Nora Sutton again and she's kind of opened my eyes to concepts and issues I'd never seriously considered. Still, I'm in a total quandary about what to say to the voters. I was starting to formulate my speech when another Rodriguez article about sex education gave me pause."

"Why? What did she say?"

"Let's talk about it at dinner. I'm really hungry."

The dining room at Best Hope House wasn't exactly elegant but it had a breathtaking view. The rugged peaks to the east were snow capped and reflecting a stunning coral color from the setting sun. "The view alone is worth the guest meal fee," Mark commented. He chose a prime ribs entrée and Lorraine ordered the Utah trout. They both sipped on tall, frosty glasses of water as each struggled with their craving for a drink.

"So tell me about the sex education article. Being cut off from news in this environment is almost as challenging as not drinking, though I have to admit, it does make for a more peaceful state of mind. The library is full of inspirational books. I've also learned there's great value in taking a morning walk as opposed to reading stock market reports, which can make you feel like you need a pill."

"Some day I'm going to have to try to not start my day with news. Having free time could be a great benefit of losing the election.

"The Rodriguez article was of course, very biased towards giving kids comprehensive sex education, but also very informative. She cited national surveys that indicate that more than ninety percent of parents don't feel they know enough to do a decent job of teaching their kids, but these folks are silent, while a tiny vocal minority dictates to school boards.

"Did you know that under our current administration, there are three federal programs that fund abstinence-only education, and no federal programs that encourage providing kids with any more teaching beyond the concept that premarital sex is wrong and harmful? Federal guidelines actually promote the idea that any youth physical contact is harmful, including holding hands."

"You've got to be kidding," Lorraine said. "I had no idea we've become that puritanical."

"Yeah, I was pretty stunned by that too. Also pretty ridiculous is that many schools that have a so-called 'sex ed' program only teach about abstinence and the AIDS virus, not even about other sexually transmitted diseases. Now I've learned that that's what Pamela's school was doing, but they're only doing that at the ninth grade level, which is obviously too late. Meanwhile, our country has much higher rates of sexually transmitted diseases and teenage pregnancy than countries like the Netherlands, where comprehensive sex education is considered essential."

"Why, I wonder, is our country so regressive?" Lorraine lamented.

"I'm actually embarrassed about what a lousy job we're doing here. Rodriguez also gave examples of schools that push untrained, unwilling teachers into classrooms with snickering students, resulting in misinformation. There were also examples of schools that have good programs with highly trained teachers. Such programs motivate teens to wait longer and to have fewer partners, and those students have a lower incidence of venereal disease and teen pregnancy."

"Mark, if Pamela's lofty private school is doing such a poor job, I'll bet the public schools in our home state aren't doing any better. It's no wonder kids don't know how to make responsible decisions about their sexuality."

"You know, Rainy, I don't think I could teach kids about contraception. I can't imagine that I could do a better job of it than a professionally trained teacher. I sure wish we had done a much better job with Pamela."

"Me too, Mark! I never questioned what she was learning in school. I guess I was so blottoed half the time, I didn't even realize she had a boyfriend, let alone that she was so involved in a relationship. I've talked to her about menstruation and told her that boys would pressure her for sex, but I sure as hell never instructed her regarding contraception or how to recognize early signs of pregnancy. Can you imagine how little teaching is done in the homes of less educated parents? Please save that article for when I get out of here."

"So what do you think about taking a hiatus from your program and coming home with me?"

"I think I'm not ready and neither are you. I need at least a few more days to consider how to cope with the alcohol-happy real world. Maybe I'll feel like I can do this about mid-week. That would give me another four or five days to work on things. I'm not even going to ask you to promise me that you'll stop drinking at this point, although I'm hoping you'll try. But I beg you, please go see Pamela and let her know that we love her."

~ Thirty-Two ~

While her parents were campaigning back home, Vivian wallowed in her turmoil alone. She worried she had scared Greg off by not taking his phone calls. Part of her wanted to accept Glenna's conclusion that he wasn't even a worthy partner, but she remained paralyzed by the thought of going for an abortion, and Greg, for all of his faults, was the father of her child. The weaker part of her wanted to salvage their relationship.

After not hearing from him for the better part of the week, she found herself even more conflicted, and she kept thinking about Glenna's sister, Shelly, and her problem child, Skyler. As much as she didn't want to terminate her pregnancy, she also didn't want to spend her life in a loveless marriage, or wind up with a child that she and maybe the rest of her family would resent.

The more she struggled with her decision, the more her feelings about Greg clouded her thoughts. Although she and her brother had never been close, there were times she had turned to him for older sibling advice. She'd never had a conversation with him about Greg, but she sensed Chris didn't like him. Not that he disliked him; he just wasn't friendly towards him. The few times they had double-dated, they seemed to get along okay, but that's as far as it went. Suddenly, she wondered what Chris really thought. She called him when she got home from school on Thursday.

"What's up, Vivian? Is everything okay with Mom and Dad?"

"As far as I know they're back home shaking hands and kissing babies. It doesn't look good for Dad though. His opponent seems to keep picking up endorsements and is running a pretty effective campaign. Dad's mood is really down. I think he's worried he's going to lose, even though the polls still show him leading by a narrow margin."

"With this election, that's possible. So is everything okay with you, Viv?"

"Well, I kind of wanted to get some big brother advice, Chris. I'm very conflicted about my relationship with Greg."

"I thought you two were the ultimate lovebirds. Aren't you running up to Delaware to visit him every other weekend?"

"I was, but not lately. He hasn't come out and said it, but I think he wants to break up, and I'm wondering if you think he's worth my trying to hold on to?"

"You've really put me on the spot, Vivian. I'm not used to your wanting my opinion on something like this. Is there something you're not telling me?"

"Just that I need your male perspective. I think he's tired of being tied down. Mom says guys your age aren't ready to make commitments. I mean, if he just wants to go play the field, do you think it might make sense for me to cut him loose, or wait until he tells me he wants to break up?"

"Come on, Viv! You know the answer to that. If he's not into the relationship anymore, why demean yourself by hanging on and allowing him to come and go as he pleases? Are you so blinded by love that you're not using your head at all, and if you are, how can I help you?"

Chris sounded just like their mother. Vivian ached to tell him that she was pregnant, but just couldn't do it. "Do you think he's a good enough guy to fight for is all I'm asking. Maybe I am too blind to see him for what he really is."

"If you really want the truth, Viv, I'll oblige, but you might not like it."

"I'm ready, Chris. I called you because I think you're a good judge of character and I want your honest opinion."

"Then I have to tell you, Vivian, I wouldn't waste my time with Greg. He's not a bad guy, but I think he's pretty materialistic, and I just feel like you could find someone with more depth of character and clearer goals. My read on Greg is that he'll just make appearances in life while he's waiting around for his trust fund to kick in. Maybe that wouldn't be a bad life for you, Vivian. Maybe that's all you'd need to be happy, but I think you've got too much on the ball to be content with Greg. I just always found him kind of superficial and wishy-washy. Sorry, Sis, but that's my honest opinion."

"Yeeesh! I was afraid you'd say something like that, but I didn't know you thought that little of him."

"Well, you wanted honesty. Sorry if I've hurt your feelings, but I think your cheating your potential if you stay tied-up with Greg. He may be rich and good-looking, but there are a lot of guys out there with a lot more important things to offer. I've got a fraternity brother I'd love to introduce you to. He's so much more dynamic and personable than Greg and he's good-looking too. Frankly, I'd be ecstatic if you'd dump Greg and get out from under whatever magic spell he's cast on you. I've wanted to tell you that for a year or so, but you've been so starry-eyed, I figured you'd have to realize it yourself."

"Boy! Maybe I have been walking around with blinders. You've opened my starry eyes, Bro. I guess I should thank you for being honest."

"Well, you're welcome. So, on a different subject, what do you think Dad could do to improve his chances? The political atmosphere here on campus makes me think his chances aren't very good right now. There's some Republican support, but the vast majority of students seem excited about change. It's interesting to see people my age realizing that if they don't get directly involved in the political process, they're leaving their futures up to leaders who are out of touch with the present, let alone the future.

"I think the final blow for Republicans though, might be the VP candidate. Her views on abortion have really mobilized people around campus, and I'm afraid Dad's views are just as extreme. It's mystifying to me how this politician can promote abstinence-only education while her seventeen-year-old unwed daughter, who doesn't even attend school, is pregnant. What's up with that?"

"So what do you think about abortion, Chris?"

"Are you kidding? I'm Pro-Choice. Aren't you?"

"It's a tough call for me but I think I'm coming around to see past Dad's views. I just don't know what I'd do myself if I was ever in that situation."

"That's the whole point of Pro-Choice, Viv. No one really knows what they'd do if it was their own personal dilemma, until they're there, which is exactly why people whose lives aren't directly affected by a pregnancy shouldn't have anything to say about it. I wouldn't even bother to discuss this with Dad, but I think the whole idea of the government deciding about anyone's pregnancy, is ridiculous. The only people who should have anything to say about whether or not to bring a child into this world are the people who are going to take care of it. As the bumper sticker goes, 'if you can't feed 'em, don't breed 'em.' Dad's not going to take care of those poor unwanted kids. I vehemently disagree with his politics on abortion and honestly, I think Mom does, too."

"Why do you say that?"

"Because a few years ago, I overheard Mom on the phone discussing a patient, and she said something like the patient was too unstable to go through with an unwanted pregnancy and needed to get to Planned Parenthood immediately. I think if you pinned Mom down, she might admit she doesn't really agree with Dad. I even wonder if Dad really believes in that platform, or that's just how he has to posture himself to get elected. He was even more caught up in Pro-Life politics some years back."

"So isn't what you're really saying is that Dad's a hypocrite?"

"Alternate definition for a successful politician, Vivian. I love our parents, but I think once someone like Dad has had the power and privileges of being a Senator for twelve years, he'll compromise his personal beliefs to stay in office. Call me a cynic, but every day I'm here studying political science, I'm more convinced that it's all hypocrisy. Very few politicians can stay committed to their ideals and rise to power at the same time. It's just the nature of the game. After I graduate, I still plan to go to law school, but not with the goal of going into politics. I think I'd like to be a judge. Politicians have to do idiotic stuff just to appeal to a bunch of know-nothing voters."

"So what are you going to do about Greg, Vivian?"

"I'm not one hundred per cent sure yet, but I think I'm going to break up with him. Thanks, Chris, I think."

~ Thirty-Three ~

Lorraine signed out of the Best Hope House on Wednesday and flew back to Washington. Mark met her at the airport with a bouquet of roses and a host of reporters following him and shouting questions about Pamela, and his views on abortion. Mark responded that he'd give a press conference on the subject on Friday, before returning to his home state to campaign.

The Wagners didn't return to their house. Their driver took them to a hotel where they donned wigs and uniforms, and exited in a laundry truck, which dropped them off at another hotel where they hunkered down. The next morning, they donned disguises, and took a cab to a hotel suite in Baltimore. Once they were certain that their whereabouts remained undetected, Jackson picked up Pamela and Gail Furness in a rental car and met them there.

Eleven days with the Furnesses had apparently been good for their daughter. She appeared less gaunt. She hugged Lorraine for a long time. Then she asked "How long do I have to stay in hiding?"

Mark shook his head. "Pamela, if you've seen even a tiny fraction of the hate on the Internet, which Jackson confessed he connected you with; you'd have to understand that there are some very ornery people out there who remain fixated on your story. The best thing you can do for the next week or so is to stay out of sight, eat well, and keep up with your schoolwork. Until the election is over, you need to keep out of the public eye."

Pamela stepped forward and looked piercingly at her father. "What about in your eyes, Daddy? Do you still think I should go to jail for choosing not to become a mother at fourteen, because I made a mistake? What are you going to say about abortion at your press conference, Daddy? Do you still think I'm a criminal like all the haters out there?"

Mark motioned for Pamela to sit across from him. "Between your experience and the advice I've received from people like Nora Sutton and even Rita Rodriguez, I think it's more important that we prevent the circumstances that made you choose abortion, Pamela. Our team is going to be working on my speech right up until I give it, so you'll just have to watch it live tomorrow, but no, Sweetheart, no. I don't believe you should go to jail."

~ ~ ~

Lorraine and Jackson joined Pamela at the home of the Furnesses on Friday at noon. "And now we take you live to the press conference being given by Congressman and Senate candidate Mark Wagner" the network announcer said, as the caption "Special News Report" rolled across the screen.

"There she is," Jackson commented as the camera paused on the stunning profile of Rita Rodriguez as it panned across a room full of reporters. With a few taps on the microphone, the buzz in the room quieted. Mark Wagner cleared his throat and began:

Good afternoon ladies and gentleman of the press and my fellow Americans. As most of you already know, in the past two weeks, my family has faced some serious crises, the kind of events that force a person to stop and re-evaluate everything he believes in.

Should there be some amongst you who do not know what's happened, I'll briefly summarize the events that have led to this press conference. My wife Lorraine and I have four children. Three are married and on their own. Our youngest child, Pamela, will turn fifteen next month and lives at home. She's a wonderful young woman. She's bright, hard working, kind, and quite self-sufficient. She was also neglected, as I was absorbed in my congressional work and my wife was secretly trying to fight addiction.

My youngest daughter made a poor decision to become intimate with a boyfriend, and then she made more poor decisions because she lacked knowledge about basic reproductive function. Then, based on miscalculations, she gave birth to a baby who was older than she thought, but still too premature to survive. Now the question is: do we blame this tragic outcome on her, her absentee parents, or an education system that works to keep young men and women ignorant? Do we send her to jail for this ignorance?

The congressman paused and wiped his brow with a handkerchief, but the room full of reporters remained silent except for the clicks of cameras. Even the little audience in the Furness's TV room seemed to be holding its collective breath as they waited for Mark to continue.

As a husband and a father, I've done an enormous amount of soul searching. Maybe I should go to prison for not providing my daughter with the care and the education she needed in order to have avoided her unfortunate situation. There are those who would say my wife belongs in jail for abusing prescriptions. Others would prosecute doctors for being conned by patients with drug problems. Who do we forgive and who do we punish for ignorance, for mistakes, or for poor judgment?

Neglectful parents can't become better parents from jail cells. Addicts can go through withdrawal in prison, but they still need rehab or they relapse. Adolescents sure don't need the education they might encounter in jail.

My wife has taken the first hard step of admitting she had a problem and seeking treatment. My children and I are committed to obtaining co-dependency counseling.

My youngest daughter is receiving therapy for anorexia, an eating disorder that may have been responsible for hormonal changes that caused her to miscalculate the term of her pregnancy. She will receive counseling to help her cope with her eating disorder, her mother's addiction, and the impact of losing her baby.

Although Rita Rodriguez wasn't present with her camera yesterday, I visited the graveside of my grandson. I will forever mourn the loss of his life. I will forever wonder how his future might have turned out had he been given a chance. It is in his honor that I will turn attention to preventing young women in my daughter's situation from making the ill-informed choices that she made. The young people of this great society, who are barraged by sexually explicit messages from multiple sources everyday, are entitled to education that would enable them to better understand their sexuality. They need help in resisting pressures to engage in premarital sex, and need to know how to prevent pregnancy. They need more accessible birth control. They also need education about adoption.

Reversal of Roe v. Wade will criminalize abortion but it will not end abortion. More fetuses will have a chance at life if more women have options that are preferable to abortion.

If my constituents should give me the chance to stay in Congress, I pledge to develop legislative initiatives to improve access to family planning, and I'll work to develop educational programs that will enable young people to make better choices regarding their health, relationships, and reproductive issues

The issue of abortion has been dangling in the realm of philosophy rather than the realm of practicality for far too long. Instead of arguing about the immorality of it, we need to make much greater effort to prevent it. All of the bickering over the definition of the beginning of life only serves to distract from the good we can do to educate our youth and insure that every child not only has an opportunity to be born, but the opportunity to be loved and provided for.

Women with unintended pregnancies don't need to be punished. They and their offspring need our compassion and support.

Thank you.

"Then you are Pro-Choice, Senator, are you not?" a reporter shouted."

"I am Anti-Abortion. Absolutely Anti-Abortion, and I want to provide assistance for desperate women so that they have better options than abortion. Call me Pro-Women and call me Pro-Children, but I am still Anti-Abortion," Mark shouted back as he exited the room.

~ Thirty-Four ~

Vivian watched the replay of Mark Wagner's speech on the evening news, and it lifted her spirits. She wondered if it would influence her father and desperately wanted to call him and ask him if he had seen it and what he thought. She rehearsed what she might say to him, but ultimately decided against getting into such a conversation. For one thing, her father was already under all kinds of pressure and she didn't want to add to it, but more importantly, if he said that Mark Wagner's opinions were wrong, it would only make it more difficult for her to consider terminating her pregnancy.

She knew she'd made the right decision about not provoking that conversation when she saw election news from their home state. The newspaper said that Senator Roger Evans had received thunderous applause when he told rally attendees that he would continue to fight for the life of the unborn from the moment of conception. Even if her brother was right and her father believed in what Mark Wagner said, he wasn't going to admit it now. She had to do what was right for herself, and as long as it didn't come to public attention like it did for poor Pamela Wagner, it would be okay.

~ ~ ~

As Greg went to leave his dormitory to see if he could score some pills from the infirmary, he saw a group of guys standing around the lobby bulletin board. The police-artist sketch of Donna drew blood to his face. When the other guys left, he got close enough to read it. Above her picture it said, "WANTED. If you know the whereabouts of this woman, please call this number immediately." Below her picture it said "WARNING. This woman has seduced and infected students with gonorrhea, chlamydia, herpes, hepatitis and AIDS. If you have had contact with this woman, you are advised to seek immediate medical attention."

"Nice girl," said a voice from behind him. "Imagine the poor chumps that hooked up with her." Greg's neck veins popped out as he turned to see an upper classman reading over his shoulder. His mouth got too dry to swallow.

When he got to the infirmary, the wanted poster was plastered on the door, on the walls of the waiting room, and at the reception desk. Seeing her face everywhere was agonizing. He knew wherever he went on campus, she'd be the topic of conversation, and even if he decided not to kill himself, he decided he had to drop out of school. He'd just say the curriculum wasn't compatible with his goals and he'd enroll elsewhere. He didn't like economics anyway.

Doctor Freitag was sympathetic and gave him prescriptions for four pain pills and one sleeping pill. Greg was pretty sure that wasn't going to result in an overdose, and he asked if he could have more to get through the weekend.

"I can't give you more than that, Greg, until you've been screened by one of our counselors for your risks for chemical dependency or suicide. Not only is that the infirmary policy for all students, but we especially worry about the risk of suicide in students who have experienced a sexual assault. Let's get you a good night's sleep, and I want you to meet with our counselor, Herb Crandle, tomorrow morning. I think you'll find him very easy to talk to and I know that if you open yourself up to him, he can help you. I'd have you see him right now but unfortunately, he's helping another one of Miss D's victims who's in crisis at this moment. Do you feel like you need to talk to someone more immediately, Greg, because if you do, I'll arrange it."

"I can wait til tomorrow, but I do really want that appointment. My mind's all messed up over this."

"That's normal, Greg. I'd be more worried about you if you weren't distraught over this, but I also need for you to assure me that you're not thinking about suicide. Can you honestly say that, Greg?"

Greg's lack of a quick response was a red flag for Doctor Freitag.

"Greg, it's very normal to think about suicide when you've been victimized like this and saddled with chronic disease. However, most people who contemplate suicide don't actually attempt it. Are you close to attempting?"

Greg hung his head and remained silent.

"I want you to sleep here tonight, Greg. You'll be in a private room with a computer and a TV, and I'll prescribe a pain reliever and a sleeping pill for you. You just have to ask the nurse for it when you're ready to go to sleep. I'll arrange for you to meet with Herb Crandle first thing in the morning. Will that work for you, Greg?"

"Thank you, Doctor Freitag. Thank you very much," Greg garbled, unable to hold back tears.

"How's your relationship with your parents, Greg? Do they know anything about your being sick?"

Greg shook his head no.

"Well, we don't have to tell them anything at this point. Does anyone on campus know about your situation or that you came here today? We don't want your fellow dorm residents to report you as a missing person because then we will have to notify your parents."

"No, no one knows I'm here. My roommate's a nice guy. He might wonder where I am because I told him I was staying on campus this weekend."

"Then we'll let the head resident and your roommate know you're here. Anyone else that might be looking for you?"

"I'll call my folks and my girlfriend back home. Other than that, I don't think there's anyone else that will miss me. Thank you, Doctor Freitag. I think you actually just saved my life."

Vivian hesitated to answer the phone when she saw it was Greg, but she decided she still needed to at least talk to him.

"How are you doing, Vivian?"

"About the same, Greg, although maybe I'm getting a little closer to making a decision about the baby."

"You mean keeping it?"

"To tell you the truth, I've been leaning more towards not having it, but I'm still undecided. How are you doing, Greg?"

"I miss you, Vivian. I was going to come home this weekend, but I caught an infection and I'm actually spending the night in the college infirmary."

"It's that bad? What kind of an infection?"

Greg hadn't planned on explaining anything, at least not over the phone, if ever. "They're not sure yet. I've had fever and a rash. They're doing some tests and keeping me here tonight to monitor things."

"Do they know what they're doing there? Wouldn't you be better off coming home and going to your family doctor? Do your parents know?"

"Don't want to worry my folks at this point. It could turn out to be nothing. It's probably better if I stay here because there are other cases on campus, so they maybe have a better chance of getting to the bottom of it. The doctor I've been seeing is pretty good, so I don't really think there'd be any advantage in coming home."

"Then maybe I should come up there and be with you."

"That wouldn't be smart, Viv. You certainly don't need to catch this, especially with the baby at stake."

"What are you saying, Greg? I thought you wanted to get rid of the baby. Now you're worried about its health?"

"I don't know what I want, Viv. To be honest, I'm so confused I can't think straight. I've been really unfair to you and I feel awful about it. You're my best friend, Vivian, and I'm sorry I haven't been a better friend to you."

"I appreciate that, Greg, but your confusion doesn't help me out as far as having to make this decision. I'm confused too, but I have to make a decision one way or another, and quickly if I'm going to terminate."

"I know. I'm so sorry I'm not giving you a more definitive answer. Give me another day to get past this illness and I promise I'll get my act together."

"You do that, Greg. Hope you feel better."

As she hung up, her brother's "wishy-washy" words echoed in her head. She could just imagine Greg vacillating back and forth about the baby for nine months while she spent her senior year throwing up in the girl's room and hiding from reporters trying to snap photos of her big belly. Just like the VP candidate's daughter, she'd be a laughing stock, fodder for comedians and political cartoons.

She had also become preoccupied by the dilemma of what would she tell her child. She had thought she could try to go for an open adoption until it occurred to her that her child would come to know that his mother was a national joke and would also suffer humiliation because of her notoriety. She didn't think she could bare closed adoption, never knowing what became of her child, and wondering if it was aching to know its real mother. She wondered if closed adoption was even possible anymore in the age of information technology. Wouldn't a determined adoptee with tomorrow's databases be able to find a biologic parent? If so, what would she tell him or her? What can you say to a child you gave away? That question drilled her brain until she felt like it was on fire. She couldn't sleep. She couldn't read. She couldn't practice piano and she couldn't even eat. And she wondered: would she forever be plagued by this pain in her heart? She made up her mind to call Doctor Fox's office in the morning.

She got an appointment within an hour of calling. She pulled her hair up and covered it with a knitted cap and put on an extra large pair of sunglasses that her father used over his reading glasses on the patio. She took her mother's car and looked for surveillance cameras as she entered the office building. She turned her face into her coat collar walking through the lobby and halls. She rummaged through her purse while waiting for an empty elevator. From a small entryway into Doctor Fox's office, she was quickly whisked into a private room.

"How would you like to pay for today's visit, Ms. Johnson?" She plunked down one hundred and fifty dollars in cash that she'd scrounged from the household emergency kitty. After she filled out a pile of papers, an older woman came into the room and introduced herself as Jeanie, a nurse practitioner. She went through Vivian's paperwork and explained in detail about Doctor Fox's office policies. She took Vivian to another room and performed a physical and an ultrasound exam.

"You do meet all the criteria for medical abortion, Sandra. How unfortunate that you became pregnant while using birth control pills. As I understand it, you wanted to have a consult before you decided on whether or not to undergo the procedure. Let me explain how it works and then you can decide whether or not you want to do this and whether you want to do it today or schedule for another time, which would have to be in the next two weeks. After seven weeks, you would no longer be eligible for medical abortion and would have to have a surgical abortion.

"Here's how medical abortion works. You'll take three doses of a pill called Mifeprex or mifepristone, here in the office. This drug, previously called RU-486, was used in Europe for more than two decades before being approved by the U.S. FDA in 2000. It has an excellent safety profile. Occasionally people feel nauseous and dizzy, so we ask that you have someone to transport you home. If you don't have someone to help, we can recommend a discreet taxi service.

"Mifepristone blocks the effect of the hormone progesterone that is needed by the uterus to maintain its lining and support the embryo. Shortly after taking this drug, the lining of the uterus starts to degenerate. After we've observed you here in the office for an hour or so, to see how you react to the mifepristone, we'll send you home with another medicine called misoprostol or Cytotec. Then, some time in the next twenty-four to seventy-two hours, you can pick a time to take the Cytotec. This medicine makes the uterus contract and expel its lining, the placenta and the embryo, usually within six to eight hours after taking the pill. Most women describe this as being like a menstrual period with cramps and heavy bleeding. Some women also report nausea, diarrhea and feeling feverish. You'll pass clumps and clots as well as typical menstrual blood, so you'll want to be somewhere with easy access to a bathroom. If you don't have a place to do this in your home, we have some rooms here that you can use, but there's a charge. Sometimes, patients do not need to take the Cytotec. The uterus spontaneously expels the embryo after the Mifeprex.

"Most of the time the procedure is completed within a few hours, but the uterus may continue to bleed for a week to several weeks afterwards. This is normal and most women can go about their regular activities. We've even had competitive athletes return to training the day after. Rarely, a woman may bleed so heavily that she requires medical attention. Also rarely, the first dose of Cytotec doesn't work and we have a hot line for you to call if there are any such problems. Sometimes, we just instruct patients to take another dose of the Cytotec, but occasionally we need to have a woman come in for further evaluation. That's very rare.

"Finally, it's essential that you return for an exam within two weeks of the procedure to check that everything that should have been expelled from the uterus, has been expelled. If there's any retained placental tissue, it must be removed or it can cause serious infection.

"Now let's answer any questions you may have."

"Do you see the baby when it's expelled?"

"At your stage of pregnancy, Sandra, the embryo is about one seventeenth of an inch long. That's about the size of the tip of a pen. If you could find it amidst the blood and placental tissue, and if you could look at it under a microscope, it would look like a tadpole. But it is highly unlikely that you would be able to distinguish the embryo from the rest of the tissue the uterus will shed at your stage of pregnancy."

"Will this have any impact on my ability to have children in the future?"

"Important question. Hundreds of thousands of women the world over have used this method and there's no evidence that their fertility has been compromised. I should point out that this method of abortion affords such a great degree of privacy, that we may not even know how many women have had the procedure, which leads me to another warning. Do *not* try to purchase these drugs on the Internet. There are websites that advertise cheap mifepristone and all they send is a sugar pill. There's also concern that some websites have sent dangerous drugs to women, resulting in illness and even death. Only qualified physicians and clinics can legally obtain the real drugs. You cannot buy them in a pharmacy and if anyone tells you they can get it for you, they are probably scamming you or selling you PLAN B, the emergency contraceptive which is not the same as mifepristone. PLAN B is a hormone that can prevent pregnancy right after intercourse, but it is not effective for terminating an existing pregnancy."

"How about the cost?"

"Mifepristone is an expensive drug. Doctor Fox charges $1,200 for the care and medicine, and if you opted not to do this today, but to come back and do it within two weeks, today's payment will be subtracted. If you waited until after the seventh week to decide, and then required *surgical* abortion, the cost is much higher. Doctor Fox doesn't provide abortion services to women who are more than twenty weeks pregnant, except for grave medical issues. Other questions?"

"I can't think of any at the moment. I don't think I'm ready to make the decision today, but I appreciate your helping me understand how this works. What if I scheduled to do it this coming week and then changed my mind?"

"You can always call and cancel if you change your mind, even at the last minute. We know how difficult a decision this is and we strongly suggest that you not go forward if you're not clear in your own mind about it."

Jeanie asked if Sandra would like information about adoption and provided her with a folder of information. "One of our counselors will be glad to sit down with you and discuss adoption options at no extra charge. Would you like an appointment?"

"Actually, I think I'd like to schedule the abortion. I'm still in high school and I don't see a future for my boyfriend and myself. I'm going to give adoption more thought, but I'm pretty sure I don't want to spend my senior year of high school pregnant, and I fear I wouldn't be able to give the baby away if I had it."

"Why don't you schedule both appointments then, and give yourself a few more days to think about it. We want you to be comfortable with the decision you make. Please call if you have more questions. Also, if you would like to speak with other women who have gone through this, we have a panel of patients who have volunteered to be available. Here's a list of their code names and phone numbers. Good luck with whatever you decide, Sandra."

~ Thirty-Five ~

Greg felt considerably better after getting a good night's sleep. He was eager to talk with the counselor Herb and found the session very helpful. Before it ended he had come to terms with his ambivalence towards his college studies and concluded that he needed to go out and work for a while and then reconsider what kind of an education and career he wanted to pursue. He was already so far behind in his course work that this decision, all by itself, took a huge load off of him. It would also get him away from the campus that he would forever think of as the scene of the attack.

Herb also helped him to understand that his infections weren't the end of a meaningful life. Doctor Freitag had found out that he'd been vaccinated against hepatitis B, which greatly reduced his risk. The other strain of hepatitis attributed to Ms. D was of less concern. The AIDS risk was relatively small and because it would be diagnosed early, and because treatment was rapidly improving, this was also less worrisome. As for the herpes issue, Greg came to appreciate that with maybe a quarter of sexually active people already infected, it wouldn't be difficult to find partners and he wouldn't automatically be perceived as a pervert. Also, there was protective medicine for the uninfected, if a relationship brought him to that crossroad.

Herb also helped him to clarify his feelings towards Vivian. "Nobody stays in love," Herb said. "No matter how passionate you feel towards someone, no matter how strong the attraction, over time, romantic love fades. It might take a few months or even years, but that hot magnetism that draws people together dissipates. If you've made a good partner choice, a deeper, more mature kind of love takes the place of the passion. If the attraction was based solely on physical feelings and not on core interests and values, then the relationship may deteriorate. For some people, love of their children keeps them together, but in our self-centered culture, too many parents put their own needs ahead of the needs of their kids.

"For most of human history and throughout most of the world, marriages haven't been based on romantic love. Instead, parents choose their children's partners based on family values, and such marriages are more durable. In our society, where individuals marry because they're *in* love, the divorce rate is at least fifty percent, and the younger the people, the higher the risk that the marriage will collapse. Second and third marriages have even worse chances of success, probably because those who keep marrying, keep clinging to the erroneous idea that marriage is about being *in* love, rather than working at loving the other person. So as soon as the romance fades away, they think the marriage is over.

"It's entirely normal that after spending more than two years in a relationship with your girlfriend, that you no longer feel that exciting spark. The question you now have to answer is: can you appreciate each other as friends and business partners, because that's ultimately what successful couples become. Another question you must answer is: Do you know what you want out of life? If not, then you need to give yourself the time and experience to figure it out, even if that means separating from your girlfriend."

Greg left his suicidal thoughts behind when he left the infirmary. He called Vivian and told her he was coming home to help her figure things out. There'd be plenty of time for him to find a way to confess about his tryst and infections. What suddenly seemed important was being a better friend to her. Herb had helped him to see that his self-respect depended on that. He packed up some clothes and his computer and arrived at the Evans house in the afternoon.

Vivian was relieved that he would be there to help her physically and financially. She was less sure about what his return meant to her emotionally. Even though he was suddenly showing some sense of responsibility, she no longer had much confidence in him. When he told her he was leaving school to check out the work world, she heard replays of her brother's assessment. For all of his intelligence and wealth, he lacked goals and a sense of purpose. Even now that he was finally there to help, he still didn't show readiness to talk about their future or share in decisions about adoption or raising a child. Just his decision to leave school seemed immature.

"Have you told your parents yet?"

He hung his head. "I want to first get our situation figured out before I tell them anything. Have you decided about the baby?"

"I made an appointment to do a medical abortion on Wednesday. My parents are coming home tomorrow night because there's a Congressional vote on Monday that my father has to partake in, but then they leave Tuesday to campaign. Barring the unexpected, they won't be back until the day after the election, which will give me a week to recover."

Greg felt another enormous weight lifted from his shoulders. They went to dinner in her favorite restaurant and rented some movies for comic relief. He spent Saturday night on the couch and went back to campus before her parents came home on Sunday.

While Vivian went to school on Monday and Tuesday, Greg went to the college administrative offices and processed his withdrawal. He got his blood drawn for the AIDS test and asked that the results be forwarded to his Email. He contacted the police investigator to let him know he was leaving school, but could be reached by email if they needed him to testify against the D girl. He told the head resident that he'd be back to get the rest of his stuff after Election Day. He thought about dropping into his old economics class and saying good-by to Colleen, but decided against it. If things didn't work out with Vivian, there'd be some other nice girl with herpes to have a relationship with.

~ Thirty-Six ~

Karida Robbins's first day working for Doctor Fox was fulfilling in many ways. She observed the nurses who counseled patients and assisted in the office surgical suite. She also checked out the computer to see if Sandra Johnson had an appointment. She was both elated and anguished to find her. She felt like T'Pol in the *Star Trek* episode where the Vulcan had to betray her own culture to insure peace in the galaxy. When the records showed that Sandra had just been in for counseling and was returning on Wednesday for medical abortion, she let Eliza know that NEB's opportunity had presented.

~ ~ ~

Everything went exactly as it should have for Vivian and Greg in Doctor Fox's office on Wednesday morning, until they stepped out into the hallway. Karida had texted the code words "How's Willie?" to Lydia, who in turn texted the code sentence "Acne doctor is suite 314" to Tracy and Daniel Abraham, so they could position themselves at just the right moment.

"Vivian? Greg?" Tracy said with her best look of surprise. She made a big show of looking at the nameplate on the office door. "That's Doctor Roland Fox's office that you just came out of."

Neither Greg nor Vivian could manage to speak.

"You guys can't be...you guys! You know, Vivian, everyone at school thought you were 'prego' anyway, but Vivian Evans! With your father out there promising to overturn *Roe v. Wade,* how can you be here seeing Doctor Fox? I can't believe this!"

"What are *you* doing here, Tracy?" Vivian stammered.

"I'm looking for the dermatologist's office. I thought it was on this floor, but it's not. My mother must have written down the wrong suite number." She waved a paper with a number on it. Vivian grabbed her hand.

"Tracy, please! You can't tell anyone you saw us here. It would destroy my father. Please, Tracy. Be a friend! Promise you won't tell anyone. Please."

"I don't know, Vivian. Nothing personal, but it just blows me away that you're here exercising the right to choose while your father's out there trying to take that right away from everyone else. My grandmother lost her life because people like your father felt it was their right to impose their beliefs on everyone else. They burned my grandmother alive, just because she was a receptionist in a clinic like this. I'm sorry, Vivian. I don't want to hurt you, but I can't promise silence where the right to choose is at stake."

Greg stepped forward. "You better really think before you go blabbing about our private business, Tracy. You know my father has…"

"Are you threatening me, Greg?" Tracy interrupted. "Maybe you better think about that yourself, because both of my parents were detectives on the D.C. police force and they wouldn't be too happy about you threatening me. In fact, I think I'll call my father right now. He's waiting for me in the car."

Greg suddenly stepped back as a big burly man appeared from out of a hallway recess and came striding towards them. "Tracy, the dermatologist is on the third floor. Mom got the suite number wrong," the big man said.

"Thanks, Daddy. I want you to meet two of my schoolmates I just happened to bump into here. This is Gregory Thatcher and Vivian Evans. This is my father, Detective Daniel Abraham."

The big man extended his hand and Greg sheepishly shook it.

"Are you okay, Miss Evans?" Daniel asked. "You look a little pale. In fact, I think you ought to sit down and put your head …."

He caught Vivian collapsing and gently lowered her to the floor. "I saw that coming. I think we need to get her back into the doctor."

Greg stood motionless with his jaw hanging.

"She just came out of this office, Daddy," Tracy pointed.

The big man scooped her up and carried her back into the office of Dr. Roland Fox, with Greg and Tracy following.

"Greg, I'm really sorry I stumbled onto your secret," Tracy said as she and her father departed. "I like Vivian and I have nothing personal against either of you. It's Vivian's father and his politics I have a problem with. Too bad this happened to you and Viv."

~ Thirty-Seven ~

Rita Rodriguez's story appeared on the front page of the Friday edition of the *Washington Chronicle*. The headline read "ABORTIONS FOR ANTI-ABORTIONISTS" and there was a picture of Roger Evans flanking the article.

Washington D.C.: Another Anti-Choice legislator's pregnant daughter has exercised the right to choose at the same time that her father is campaigning to take that right away from American women.

Detective Daniel Abraham, formerly of the Washington D.C. police force, told me that while taking his own daughter to see a physician on Wednesday, he met his daughter's schoolmates, Vivian Evans and Gregory Thatcher, as they exited from an abortion clinic. Apparently Miss Evans fainted upon being recognized, and Detective Abraham had to carry her back into the clinic for additional assistance.

Miss Evans' father, Roger Evans, is currently campaigning for his third term in the US Senate. He has been an Anti-Choice voice throughout his political career, and is currently telling voters in his state that he will seek to overturn *Roe v. Wade*, the 1973 supreme court decision that legalized abortion.

Senator Evans was also one of the architects of the federal government's defunding of UNFPA, the United Nations Fund for Population Activities. This organization is an international relief agency for women and children living in the most dangerous places on Earth. It works to insure child and maternal health so mothers can care for their children.

Leaders around the world cite UNFPA as one of the most successful UN programs in history, while Roger Evans and his Anti-Choice collaborators have conducted a campaign to defame this organization, based on trumped-up propaganda. According to UN sources, when UNPFA tried to provide emergency contraception to rape victims in Kosovo, Senator Evans claimed that the UN was committing genocide and ethnic cleansing. When UNPFA tried to establish emergency obstetric clinics in Iraq, Senator Evans and friends called it abortion jihad. Defunding of the clinics left Iraqi women to give birth in cluster bomb rubble.

UNFPA has never provided abortion services. One of its principal goals is to prevent abortion by providing family planning options for women who are unable to provide for children, such as impoverished rape victims and starving refugees. UNPFA was established in 1969 and operates in one hundred forty countries. Experts at Johns Hopkins University estimate that the withdrawal of US support for UNFPA by the Bush administration has resulted in approximately two million infant deaths, one hundred and twenty-five thousand maternal deaths, sixty million unintended pregnancies, and twenty-five million abortions.

Senator Evans, his daughter Vivian and her boyfriend, Mr. Thatcher, could not be reached for comment. Classmates of Miss Evans have verified that she and Mr. Thatcher have been a couple for several years. She's a senior at the Lincoln Wilson Academy from which Mr. Thatcher graduated last year.

Child welfare advocates are encouraged by Congressman Wagner's recent promise to provide women burdened with unintended pregnancies, better options than abortion, rather than to criminalize them. They now look to Senator Evans to tell the nation why he would deny other women the right to choose that his own daughter has just exercised.

Ferris Thatcher called Greg as soon as he saw the newspaper.

"Where the devil are you, Son?"

"I'm with Vivian, Dad."

He told Greg about the article on the front page of the *Chronicle.* "But *where* are you, for crying out loud?"

"We're at Vivian's house. Her parents are campaigning back home."

"Well you better get out of there right now. Is she okay?"

"Actually Dad, she's expelling the embryo as we speak."

"What? The paper said she was in an abortion clinic two days ago."

"It's medical abortion, Dad. They give you the first pills in the clinic, which starts the process, and you take the next pill in a day or so, which makes the uterus expel the embryo. She took the second pill last night and it started to work early this morning."

"Well, Greg, as we speak, there are TV news vans pulling up to our house, and I'll bet if you look out the window, they're pulling up to the Evans house as well. The demonstrators will probably be descending on you momentarily. I'm going to get a security team to get you out of there. I'll arrange for a pilot to get you to a villa in Bermuda before these wolves eat you alive. Have Vivian call her mother to let her know you kids will be safe. Better yet, get me her father's number. I'll deal with the senator. Keep your cell phone on you, and do not take any calls unless they're from me. How can a rescue vehicle get to you? What's the security system like on that house?"

Greg looked out the window but could see little. The house was screened from the street by a wall of pine trees. From upstairs he could sense an unusual amount of activity beyond the trees. "The Evans have a gated driveway. The code is 7716. There's an intercom at the front door."

"Do not open the door for anyone who does not give you the code word 'perfidia.' Understand?"

"Perfidia. Got it. Thanks, Dad. I guess we should have anticipated this."

"No time for regrets. Get yourselves ready and let me get to work."

Vivian was still sitting on the toilet with a cramping belly when Greg heard a man's voice say "perfidia" through the intercom. He opened the door to see a six-foot-five ex-football player wearing military garb. Vivian barely got her pants pulled up before the bodyguard scooped her up with her cat Nutmeg in her arms and carried her to a chauffeured limo in the Evans's circular driveway, while another armed man in military garb ushered Greg into the back seat next to her. The security team got into a Hummer parked in front of the limo. The two-car procession had to move slowly to avoid crashing into the reporters and demonstrators that were rapidly converging on the street in front of the gate. They'd just barely reached the corner of the next block when shots rang out. The limo lurched and the chauffeur slumped forward. Vivian heard breaking glass and felt a searing pain in her neck.

~ ~ ~

Fritz Anders of the *Baltimore Record* got the best eyewitness account. The front-page headline of Saturday's paper read "SENATOR'S DAUGHTER TARGETED BY PRO-LIFE ACTIVISTS."

> Washington D.C.: Senator Roger Evans's seventeen-year-old daughter Vivian, and her eighteen-year-old boyfriend, Gregory Thatcher, were shot and injured, presumably by persons who were enraged by their decision to terminate an unintended pregnancy.
>
> The couple was being transported away from the home of the senator when their vehicle was ambushed. Witnesses report seeing an old brown sedan parked at the end of the street where the Evans reside. When the transport car drove by it, bullets hit Mr. Thatcher in the shoulder and Miss Evans in the neck. The driver was shot in the arm and the car was disabled with two flat tires. The brown car sped away and was found abandoned a few blocks from the

shooting. The security team accompanying the transport vehicle gave first aid to the injured, instead of pursuing the perpetrators.

The victims were taken to D.C. Memorial Hospital. Mr. Thatcher and the driver are expected to make a full recovery. Miss Evans has a bullet lodged close to her spinal cord, but surgeons report that the cord was not injured and they expect her to do well once she recovers from surgery. A policeman said it was miraculous that the gunmen missed their heads.

Senator Evans has been at his daughter's bedside along with an entourage of security personnel. In a brief statement, he asked the public to realize that the majority of persons and organizations that seek to protect the rights of the unborn are not violent. Most are devoting their efforts to helping women to avoid abortion, and the radical element of the Pro-Life movement does not speak for the peaceful majority of people who believe that abortion is murder.

When asked if he would support Congressman Mark Wagner's new platform to reduce abortion without criminalizing it, he said he would work hard to promote adoption. He did not respond to questions about his daughter's right to choose, or his campaign against the UNPFA.

Any persons with information as to the identity of the occupants of the brown car are asked to notify police.

~ Thirty-Eight ~

Karida and Peter Robbins joined the other NEB members at the home of cleaning tycoon Sherry to watch the results of the election. Karida was struggling with her conscience for having been part of the plot that exposed Vivian Evans to the wrath of the radicals, and she wondered how Tracy was handling the guilt.

"I don't feel guilty at all," Tracy said. "I feel badly about what happened to Vivian, but not guilty. I'd feel much worse about all the suffering that would be caused if politicians like Roger Evans succeeded in taking away the right to choose. Dad, tell Karida what your friend from the police department told you."

Daniel Abraham said, "this is very inside information, Karida, but before you go beating up on yourself, let me tell you about the two thugs that shot Vivian. It hasn't hit the news yet, because they just arrested these guys yesterday and the interrogations are still ongoing, but I spoke to the lead investigator this afternoon. He was once my partner. Each of these suspects has been eager to blame the other, so the interrogators have been able to pump quite a lot of information out of them. They're white supremacists and members of a para-military organization that sanctions violent means to reverse *Roe v Wade*. This group has been associated with more than two thousand acts of violence against clinics, doctors and individuals. They actually publish detailed instructions on how to make bombs, attack clinics, and cut off the hands of doctors who perform abortions.

"The older guy is thirty-four and has a long rap sheet. The younger guy is twenty-six. I could go on for a long time telling you about the evil deeds they've done, but the bottom line is that each of them seemingly came into this life as an unwanted child. The young guy grew up in foster care until he got sent to juvenile detention for assault. The older guy grew up on the street when his heroin-dealing mother was incarcerated. He survived by prostituting himself and running drugs for gangs. According to their crime histories, they're both hardcore haters of women, blacks, gays, Jews, Latinos, and a host of other human beings. But, they love the unborn?

"You, Karida, did not cause harm to Vivian. Had you done absolutely nothing, her secret would have come out anyway. Tracy says most everyone in school assumed she was pregnant, and they would have figured it out when she was no longer pregnant. The role we played in exposing her story just caused that to happen in a way that we hope will impact her Anti-Choice father. We had nothing to do with her getting pregnant or choosing to terminate her pregnancy. She made those decisions herself. Instead of fretting about her unfortunate outcome, try to focus on how the exposure of Pamela Wagner's case has turned her father around. Not only is he no longer against freedom to choose, but if he wins, he says he'll work to influence others in Congress to give women better options. That's a major accomplishment."

As Daniel Abraham got up, his wife Roxanne sat down across from Karida. "We all struggle with the ethics of what NEB does, Karida. You wouldn't be an ethical person if you didn't. When I'm questioning myself, I'm consoled by what Daniel and I have learned as police officers, and that's that bad criminals are very often unwanted children. I'm not talking about adopted children; most kids who are fortunate enough to be adopted are very wanted. And, sometimes criminals do emerge from good homes; but when you look at the backgrounds of people who go out and hurt other people, over and over again you learn that they were unwanted children who grew up in unstable or abusive environments without love or a sense of security, and they're angry. In your nursing training, Karida, were you ever exposed to the research of Levitt and Donahue?"

Karida shook her head no.

"In 1999, they published data showing that the incidence of violent crime steadily decreased after the passage of *Roe v. Wade*. In other words, once abortion was legalized in 1973, thousands of unwanted children were no longer being born to grow up to be violent criminals. Their theory has been challenged, but as a former police profiler, I think they're one hundred percent correct."

"No one would blame you, Karida, if you wanted to dissociate from NEB," Nora said. "None of us should be here if our consciences disallow our continued participation. It really does boil down to: does the end justify the means? For me, if even one unwanted child isn't born, because of the choices that Pamela and Vivian made, the means are justified. In reality, I think thousands of unwanted children might not be born because of Pamela and Vivian, and these cases might not have come to public attention without our intervention. You can consider that to be a burden of guilt or a proud accomplishment, but I think in the long term, you will see that you positively contributed to one of the most important issues in history, and perhaps, saved the lives of hundreds of thousands of women."

"I hadn't thought of it that way," Karida said, but Eliza sensed she still had doubts. She was about to try to console her a little more when their conversation was interrupted by the arrival of the pizzas they had ordered. As she chomped on her piece, Eliza wondered if NEB's newest member was still with them. They were all eating when the election results were cut into by a special news report.

We interrupt this programming to inform you that one of the suspects in the shooting of Senator Roger Evans' daughter, Vivian, and her boyfriend, Gregory Thatcher, has confessed to driving the ambush vehicle and accused his accomplice, also in police custody, of being the shooter. We are also now informed

that surgeons at D.C. Memorial Hospital have successfully
removed the bullet from Vivian Evans's neck without
damaging her spinal cord, and they are optimistic about her
recovery. We return you now to tonight's election coverage.

Sherry broke out bottles of champagne when the network projected that Barak Obama was the President-Elect. Their celebration became even more jubilant when a network predicted that Mark Wagner would win his Senate seat, while Roger Evans would be defeated. As the group continued to savor that, Lydia found more good news on the Internet: the voters in South Dakota rejected Proposition Eleven that would have banned almost all abortions, and Colorado voters defeated Proposition Forty-Eight, which would have provided full legal status to fertilized eggs. Seventy-three percent of Colorado voters said no.

After the popping corks and clinking glasses ceased, Karida asked if its mission was so well accomplished, that NEB no longer needed to exist.

"Wonderful question, Karida," Nora answered. "How I wish that were the case. We can rest easier for at least the next four years, assuming that Anti-Choice judges won't be appointed to the Supreme Court. And we can take heart from the tendency of many moderate Pro-Life leaders to be moving towards compromise. But, we can't let our guard down just yet. The more radical Anti-Choice movement will mobilize. Even though decades of debate since the '73 Roe decision haven't changed public opinion, and the majority of Americans believe that restricted abortion should continue to be legal, abortion foes will continue to try to impose their views on the majority. Strong backlash is expected to arise in states like Oklahoma, Utah, South Dakota, Mississippi, Montana, Missouri, and Georgia. Militants might become more militant. Imagine how much money and energy they'll waste on advancing their agenda, instead of using it to help poor women and abandoned children.

"We've won a major battle tonight, but the war is not over. Unintended pregnancies will continue to occur, even if we provide all citizens with the knowledge and resources they need to prevent them. The biologic imperative to procreate that drives human sexuality and makes males constantly fertile isn't going to go away. We still need to promote the idea that the life of a victim of an unintended pregnancy isn't less valuable then the potential life of the unborn. How the victim of an unwanted pregnancy handles her burden really is nobody else's business.

"Today, many young women take access to safe abortion for granted, while people who have first-hand experience with the tragedy that can result when legal abortion isn't available, will be fading away. If younger people don't take up the cause, the right to choose could be lost. That is why people like Harriet, Sherry, Eliza, Lydia, Roxanne, and the rest of us are sharing our stories with women like you, Karida. You, Tracy, Pamela, and Vivian, and the people of your generation must continue the fight, or it could be one of your daughters that winds up waiting on a street corner for someone to take her money, and maybe mutilate or kill her. This election has been a great victory for reproductive rights. We just have to be sure that it doesn't lead to complacency."

THE END

~ Acknowledgments ~

This story was published with the invaluable assistance of Nancy Costo, Julie Doerr-Arenson, Audrey Siegel, Barbara Podstawski, Catherine Hiller, and Katie Mullaly.

~ About the Author ~

Dr. Beverly Hurwitz, originally from Brooklyn, New York, has spent her professional life as a physician, educator, and author.

In her youth she won awards for scholastic journalism and she served as copy editor for her college newspaper. Before attending medical school, she spent nine years as a health and physical education teacher in rural public schools.

As a medical fellow, Beverly specialized in the care of children with neurologic disability. After three decades of clinical practice, she spent eight years as a medical case analyst/writer for administrative law judges in federal and state court systems. In recent years, she has been writing this and other novels. She published two hiking books in 2017-18.

Beverly divides her personal time between reading, writing, golfing, hiking, skiing, and ice-skating.

52905611R00167

Made in the USA
Columbia, SC
10 March 2019